MONSTER HIGH™

I Only Have EYE for You

An ORIGINAL Graphic Novel

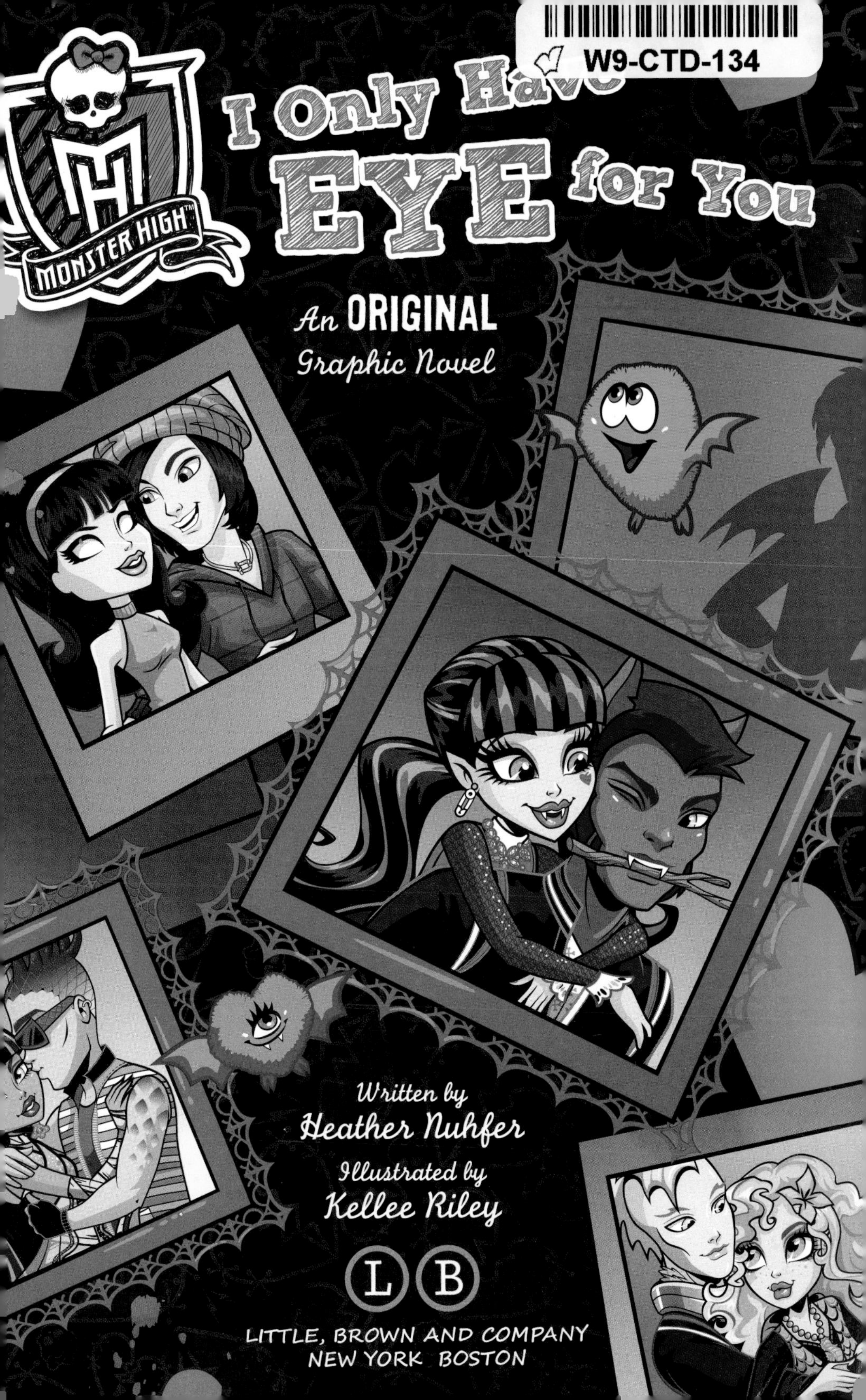

Written by
Heather Nuhfer
Illustrated by
Kellee Riley

LB
LITTLE, BROWN AND COMPANY
NEW YORK BOSTON

Special thanks to Venetia Davie, Tanya Mann, Darren Sander, Julia Phelps, Garrett Sander, Charnita Belcher, Sharon Woloszyk, and Andrea Isasi.
Cover art by Kellee Riley
Cover design by Christina Quintero
Interior inks and colors by Kellee Riley
Bubbles and lettering by Kellee Riley and Ching Nga Chan

Little, Brown and Company

Hachette Book Group
1290 Avenue of the Americas, New York, NY 10104
Visit us at lb-kids.com
monsterhigh.com

Little, Brown and Company is a division of Hachette Book Group, Inc.
The Little, Brown name and logo are trademarks of Hachette Book Group, Inc.

The publisher is not responsible for websites (or their content) that are not owned by the publisher.

First Edition: December 2014

Library of Congress Control Number: 2014943618

ISBN 978-0-316-28286-4

10 9 8 7 6 5 4 3 2 1

CW

Printed in the United States of America

TABLE OF
CONTENTS

WHO'S WHO

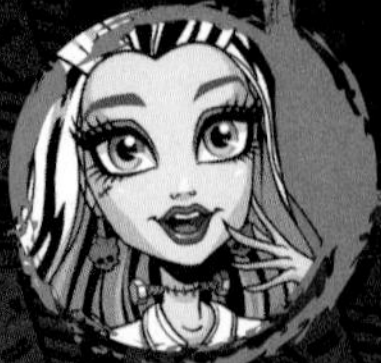

FRANKIE STEIN

MONSTER PARENTS: FRANKENSTEIN AND HIS BRIDE

AGE: HOW MANY DAYS HAS IT BEEN?

FRANKIE IS SPARKING WITH ENTHUSIASM FOR UNLIFE AT MONSTER HIGH. SHE MAY SOMETIMES FALL APART AT THE SEAMS, BUT SHE IS ALWAYS THERE TO LEND A HELPING HAND.

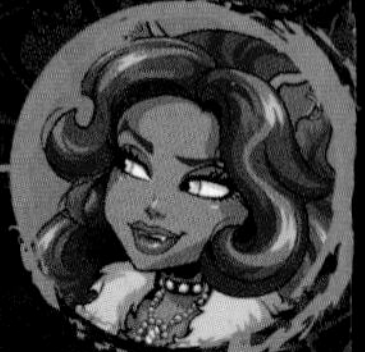

CLAWDEEN WOLF

MONSTER PARENTS: THE WEREWOLVES

AGE: 15

CLAWDEEN IS BOLD, OPINIONATED, AND FIERCELY LOYAL TO HER FRIENDS. SHE IS THE YOUNGER SISTER OF CLAWDIA AND CLAWD, AND SHE IS HOWLEEN'S OLDER SISTER.

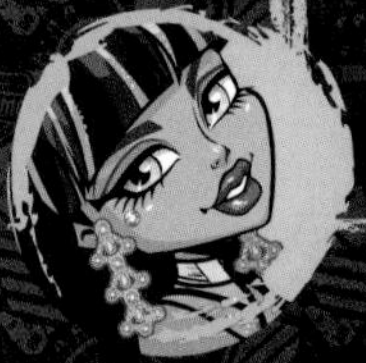

CLEO DE NILE

MONSTER PARENT: THE MUMMY

AGE: 5,842 (GIVE OR TAKE A FEW YEARS)

AN ACTUAL EGYPTIAN PRINCESS, CLEO RULES THE HALLS OF MONSTER HIGH AS CAPTAIN OF THE FEAR SQUAD. WHILE A BIT SELF-CENTERED, CLEO IS A TRUE FRIEND.

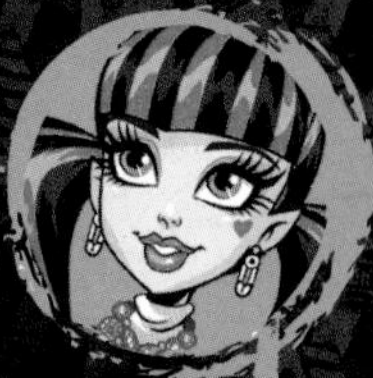

DRACULAURA

MONSTER PARENT: DRACULA

AGE: 1,600

DRACULAURA IS KIND, GENEROUS, AND SCARY-SWEET. SHE IS A VEGETARIAN VAMPIRE AND A HOPELESS ROMANTIC.

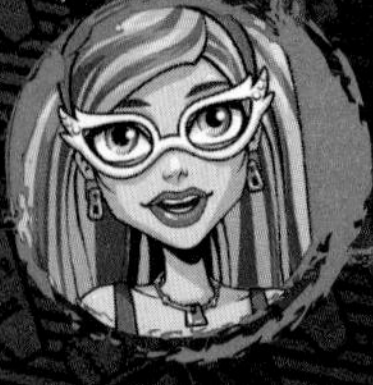

GHOULIA YELPS

MONSTER PARENTS: ZOMBIES

AGE: 16

GHOULIA MAY MOVE A BIT SLOWLY, BUT SHE'S THE SMARTEST GHOUL AT MONSTER HIGH. SHE SPEAKS ONLY IN ZOMBESE, WHICH MOST MONSTERS CAN EASILY UNDERSTAND.

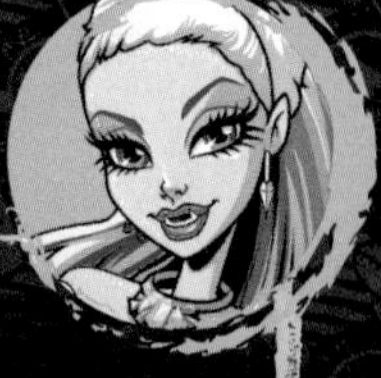

ABBEY BOMINABLE

MONSTER PARENT: THE YETI

AGE: 16

ABBEY IS ENORMOUSLY STRONG AND AS BLUNT AS A HAMMER. HER WORDS CAN COME ACROSS AS COLD AND HARSH, BUT SHE HAS A WARM HEART.

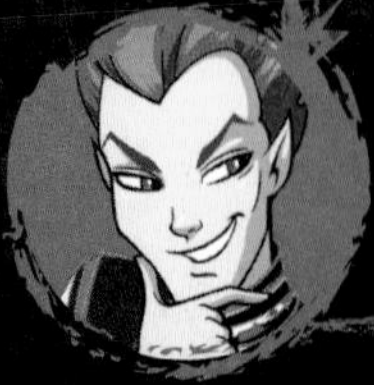

HEATH BURNS

MONSTER PARENTS: FIRE ELEMENTALS

AGE: 15

HEATH HAS A GOOD HEART, BUT HE TENDS TO CAUSE A LITTLE CHAOS WHEN THINGS HEAT UP!

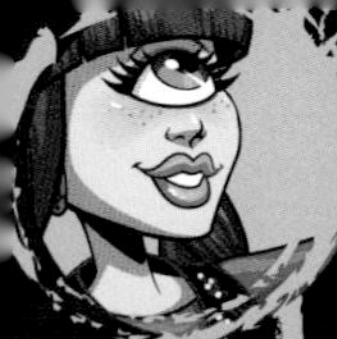

IRIS CLOPS

MONSTER PARENT: THE CYCLOPS

AGE: 15

IRIS IS A LITTLE BIT SHY AND A LITTLE BIT CLUMSY—PROBABLY DUE TO HER LACK OF DEPTH PERCEPTION! BUT SHE HAS A KEEN EYE FOR FASHION.

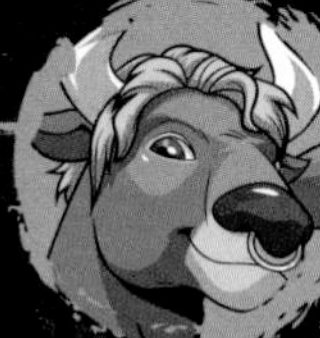

MANNY TAUR

MONSTER PARENT: THE MINOTAUR

AGE: 16

MANNY IS LARGER THAN YOUR AVERAGE MONSTER AND TENDS TO KNOCK THINGS OVER, WHICH EMBARRASSES HIM. BUT HE'S UP FOR ANY COMPETITION, WHETHER IT'S FOOTBALL, CASKETBALL, OR SKRM!

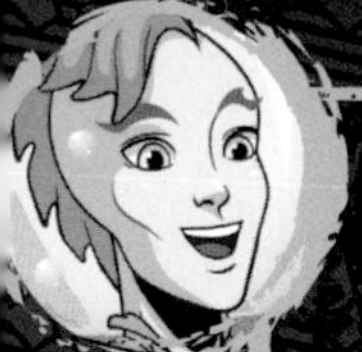

GILLINGTON "GIL" WEBBER

MONSTER PARENT: THE RIVER MONSTER

AGE: 16

GIL CAN'T HELP LOVING HIS SEA MONSTER GAL, LAGOONA, DESPITE HIS FEAR OF THE OCEAN. HIS HELMET KEEPS HIS HEAD HYDRATED WHEN HE'S NOT SWIMMING.

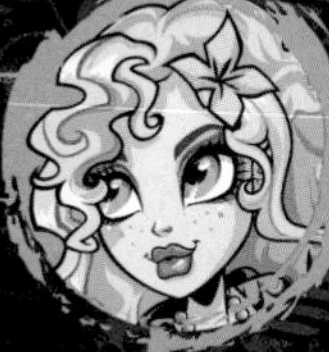

LAGOONA BLUE

MONSTER PARENT: THE SEA MONSTER

AGE: 15

LAGOONA'S LAID-BACK STYLE PLAYS WELL WITH HER LOVE OF SPORTS. SHE'D LOVE TO BE SWIMMING ALL THE TIME!

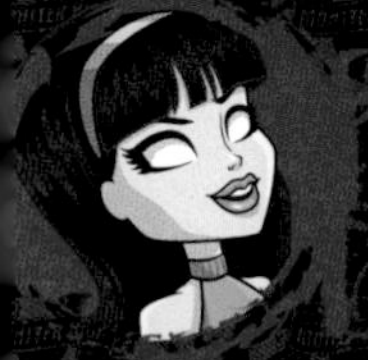

SCARAH SCREAMS

MONSTER PARENT: THE BEAN SÍ (BANSHEE)

AGE: 15

SCARAH CAN READ OTHER PEOPLE'S MINDS, BUT SHE TRIES TO BE POLITE ABOUT IT.

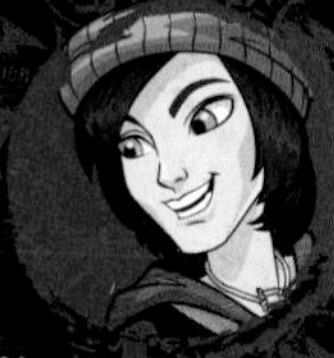

INVISI BILLY

MONSTER PARENT: THE INVISIBLE MAN

AGE: 15

BILLY CAN HIDE IN PLAIN SIGHT IF HE WANTS TO, WHICH COMES IN HANDY WHEN HE'S WORKING BACKSTAGE FOR MONSTER HIGH THEATER PRODUCTIONS!

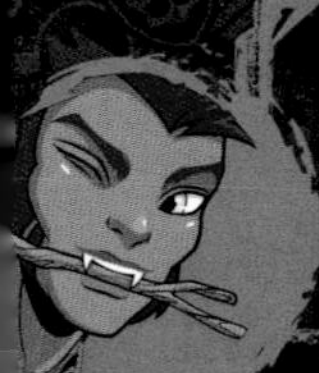

CLAWD WOLF

MONSTER PARENTS: THE WEREWOLVES

AGE: 17

CLAWD IS THE QUARTERBACK OF THE FOOTBALL TEAM AND THE CAPTAIN OF THE CASKETBALL TEAM, BUT HE'S NO DUMB JOCK. HE IS THE OLDER BROTHER OF CLAWDEEN AND HOWLEEN, AND HE'S DATING DRACULAURA.

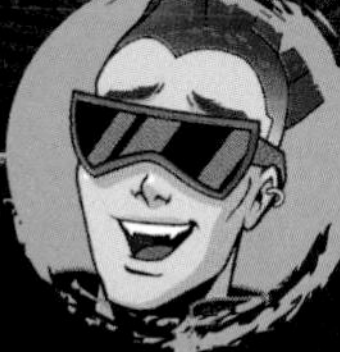

DEUCE GORGON

MONSTER PARENT: MEDUSA

AGE: 16

THIS CHILL CASKETBALL PLAYER LOVES TO COOK AND IS ONE-HALF OF THE POWER COUPLE ON CAMPUS WITH CLEO DE NILE.

IRIS and MANNY

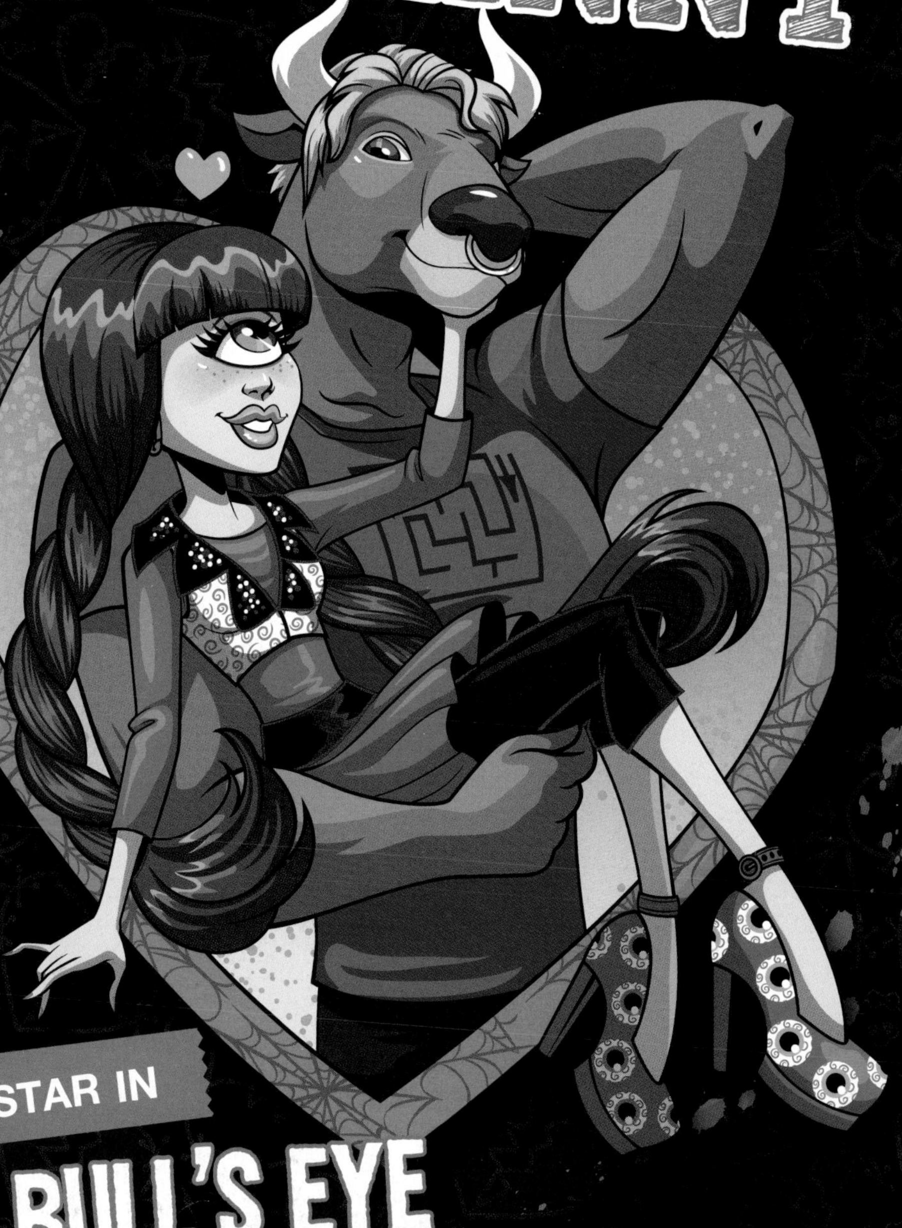

STAR IN

BULL'S EYE

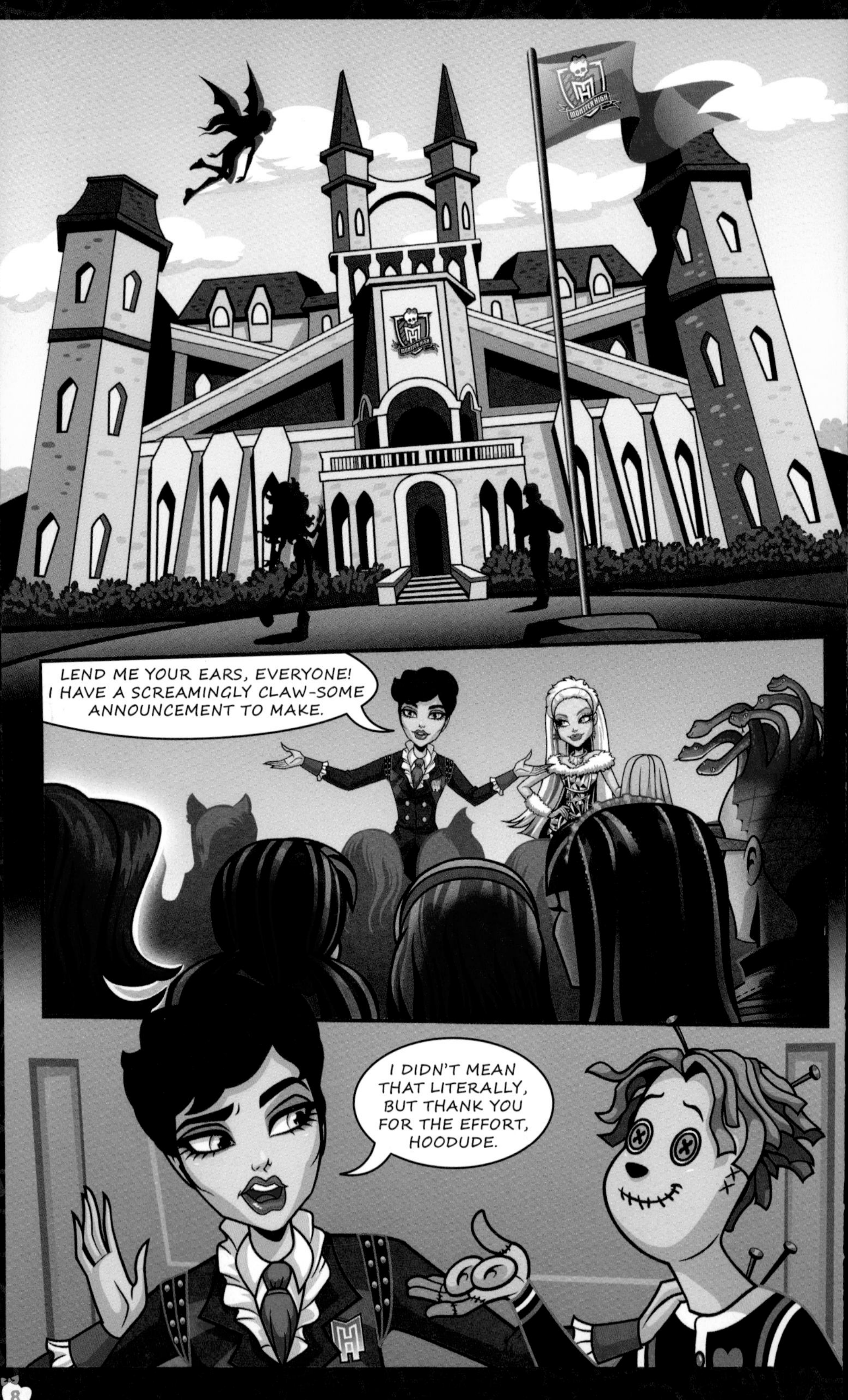
LEND ME YOUR EARS, EVERYONE! I HAVE A SCREAMINGLY CLAW-SOME ANNOUNCEMENT TO MAKE.
I DIDN'T MEAN THAT LITERALLY, BUT THANK YOU FOR THE EFFORT, HOODUDE.

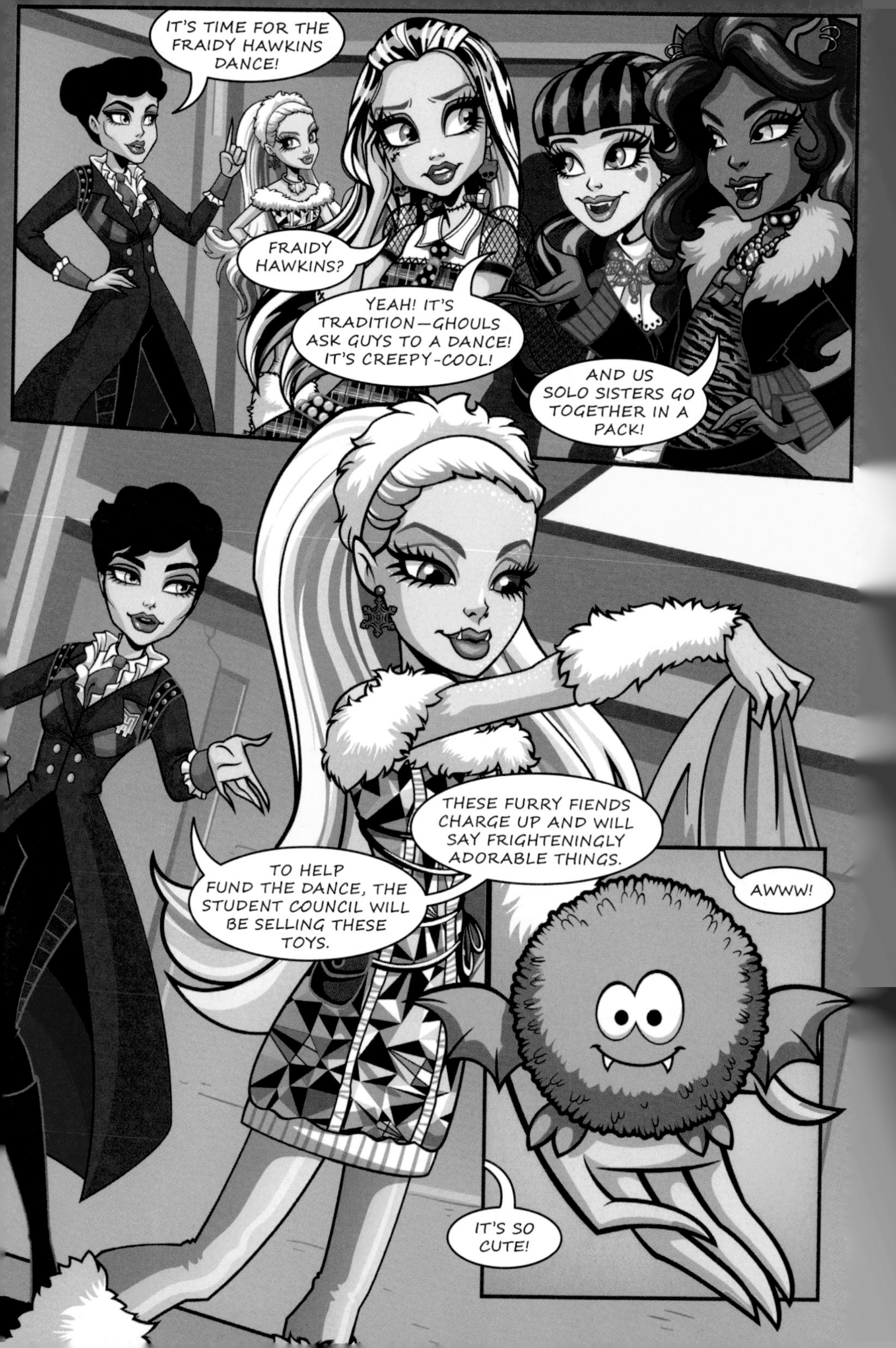
IT'S TIME FOR THE FRAIDY HAWKINS DANCE!
FRAIDY HAWKINS?
YEAH! IT'S TRADITION—GHOULS ASK GUYS TO A DANCE! IT'S CREEPY-COOL!
AND US SOLO SISTERS GO TOGETHER IN A PACK!
TO HELP FUND THE DANCE, THE STUDENT COUNCIL WILL BE SELLING THESE TOYS.
THESE FURRY FIENDS CHARGE UP AND WILL SAY FRIGHTENINGLY ADORABLE THINGS.
AWWW!
IT'S SO CUTE!

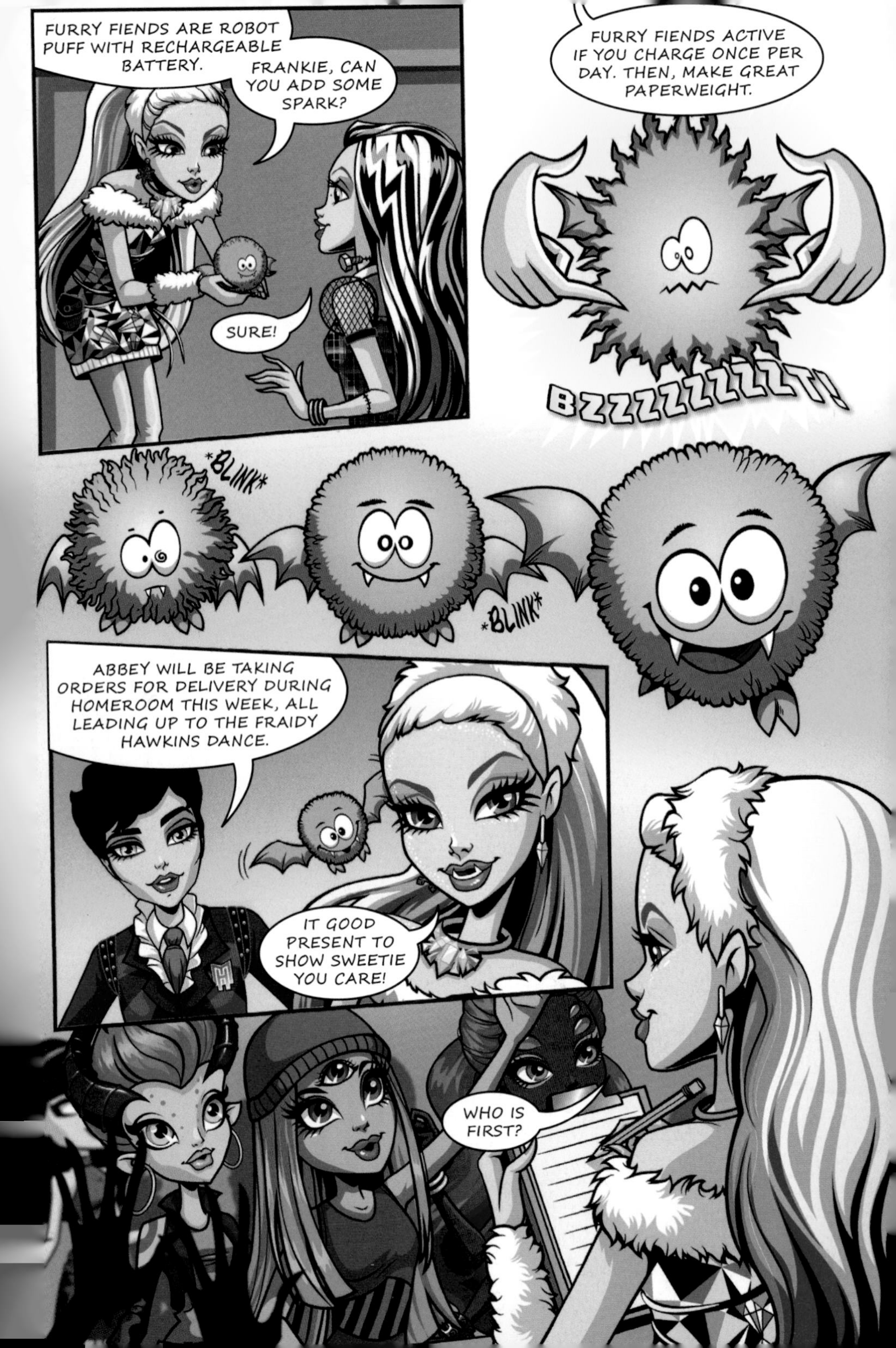
FURRY FIENDS ARE ROBOT PUFF WITH RECHARGEABLE BATTERY.
FRANKIE, CAN YOU ADD SOME SPARK?
SURE!
FURRY FIENDS ACTIVE IF YOU CHARGE ONCE PER DAY. THEN, MAKE GREAT PAPERWEIGHT.
BZZZZZZZZT!
BLINK
BLINK
ABBEY WILL BE TAKING ORDERS FOR DELIVERY DURING HOMEROOM THIS WEEK, ALL LEADING UP TO THE FRAIDY HAWKINS DANCE.
IT GOOD PRESENT TO SHOW SWEETIE YOU CARE!
WHO IS FIRST?

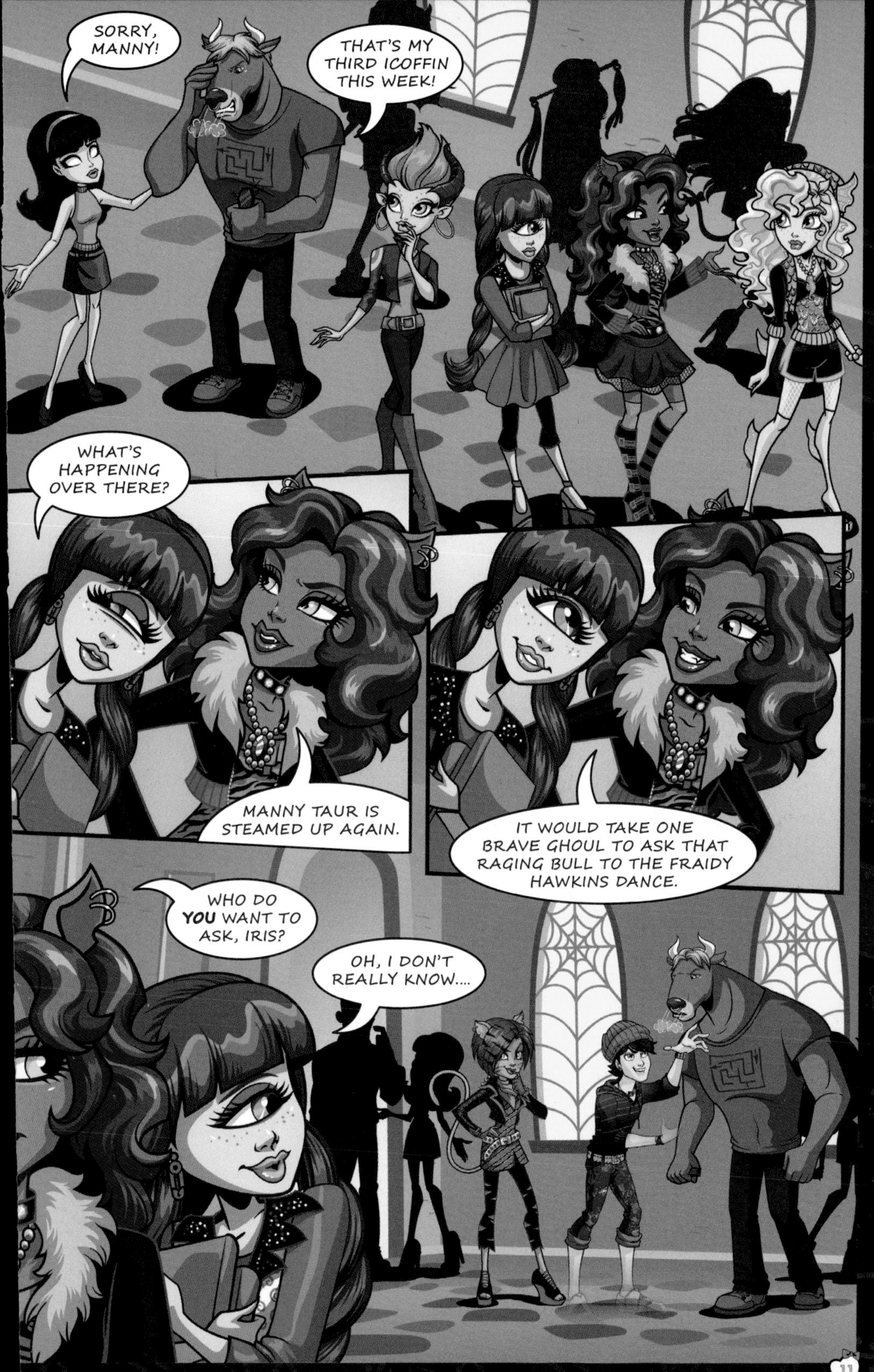
SORRY, MANNY!
THAT'S MY THIRD ICOFFIN THIS WEEK!
WHAT'S HAPPENING OVER THERE?
MANNY TAUR IS STEAMED UP AGAIN.
IT WOULD TAKE ONE BRAVE GHOUL TO ASK THAT RAGING BULL TO THE FRAIDY HAWKINS DANCE.
WHO DO **YOU** WANT TO ASK, IRIS?
OH, I DON'T REALLY KNOW....

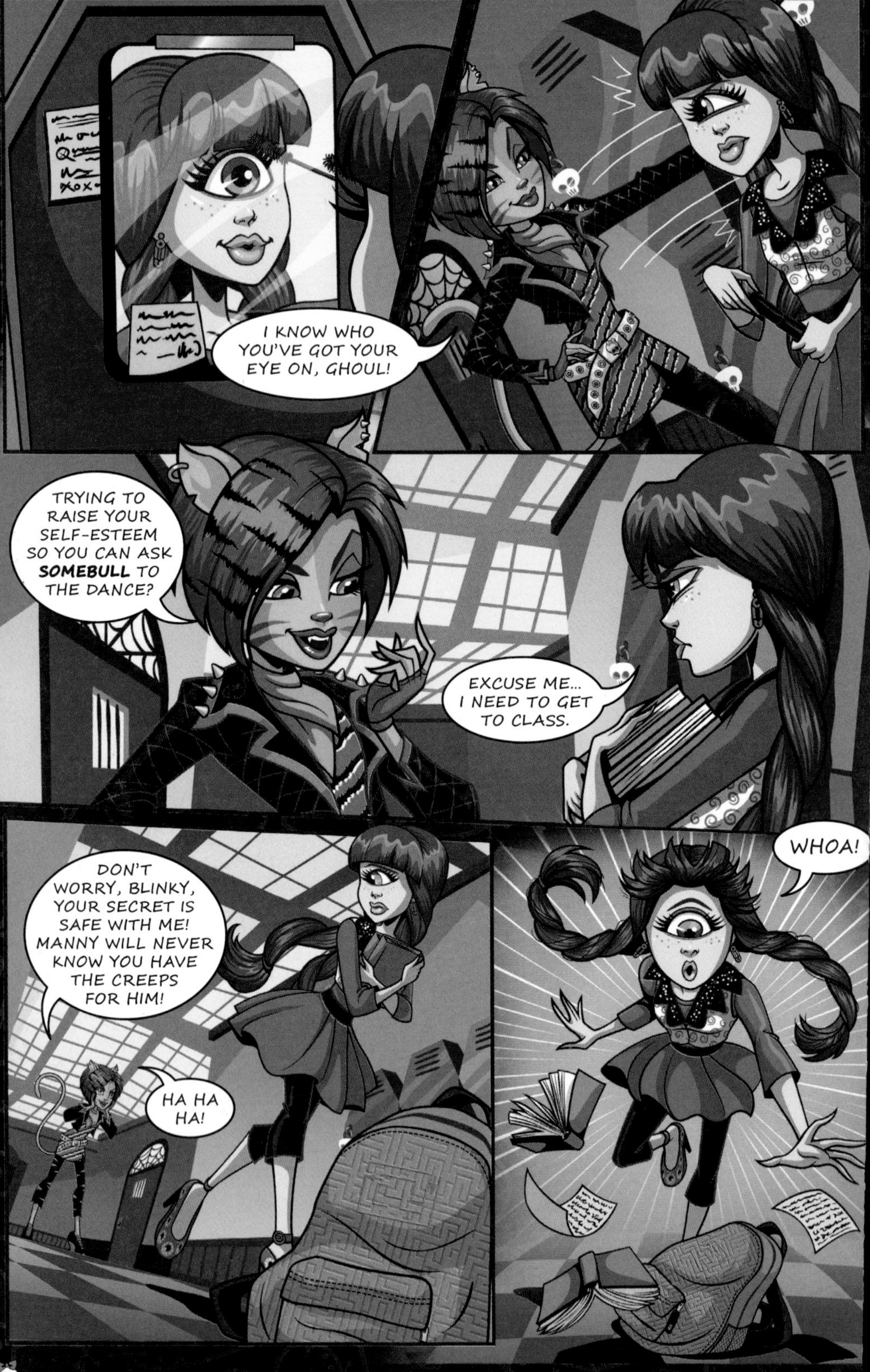
I KNOW WHO YOU'VE GOT YOUR EYE ON, GHOUL!
TRYING TO RAISE YOUR SELF-ESTEEM SO YOU CAN ASK **SOMEBULL** TO THE DANCE?
EXCUSE ME... I NEED TO GET TO CLASS.
DON'T WORRY, BLINKY, YOUR SECRET IS SAFE WITH ME! MANNY WILL NEVER KNOW YOU HAVE THE CREEPS FOR HIM!
HA HA HA!
WHOA!

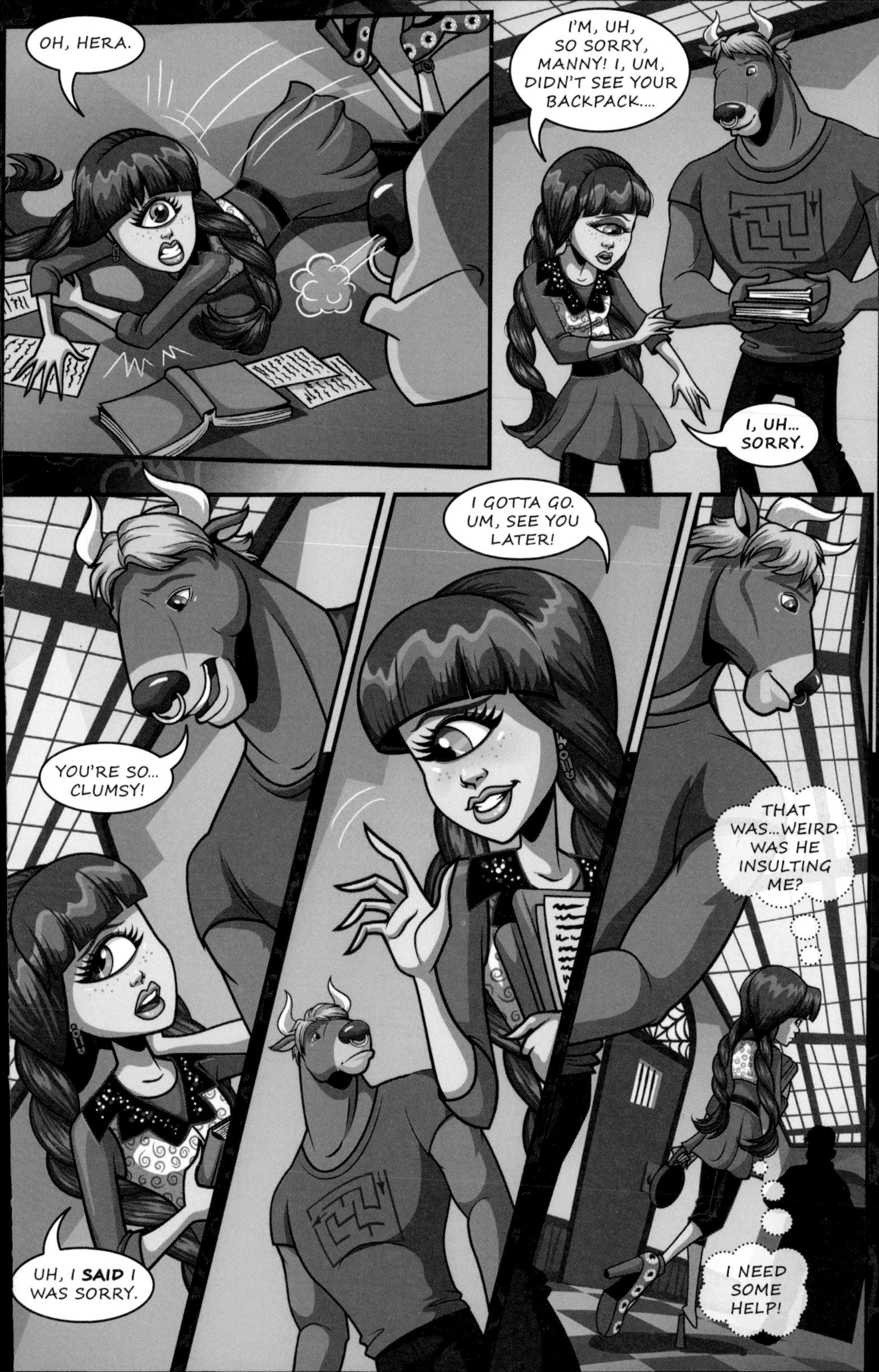
OH, HERA.
I'M, UH, SO SORRY, MANNY! I, UM, DIDN'T SEE YOUR BACKPACK....
I, UH... SORRY.
YOU'RE SO... CLUMSY!
UH, I **SAID** I WAS SORRY.
I GOTTA GO. UM, SEE YOU LATER!
THAT WAS...WEIRD. WAS HE INSULTING ME?
I NEED SOME HELP!

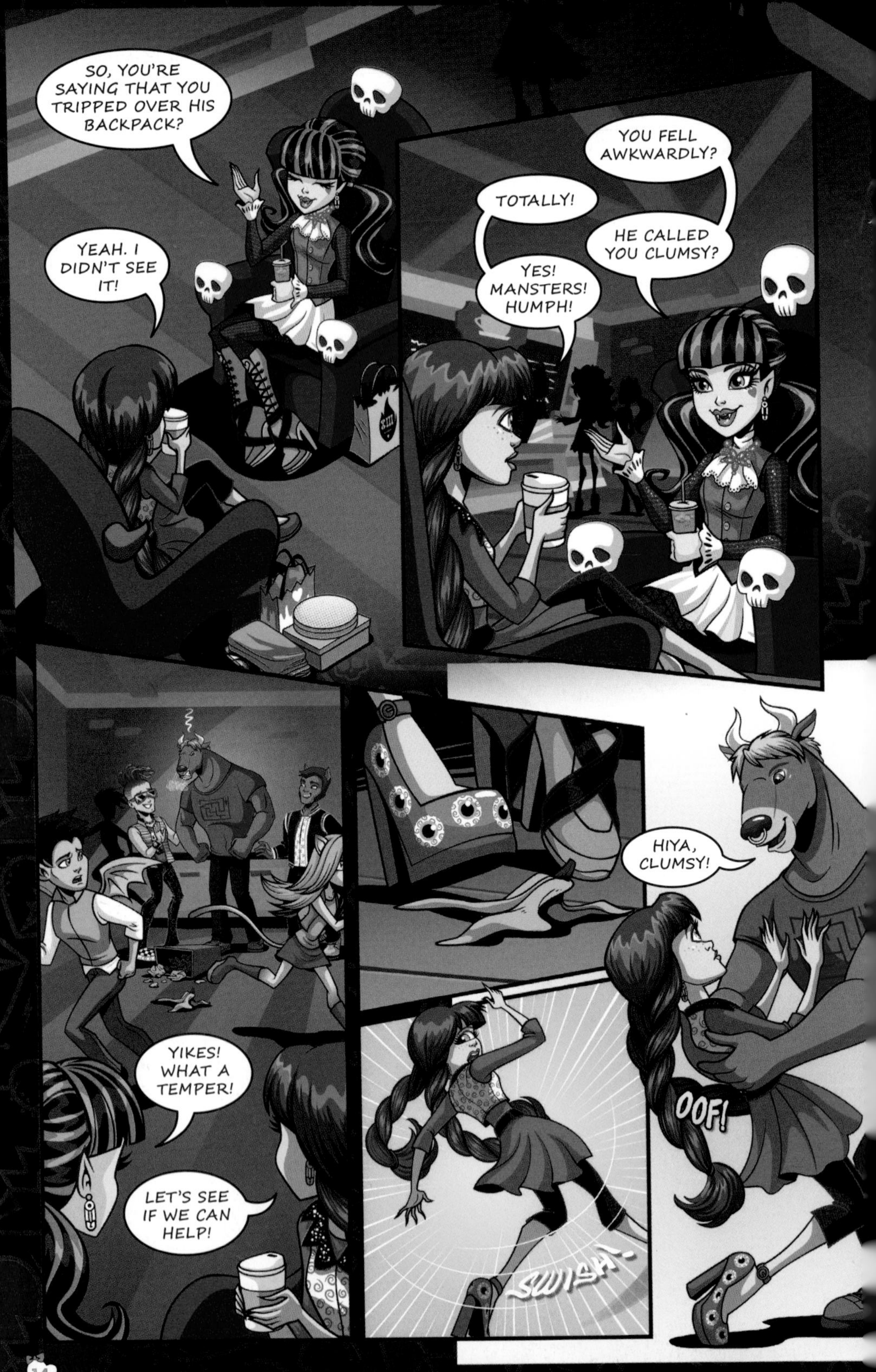
SO, YOU'RE SAYING THAT YOU TRIPPED OVER HIS BACKPACK?
YEAH. I DIDN'T SEE IT!
YOU FELL AWKWARDLY?
TOTALLY!
HE CALLED YOU CLUMSY?
YES! MANSTERS! HUMPH!
HIYA, CLUMSY!
OOF!
SWISH!
YIKES! WHAT A TEMPER!
LET'S SEE IF WE CAN HELP!

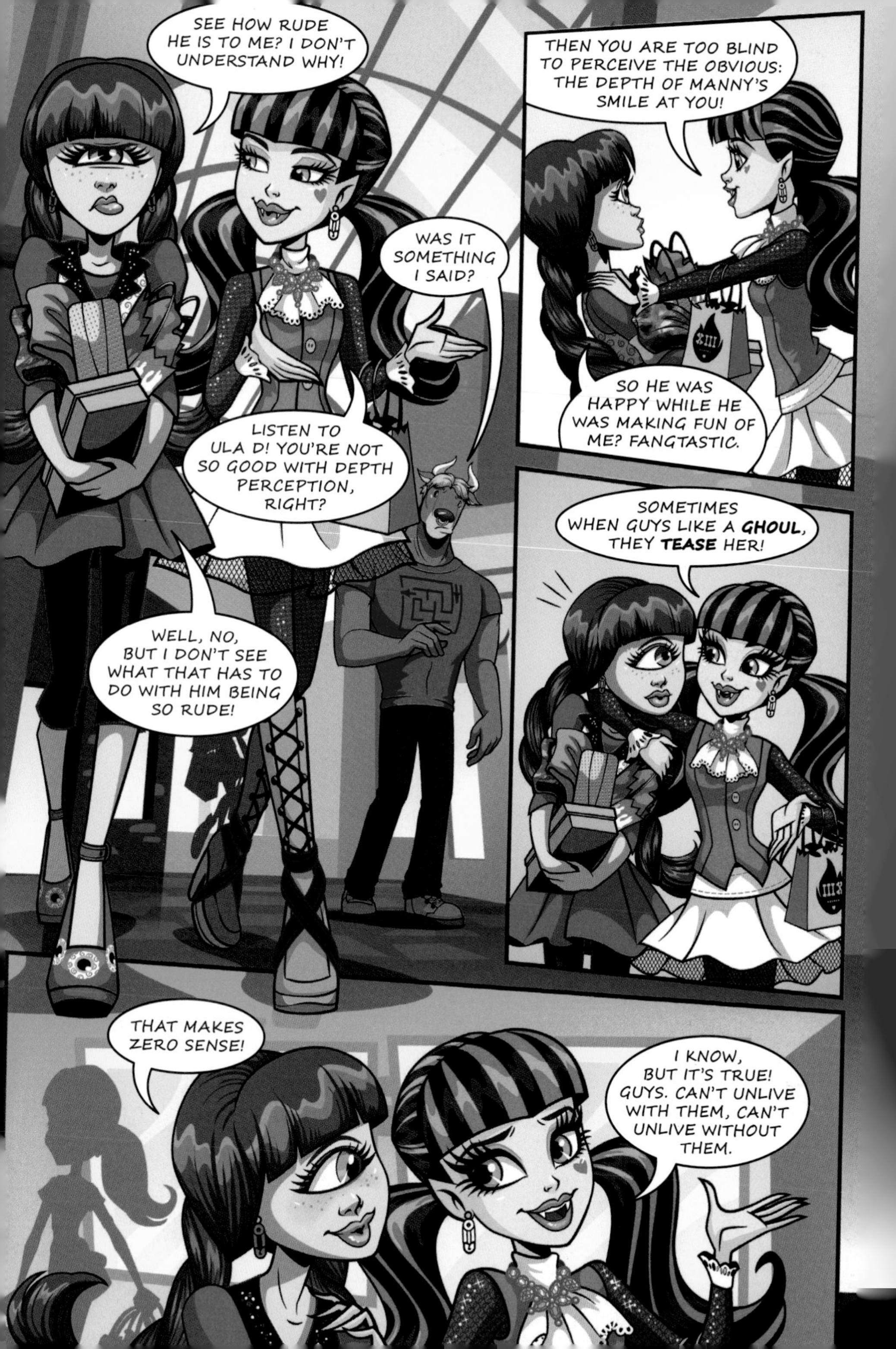
SEE HOW RUDE HE IS TO ME? I DON'T UNDERSTAND WHY!
WAS IT SOMETHING I SAID?
LISTEN TO ULA D! YOU'RE NOT SO GOOD WITH DEPTH PERCEPTION, RIGHT?
WELL, NO, BUT I DON'T SEE WHAT THAT HAS TO DO WITH HIM BEING SO RUDE!
THEN YOU ARE TOO BLIND TO PERCEIVE THE OBVIOUS: THE DEPTH OF MANNY'S SMILE AT YOU!
SO HE WAS HAPPY WHILE HE WAS MAKING FUN OF ME? FANGTASTIC.
SOMETIMES WHEN GUYS LIKE A **GHOUL**, THEY **TEASE** HER!
THAT MAKES ZERO SENSE!
I KNOW, BUT IT'S TRUE! GUYS. CAN'T UNLIVE WITH THEM, CAN'T UNLIVE WITHOUT THEM.

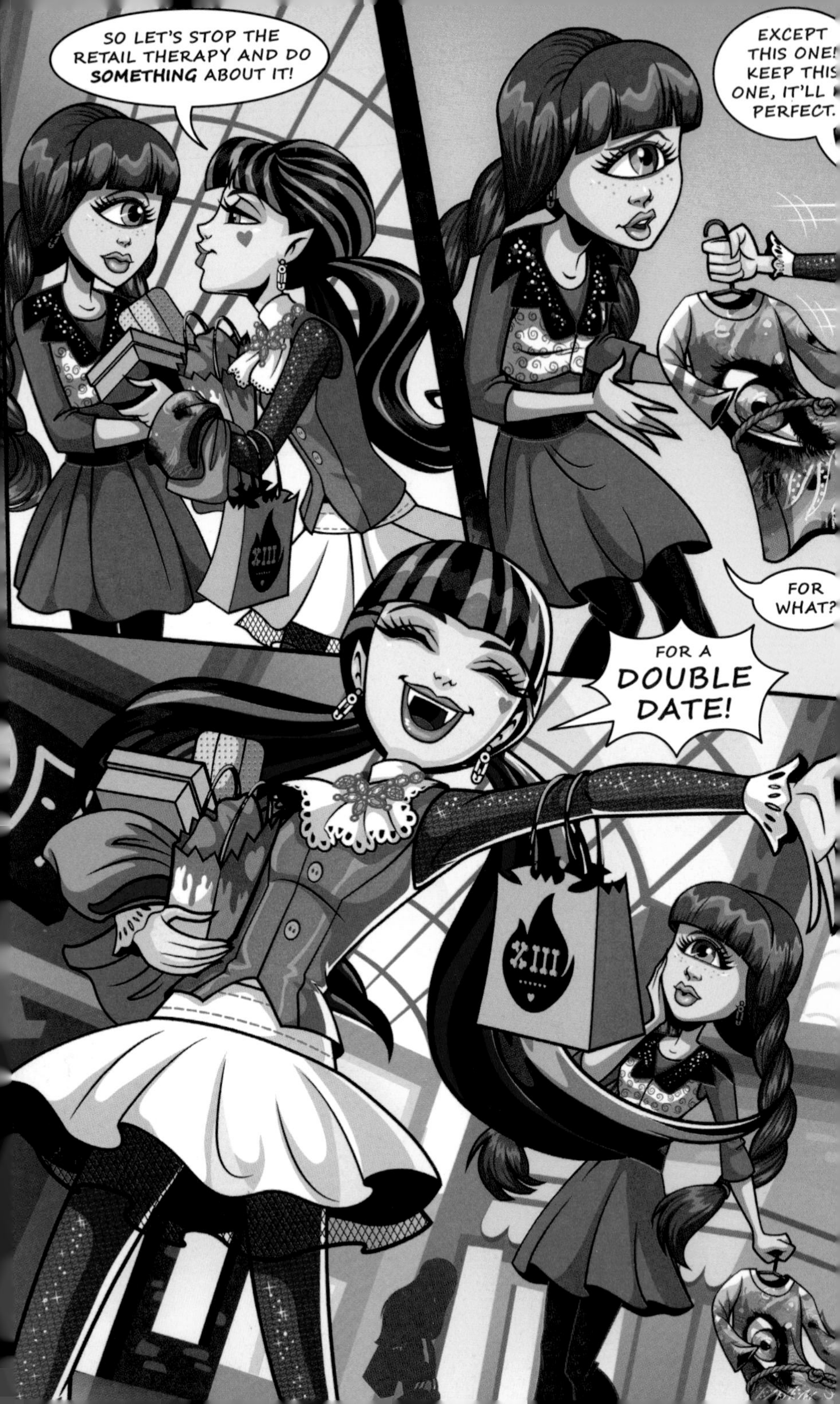
SO LET'S STOP THE RETAIL THERAPY AND DO **SOMETHING** ABOUT IT!
EXCEPT THIS ONE! KEEP THIS ONE, IT'LL PERFECT.
FOR WHAT?
FOR A DOUBLE DATE!

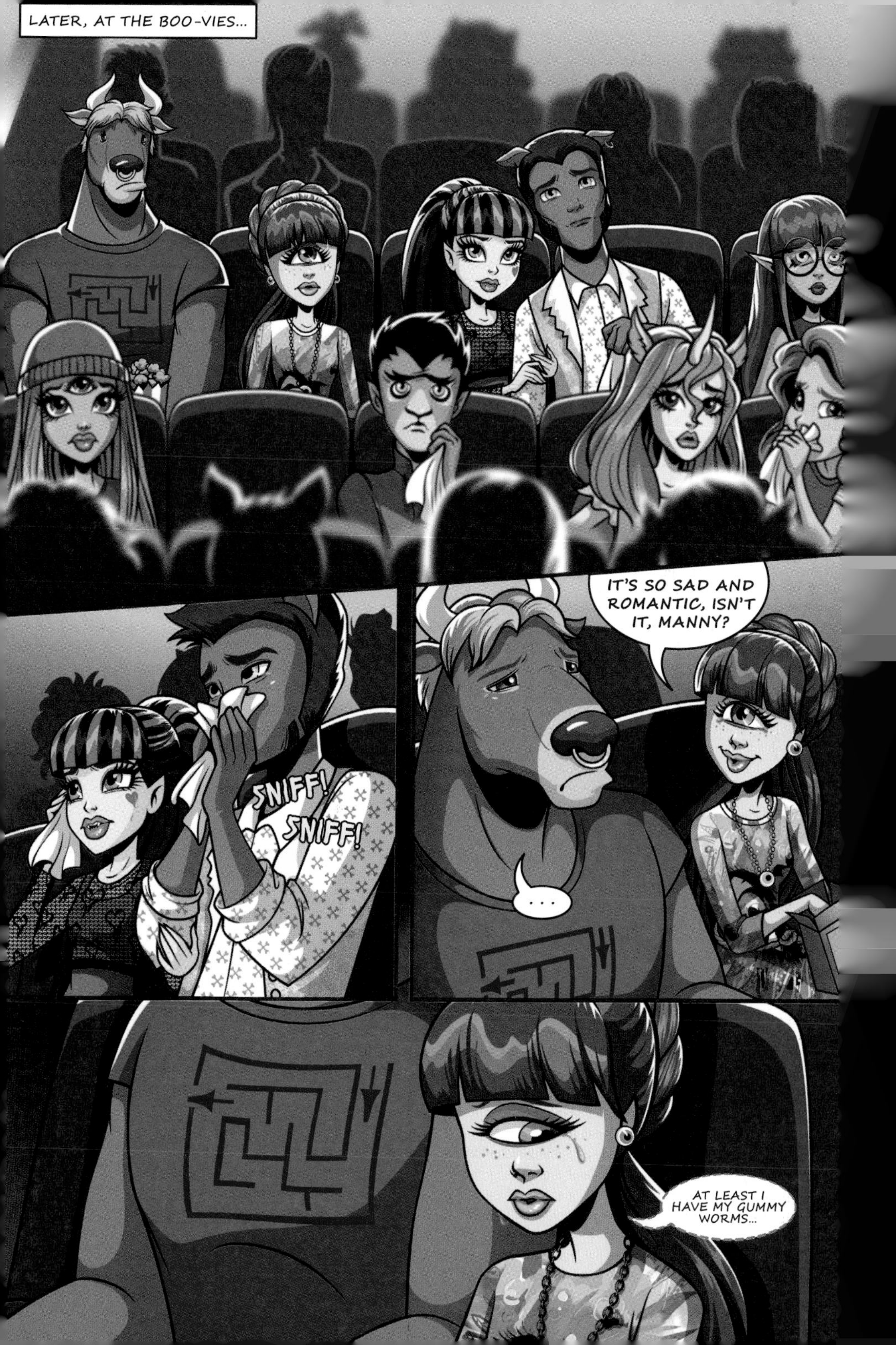
LATER, AT THE BOO-VIES...
SNIFF!
SNIFF!
IT'S SO SAD AND ROMANTIC, ISN'T IT, MANNY?
...
AT LEAST I HAVE MY GUMMY WORMS...

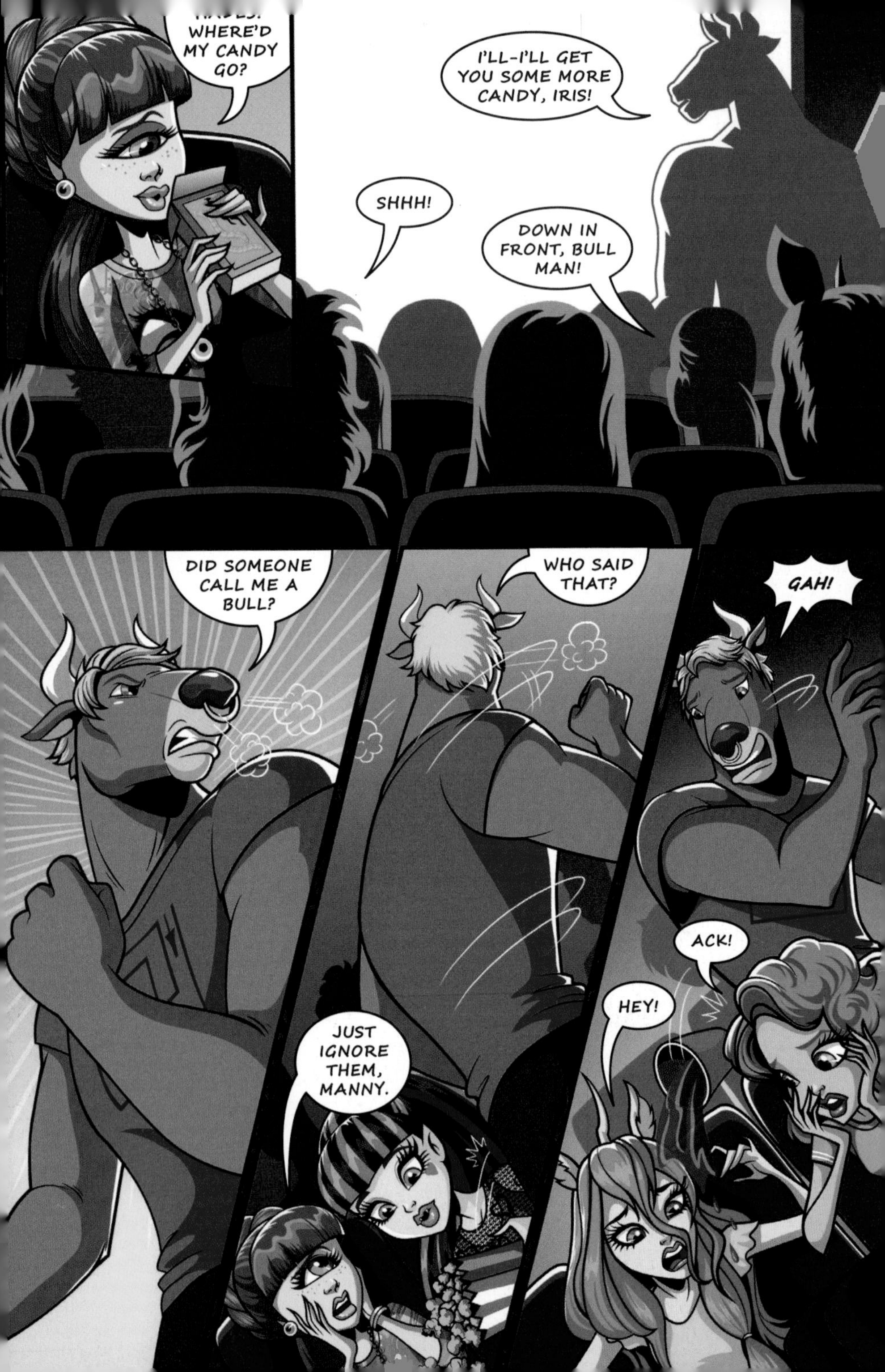
WHERE'D MY CANDY GO?
I'LL-I'LL GET YOU SOME MORE CANDY, IRIS!
SHHH!
DOWN IN FRONT, BULL MAN!
DID SOMEONE CALL ME A BULL?
WHO SAID THAT?
JUST IGNORE THEM, MANNY.
GAH!
ACK!
HEY!

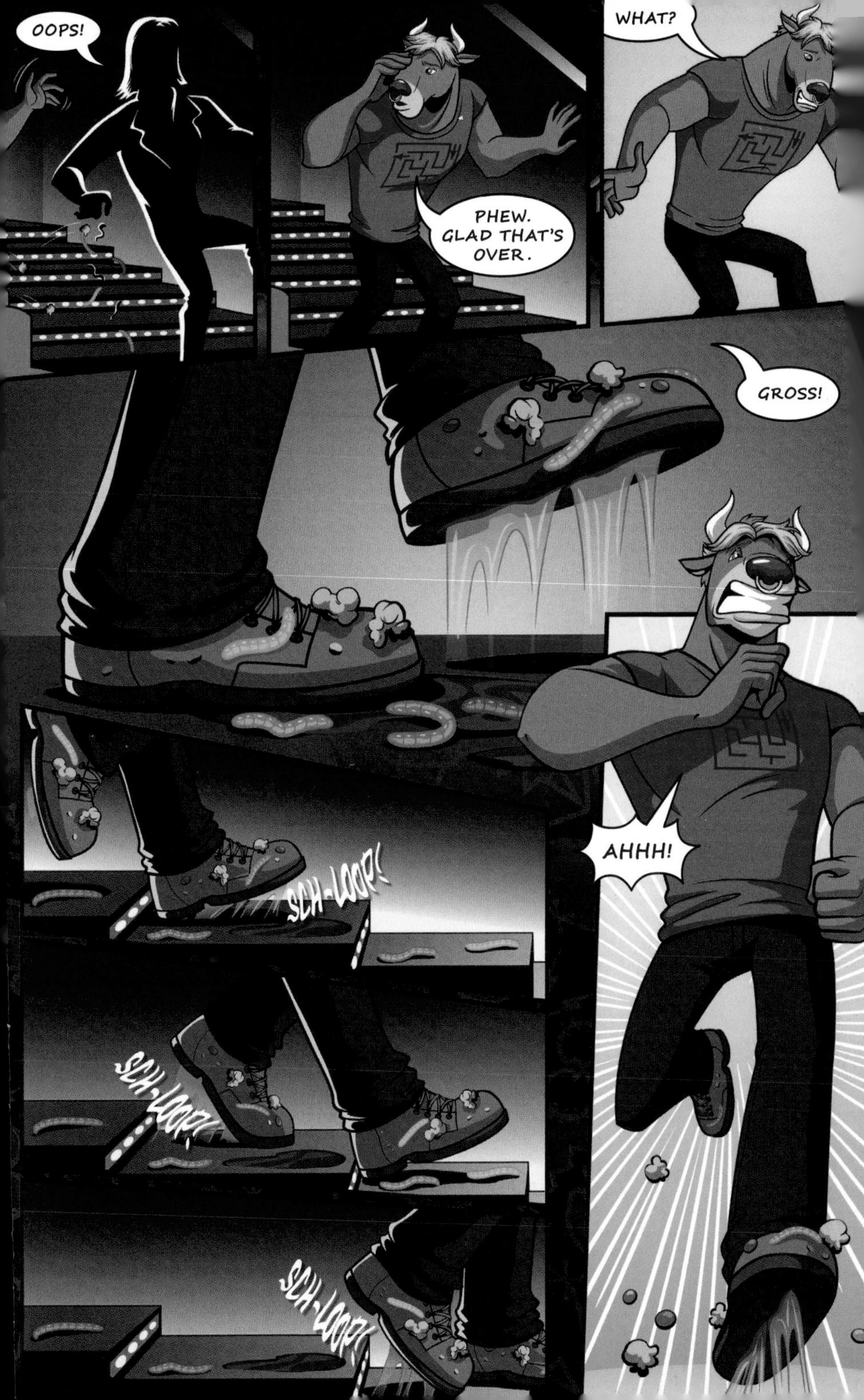
OOPS!
PHEW. GLAD THAT'S OVER.
WHAT?
GROSS!
SCH-LOOP!
SCH-LOOP!
SCH-LOOP!
AHHH!

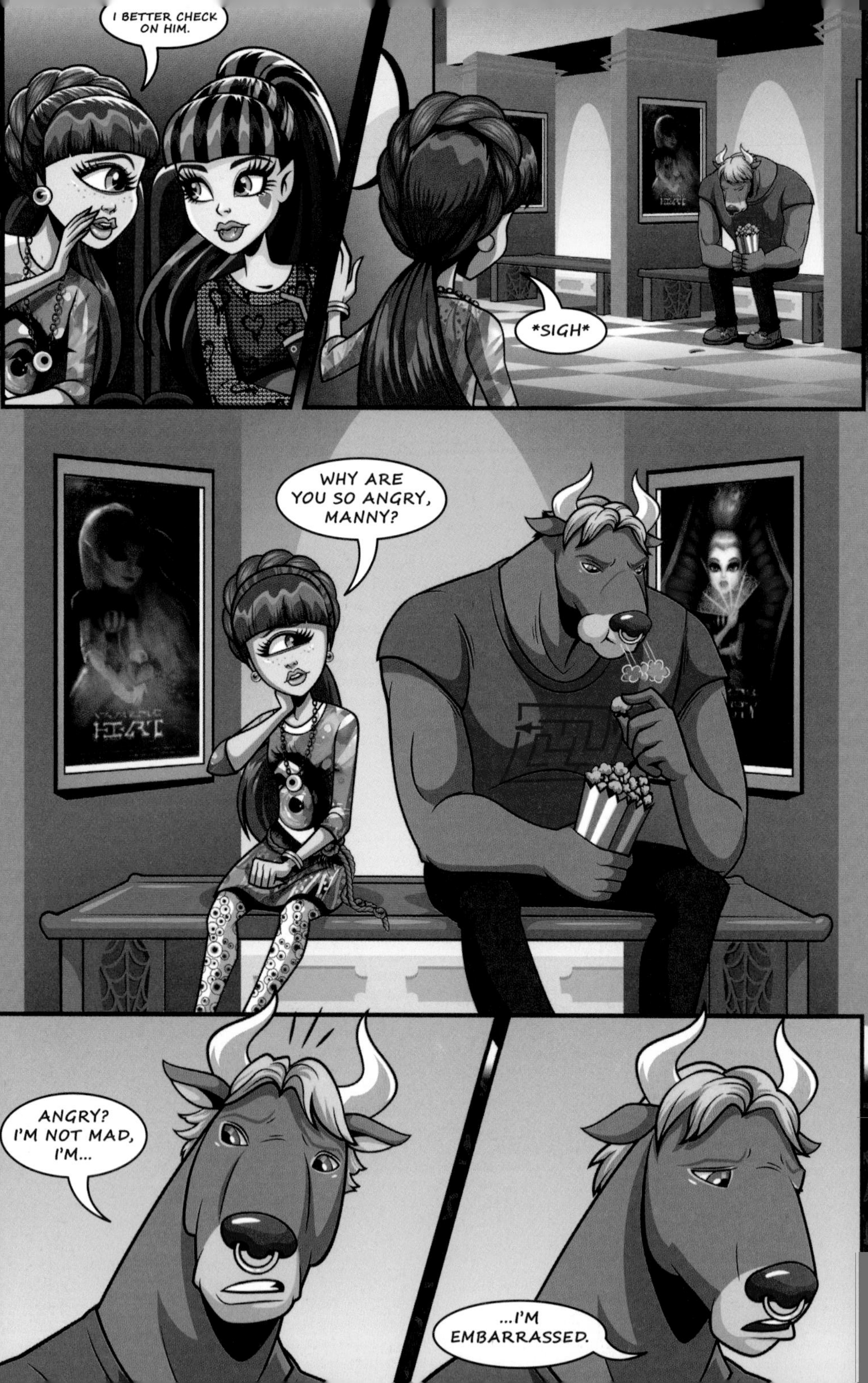
I BETTER CHECK ON HIM.
SIGH
WHY ARE YOU SO ANGRY, MANNY?
ANGRY? I'M NOT MAD, I'M...
...I'M EMBARRASSED.

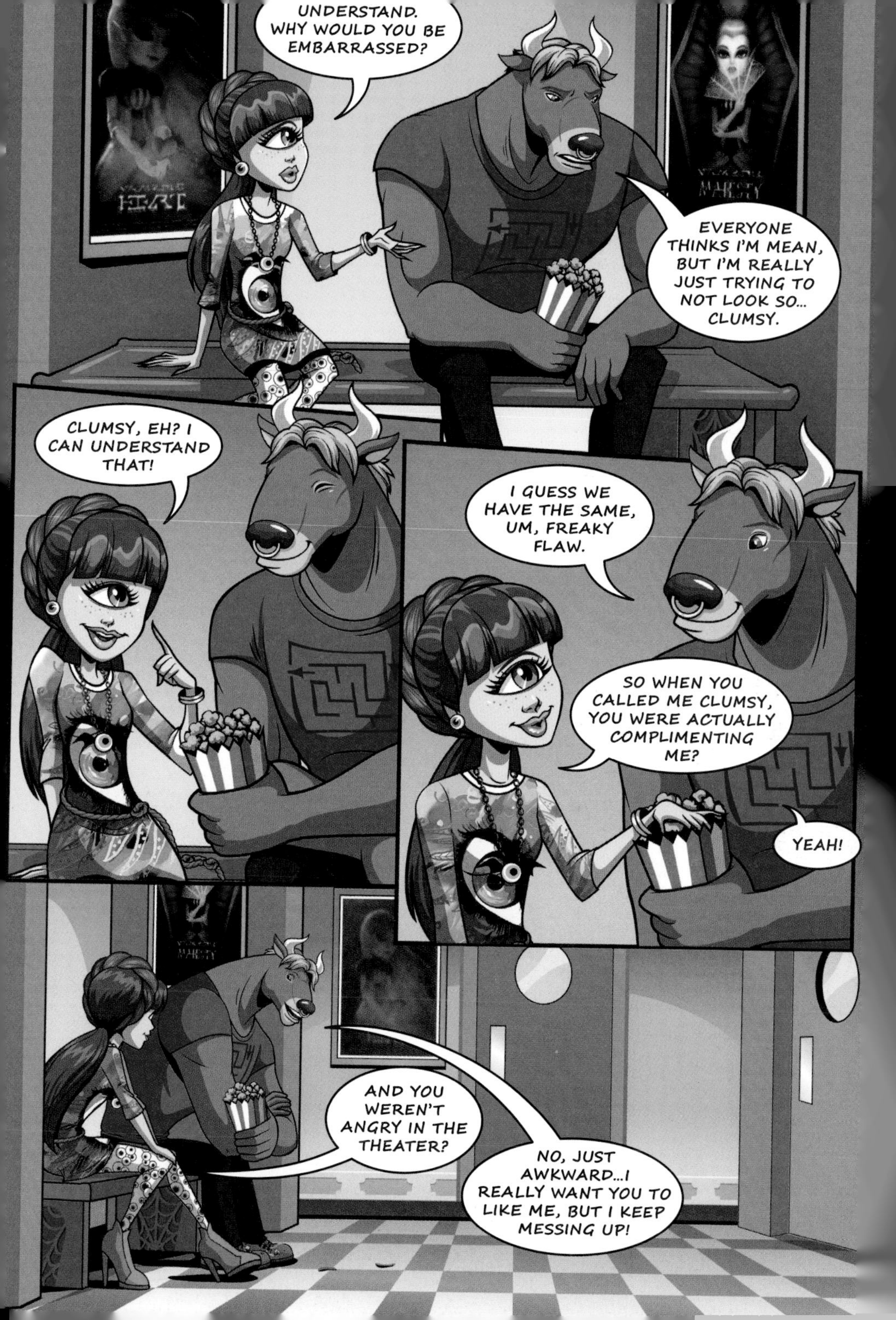
UNDERSTAND. WHY WOULD YOU BE EMBARRASSED?
EVERYONE THINKS I'M MEAN, BUT I'M REALLY JUST TRYING TO NOT LOOK SO... CLUMSY.
CLUMSY, EH? I CAN UNDERSTAND THAT!
I GUESS WE HAVE THE SAME, UM, FREAKY FLAW.
SO WHEN YOU CALLED ME CLUMSY, YOU WERE ACTUALLY COMPLIMENTING ME?
YEAH!
AND YOU WEREN'T ANGRY IN THE THEATER?
NO, JUST AWKWARD...I REALLY WANT YOU TO LIKE ME, BUT I KEEP MESSING UP!

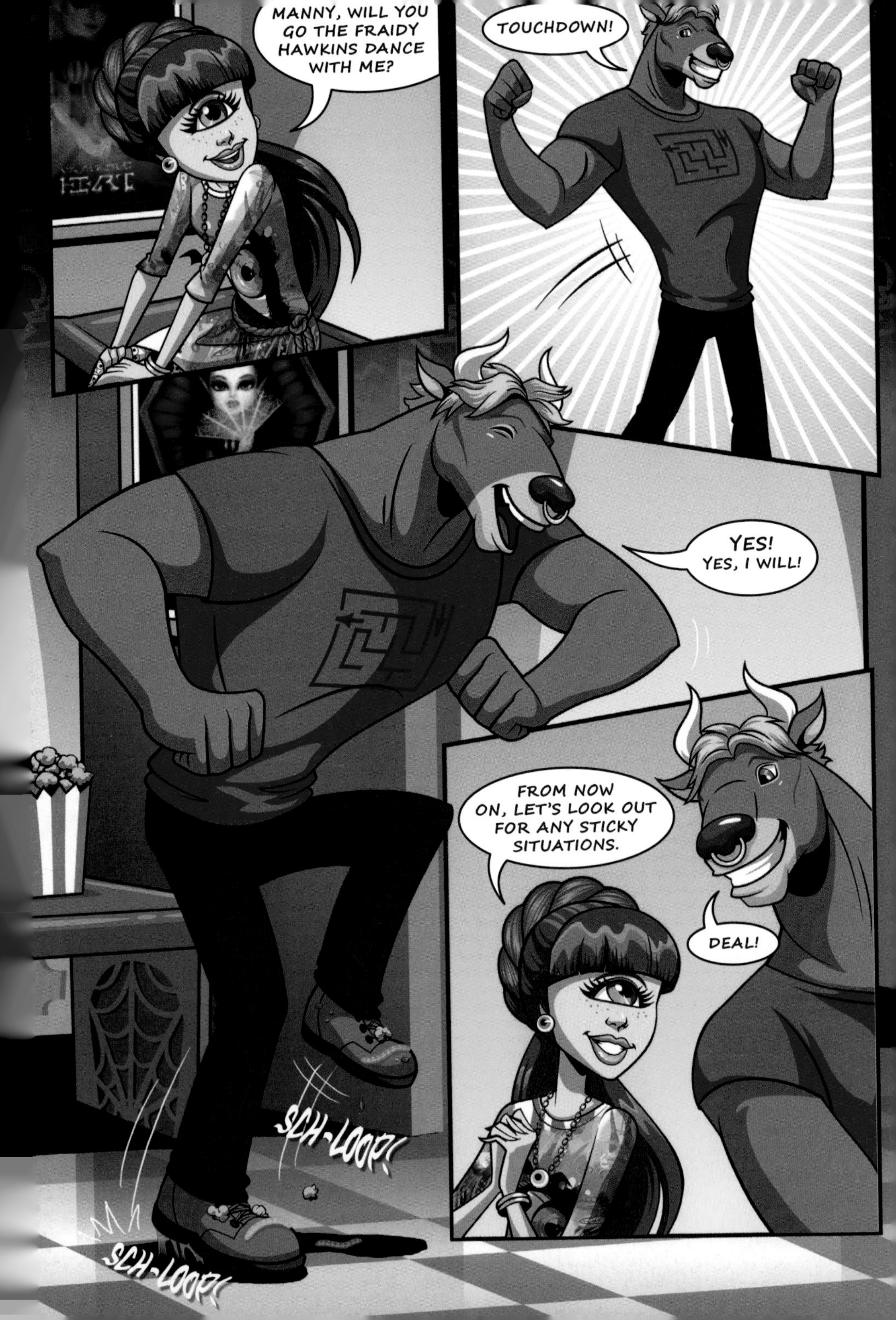
MANNY, WILL YOU GO THE FRAIDY HAWKINS DANCE WITH ME?
TOUCHDOWN!
YES! YES, I WILL!
SCH-LOOP!
SCH-LOOP!
FROM NOW ON, LET'S LOOK OUT FOR ANY STICKY SITUATIONS.
DEAL!

LAGOONA and GIL

STAR IN

LOCKETNESS MONSTER

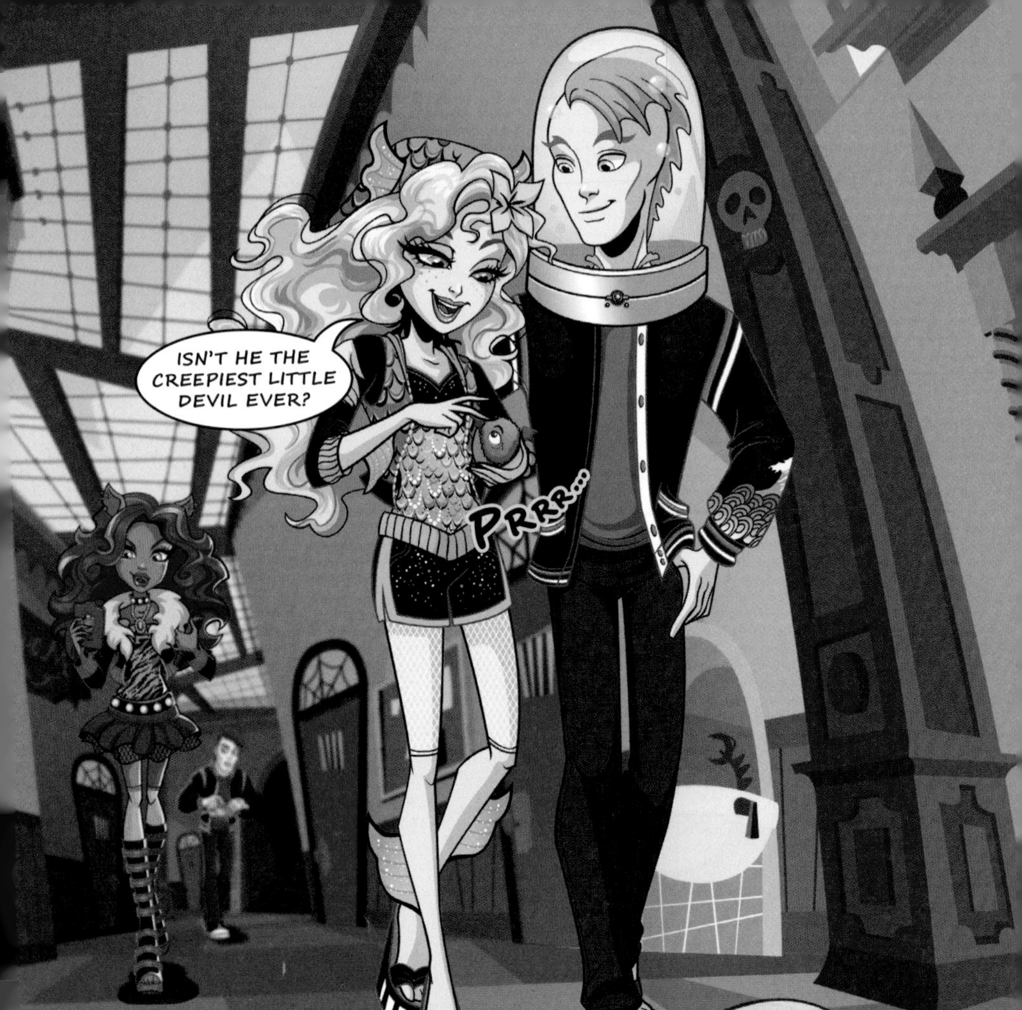
ISN'T HE THE CREEPIEST LITTLE DEVIL EVER?
PRRR...

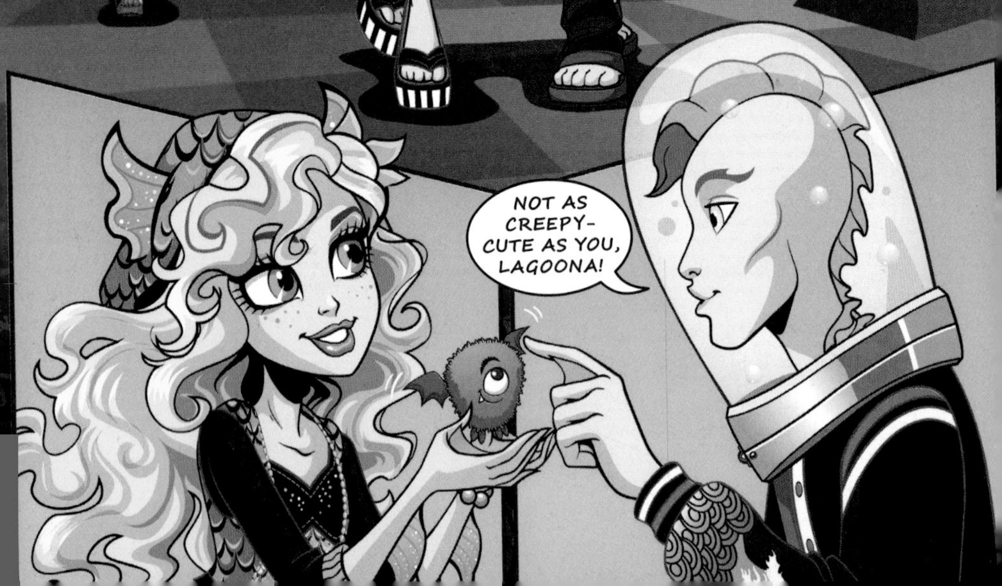
NOT AS CREEPY-CUTE AS YOU, LAGOONA!

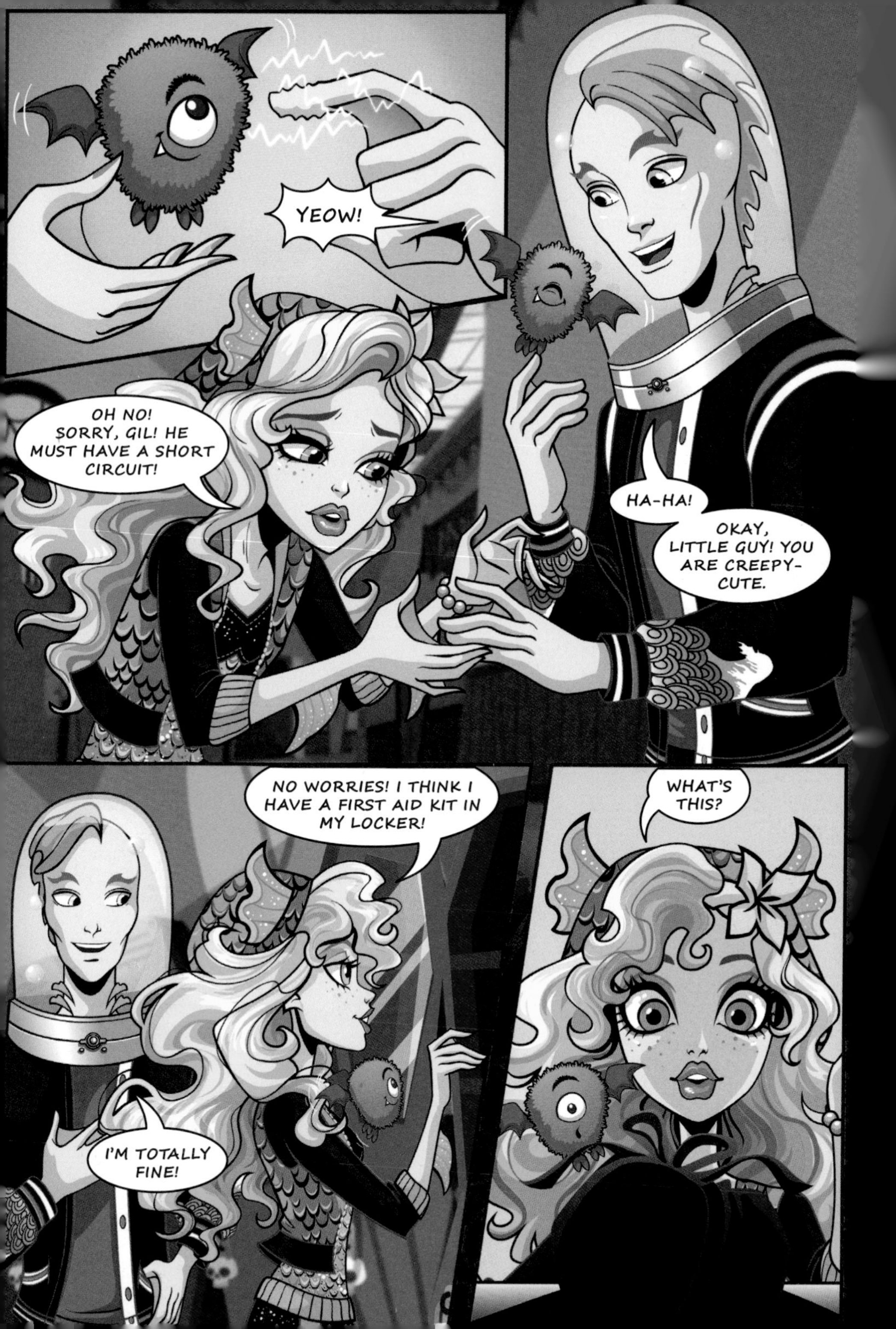
YEOW!
OH NO! SORRY, GIL! HE MUST HAVE A SHORT CIRCUIT!
HA-HA!
OKAY, LITTLE GUY! YOU ARE CREEPY-CUTE.
NO WORRIES! I THINK I HAVE A FIRST AID KIT IN MY LOCKER!
I'M TOTALLY FINE!
WHAT'S THIS?

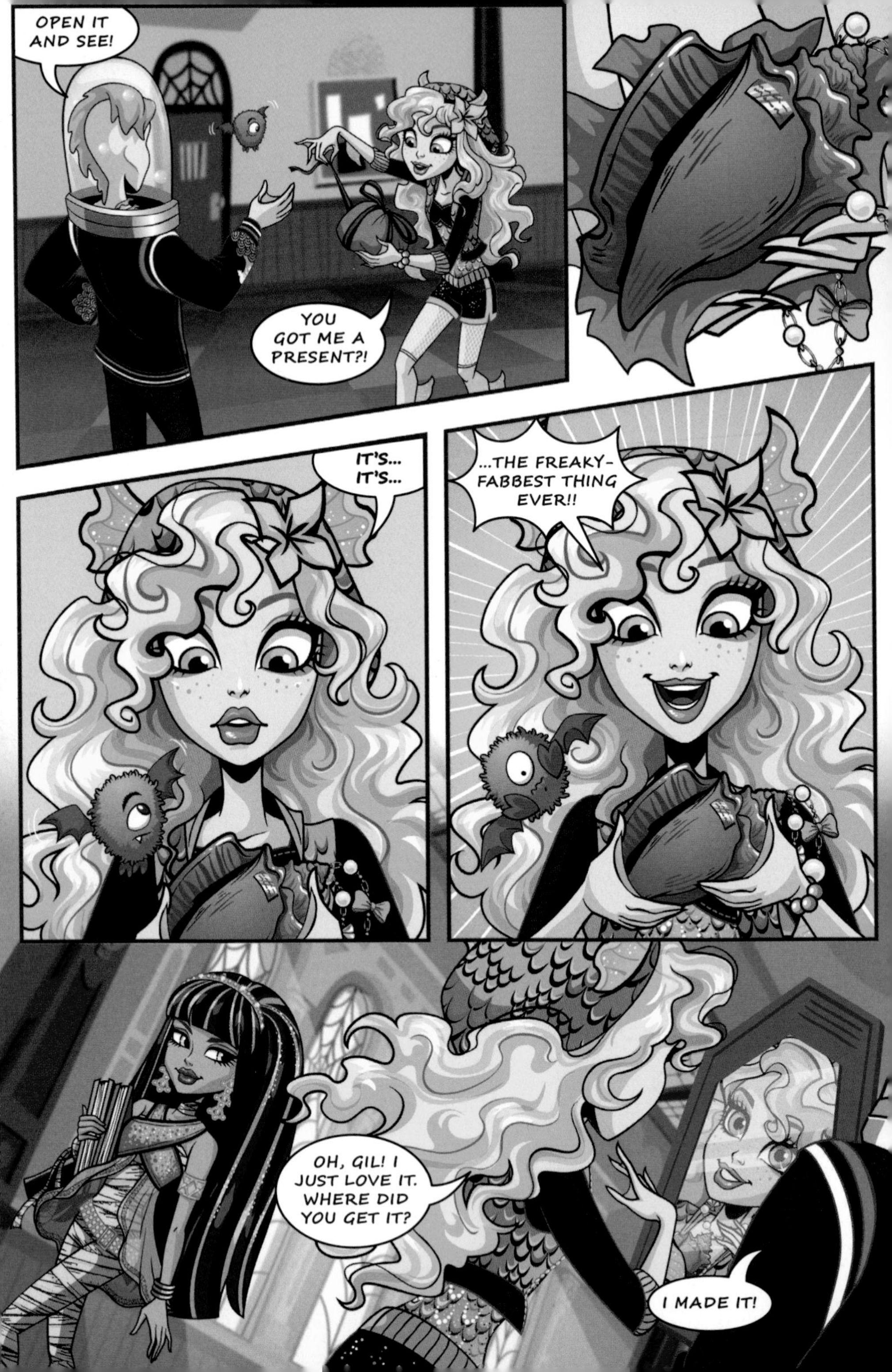
OPEN IT AND SEE!
YOU GOT ME A PRESENT?!
IT'S... IT'S...
...THE FREAKY-FABBEST THING EVER!!
OH, GIL! I JUST LOVE IT. WHERE DID YOU GET IT?
I MADE IT!

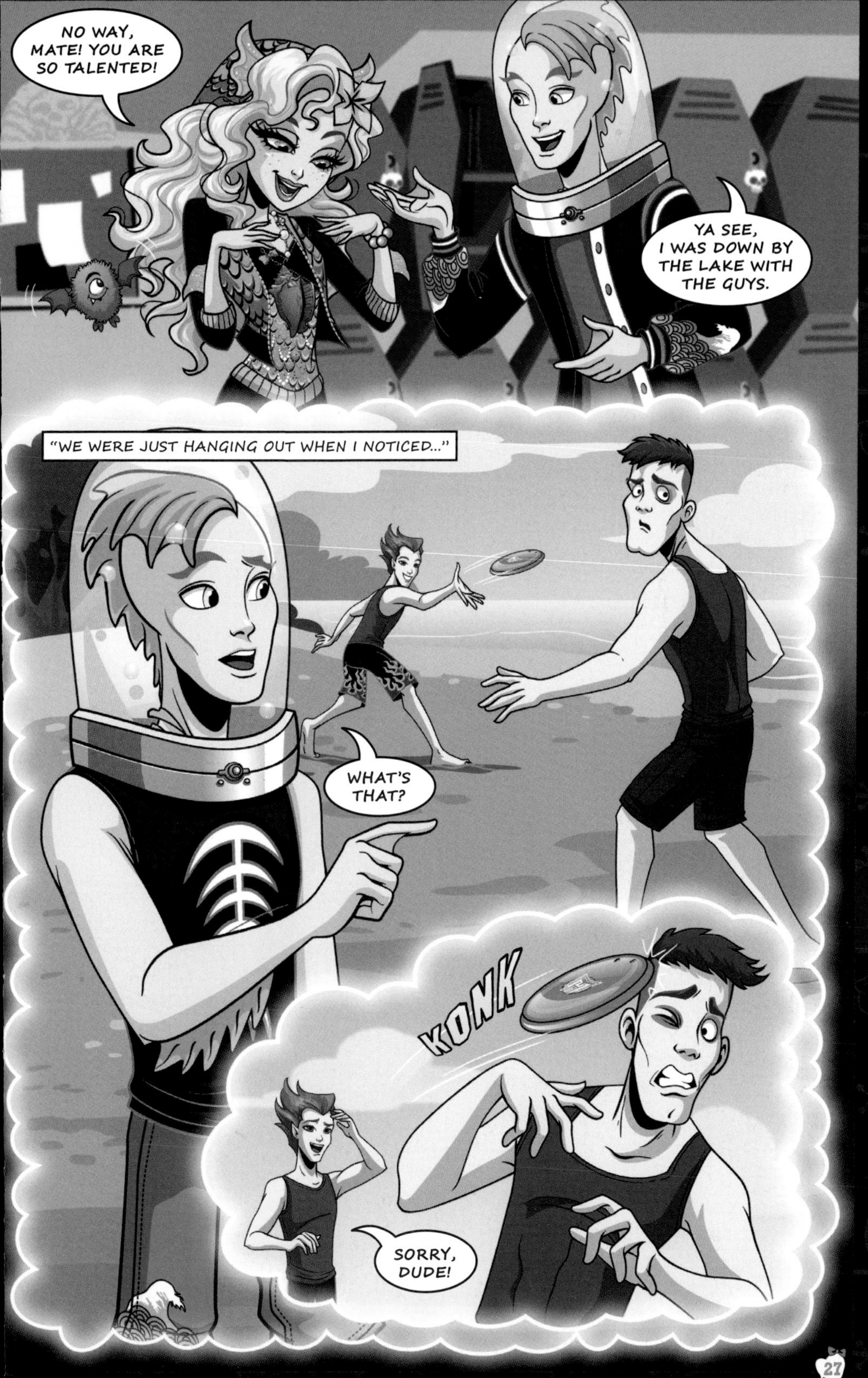
NO WAY, MATE! YOU ARE SO TALENTED!
YA SEE, I WAS DOWN BY THE LAKE WITH THE GUYS.
"WE WERE JUST HANGING OUT WHEN I NOTICED..."
WHAT'S THAT?
KONK
SORRY, DUDE!

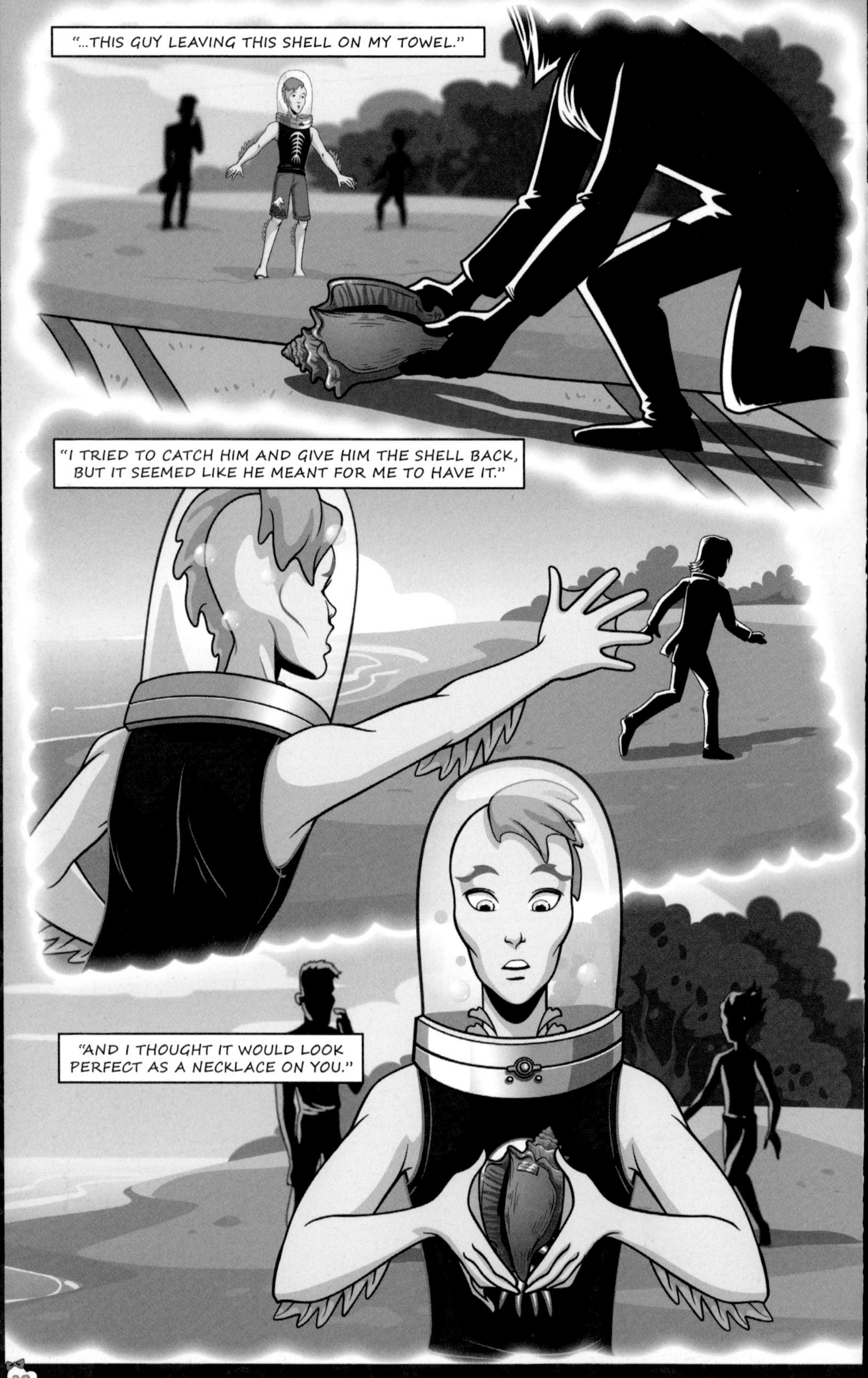
"...THIS GUY LEAVING THIS SHELL ON MY TOWEL."
"I TRIED TO CATCH HIM AND GIVE HIM THE SHELL BACK, BUT IT SEEMED LIKE HE MEANT FOR ME TO HAVE IT."
"AND I THOUGHT IT WOULD LOOK PERFECT AS A NECKLACE ON YOU."

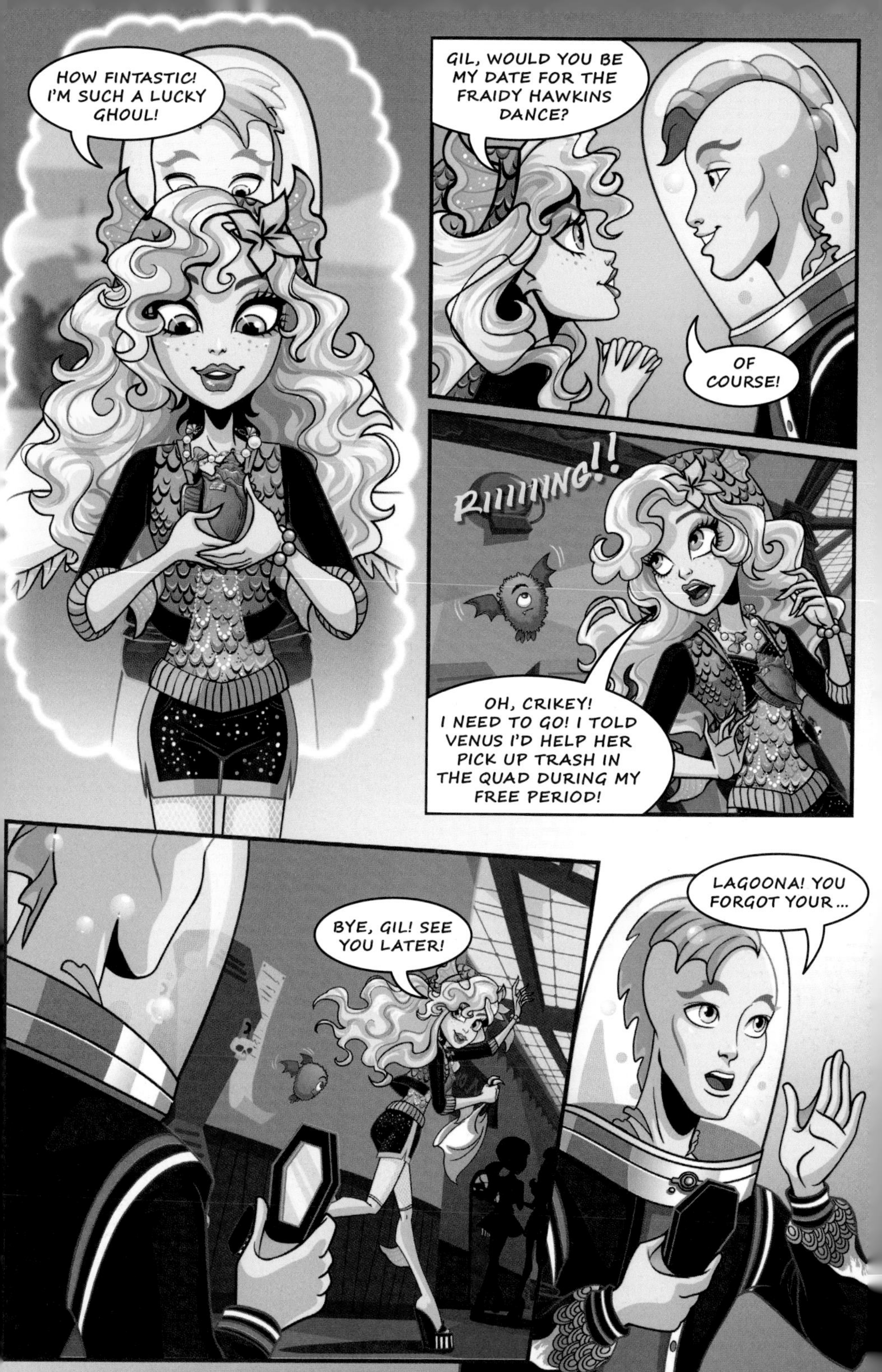
HOW FINTASTIC! I'M SUCH A LUCKY GHOUL!
GIL, WOULD YOU BE MY DATE FOR THE FRAIDY HAWKINS DANCE?
OF COURSE!
RIIIIING!!
OH, CRIKEY! I NEED TO GO! I TOLD VENUS I'D HELP HER PICK UP TRASH IN THE QUAD DURING MY FREE PERIOD!
BYE, GIL! SEE YOU LATER!
LAGOONA! YOU FORGOT YOUR...

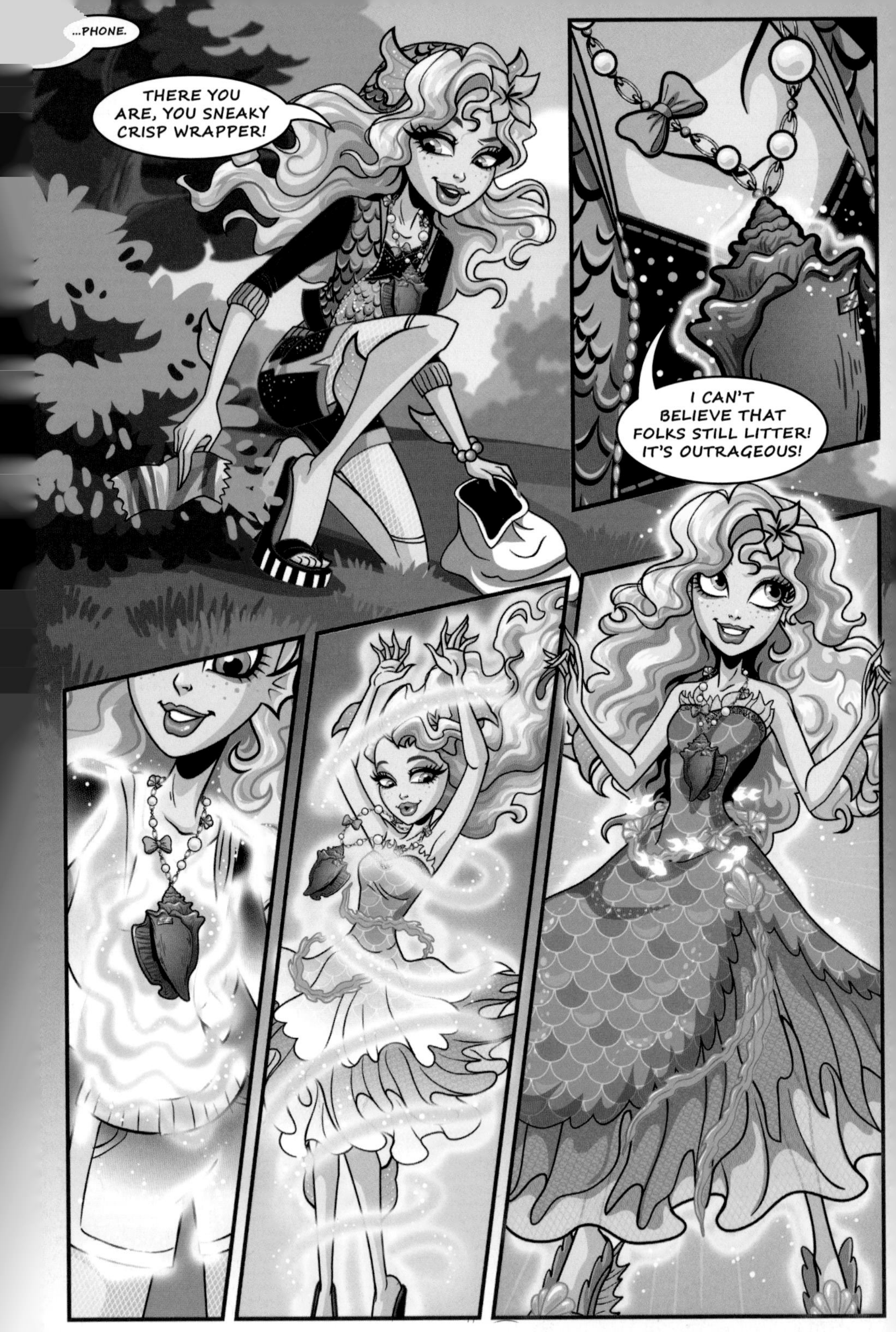
...PHONE.
THERE YOU ARE, YOU SNEAKY CRISP WRAPPER!
I CAN'T BELIEVE THAT FOLKS STILL LITTER! IT'S OUTRAGEOUS!

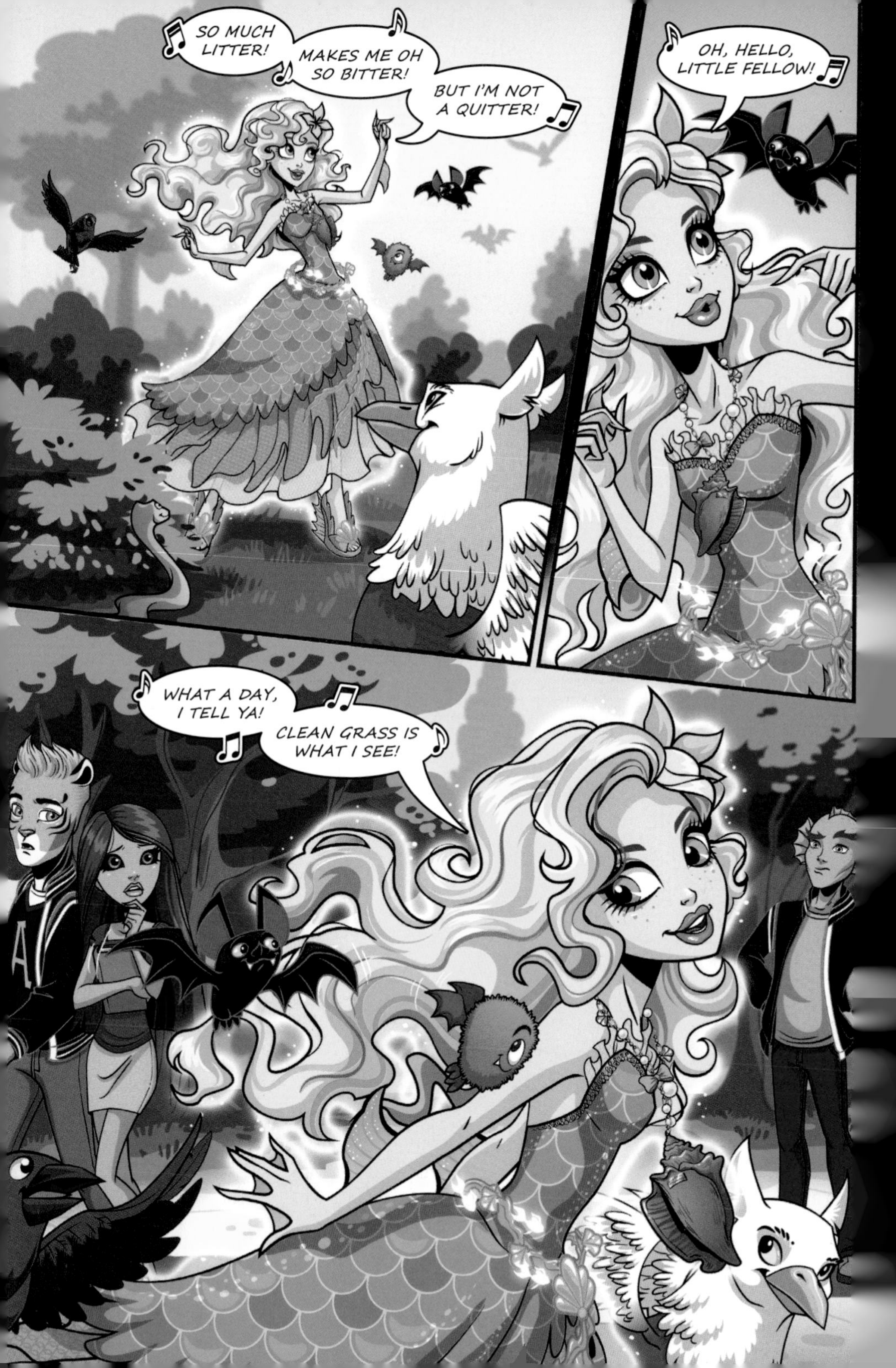
SO MUCH LITTER!
MAKES ME OH SO BITTER!
BUT I'M NOT A QUITTER!
OH, HELLO, LITTLE FELLOW!
WHAT A DAY, I TELL YA!
CLEAN GRASS IS WHAT I SEE!

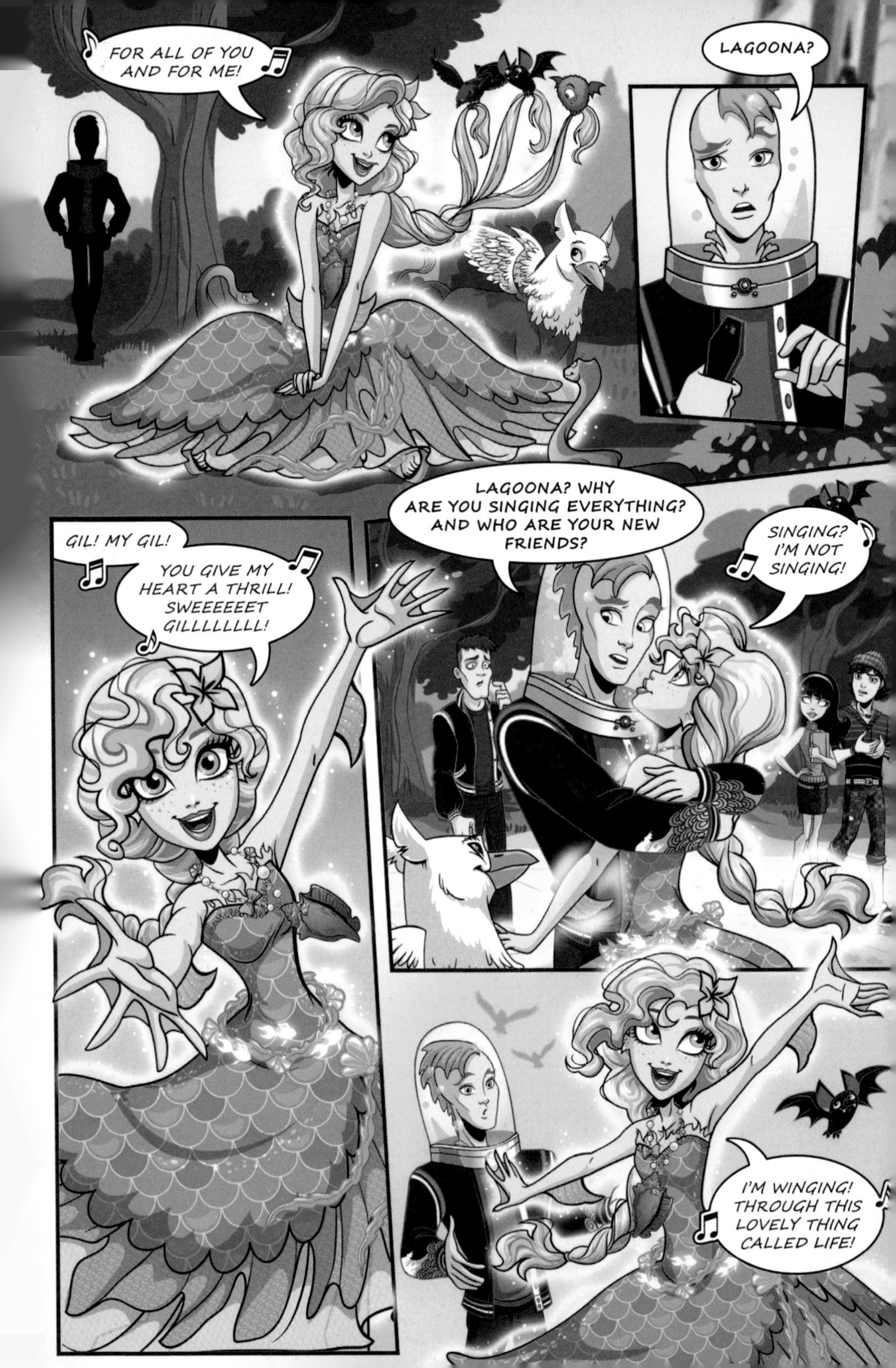
FOR ALL OF YOU AND FOR ME!
LAGOONA?
LAGOONA? WHY ARE YOU SINGING EVERYTHING? AND WHO ARE YOUR NEW FRIENDS?
GIL! MY GIL!
YOU GIVE MY HEART A THRILL! SWEEEEEET GILLLLLLLL!
SINGING? I'M NOT SINGING!
I'M WINGING! THROUGH THIS LOVELY THING CALLED LIFE!

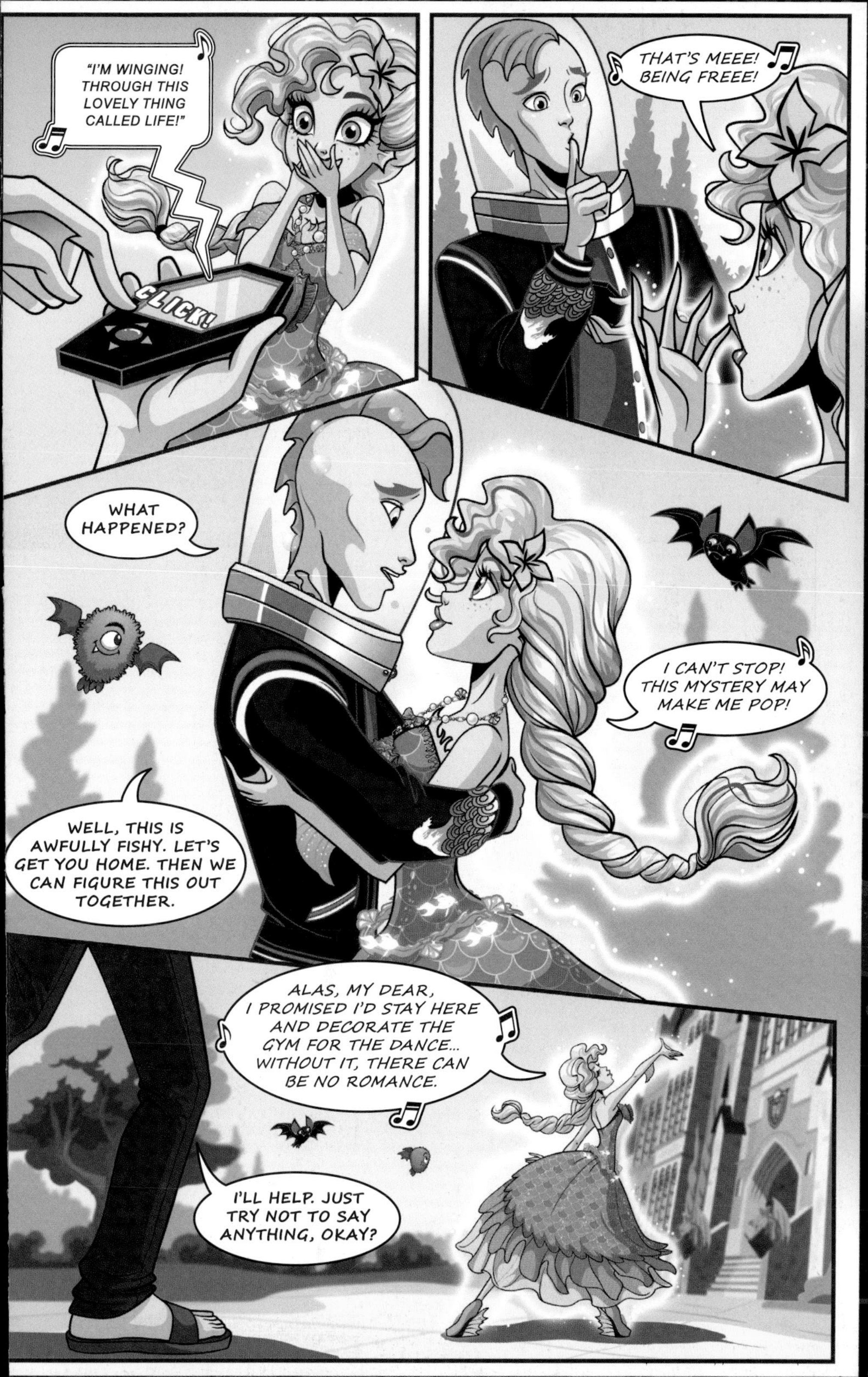
"I'M WINGING! THROUGH THIS LOVELY THING CALLED LIFE!"
CLICK!
THAT'S MEEE! BEING FREEE!
WHAT HAPPENED?
I CAN'T STOP! THIS MYSTERY MAY MAKE ME POP!
WELL, THIS IS AWFULLY FISHY. LET'S GET YOU HOME. THEN WE CAN FIGURE THIS OUT TOGETHER.
ALAS, MY DEAR, I PROMISED I'D STAY HERE AND DECORATE THE GYM FOR THE DANCE... WITHOUT IT, THERE CAN BE NO ROMANCE.
I'LL HELP. JUST TRY NOT TO SAY ANYTHING, OKAY?

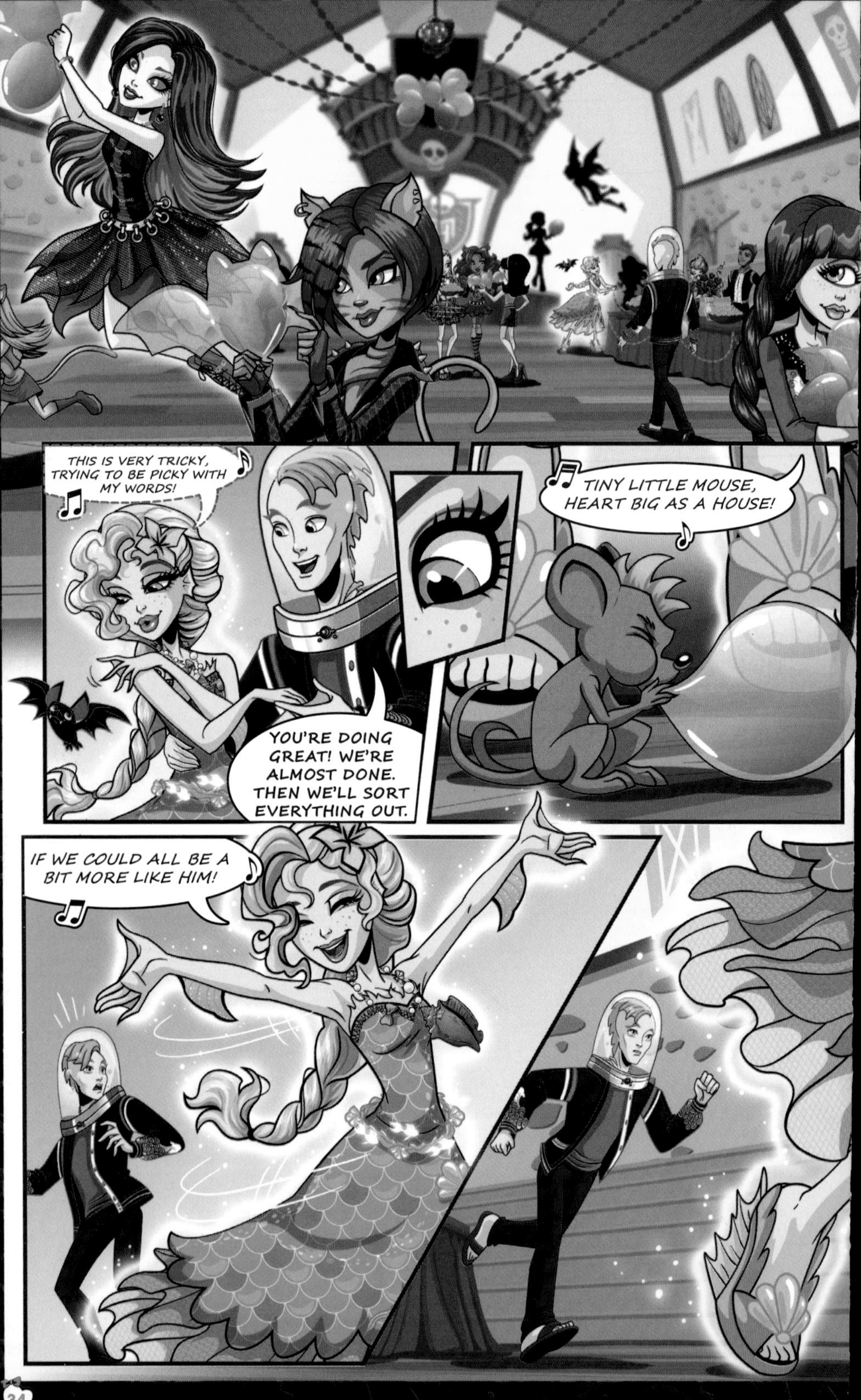
THIS IS VERY TRICKY, TRYING TO BE PICKY WITH MY WORDS!
YOU'RE DOING GREAT! WE'RE ALMOST DONE. THEN WE'LL SORT EVERYTHING OUT.
TINY LITTLE MOUSE, HEART BIG AS A HOUSE!
IF WE COULD ALL BE A BIT MORE LIKE HIM!

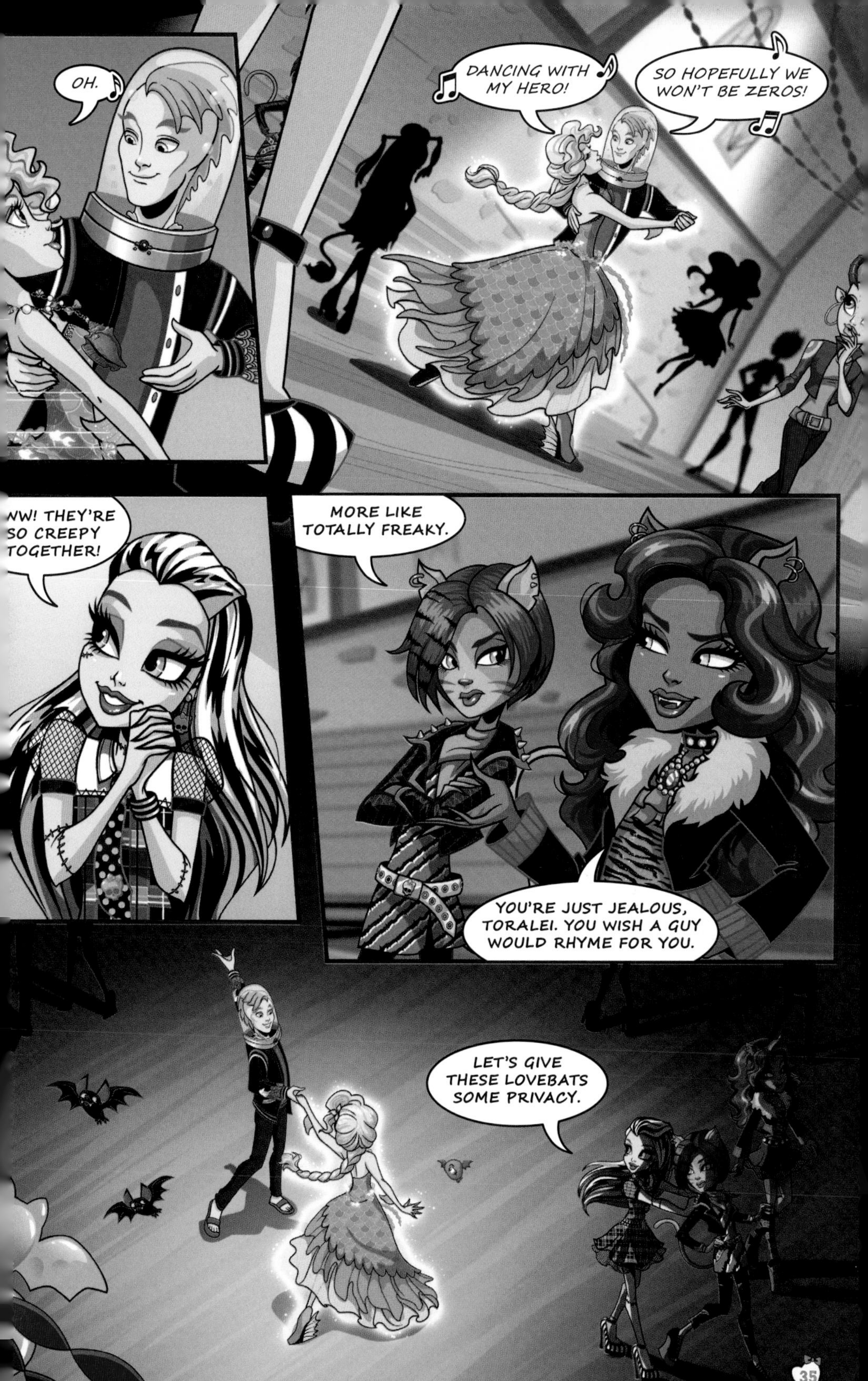
OH.
DANCING WITH MY HERO!
SO HOPEFULLY WE WON'T BE ZEROS!
NW! THEY'RE SO CREEPY TOGETHER!
MORE LIKE TOTALLY FREAKY.
YOU'RE JUST JEALOUS, TORALEI. YOU WISH A GUY WOULD RHYME FOR YOU.
LET'S GIVE THESE LOVEBATS SOME PRIVACY.

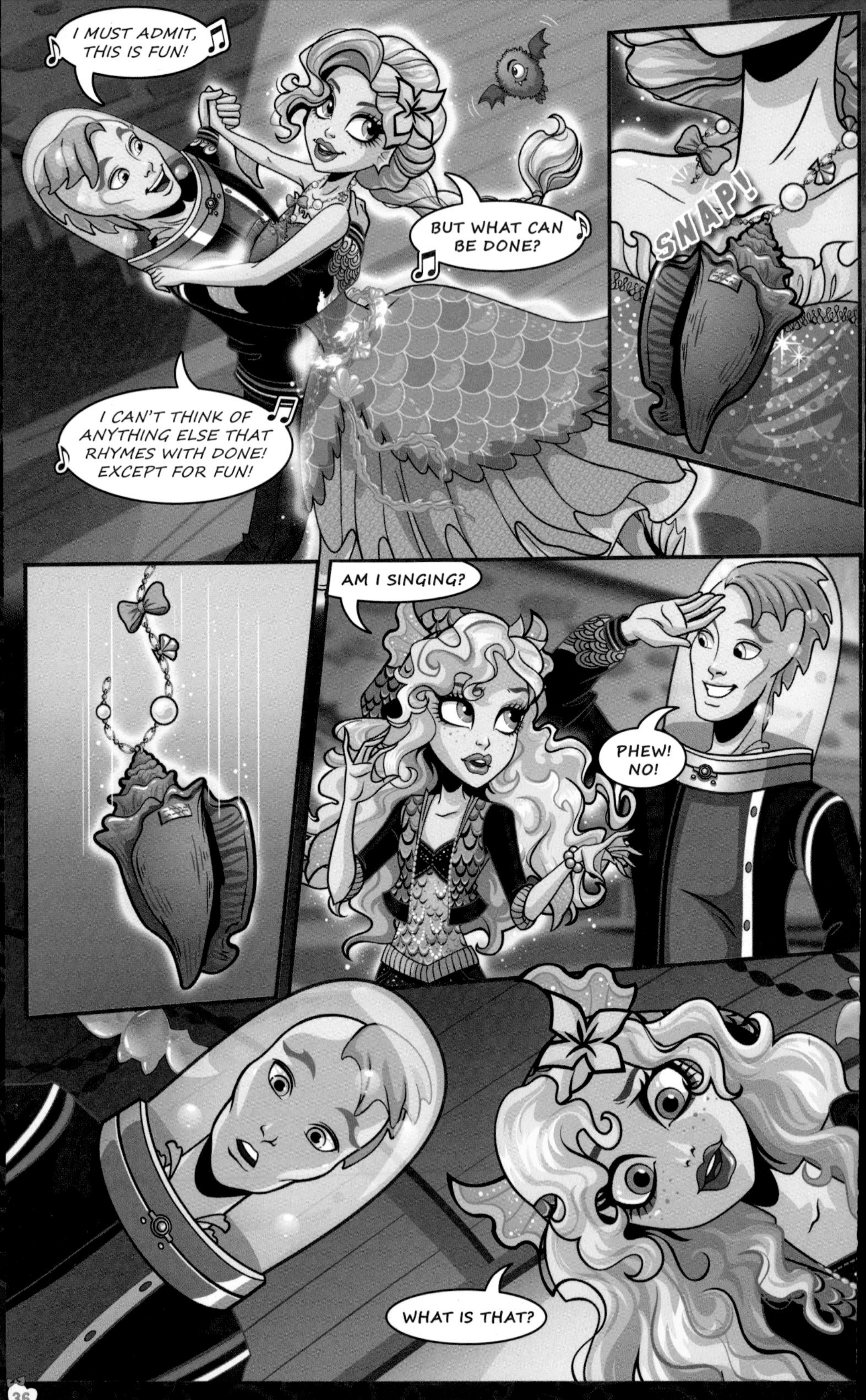
I MUST ADMIT, THIS IS FUN!
BUT WHAT CAN BE DONE?
I CAN'T THINK OF ANYTHING ELSE THAT RHYMES WITH DONE! EXCEPT FOR FUN!
SNAP!
AM I SINGING?
PHEW! NO!
WHAT IS THAT?

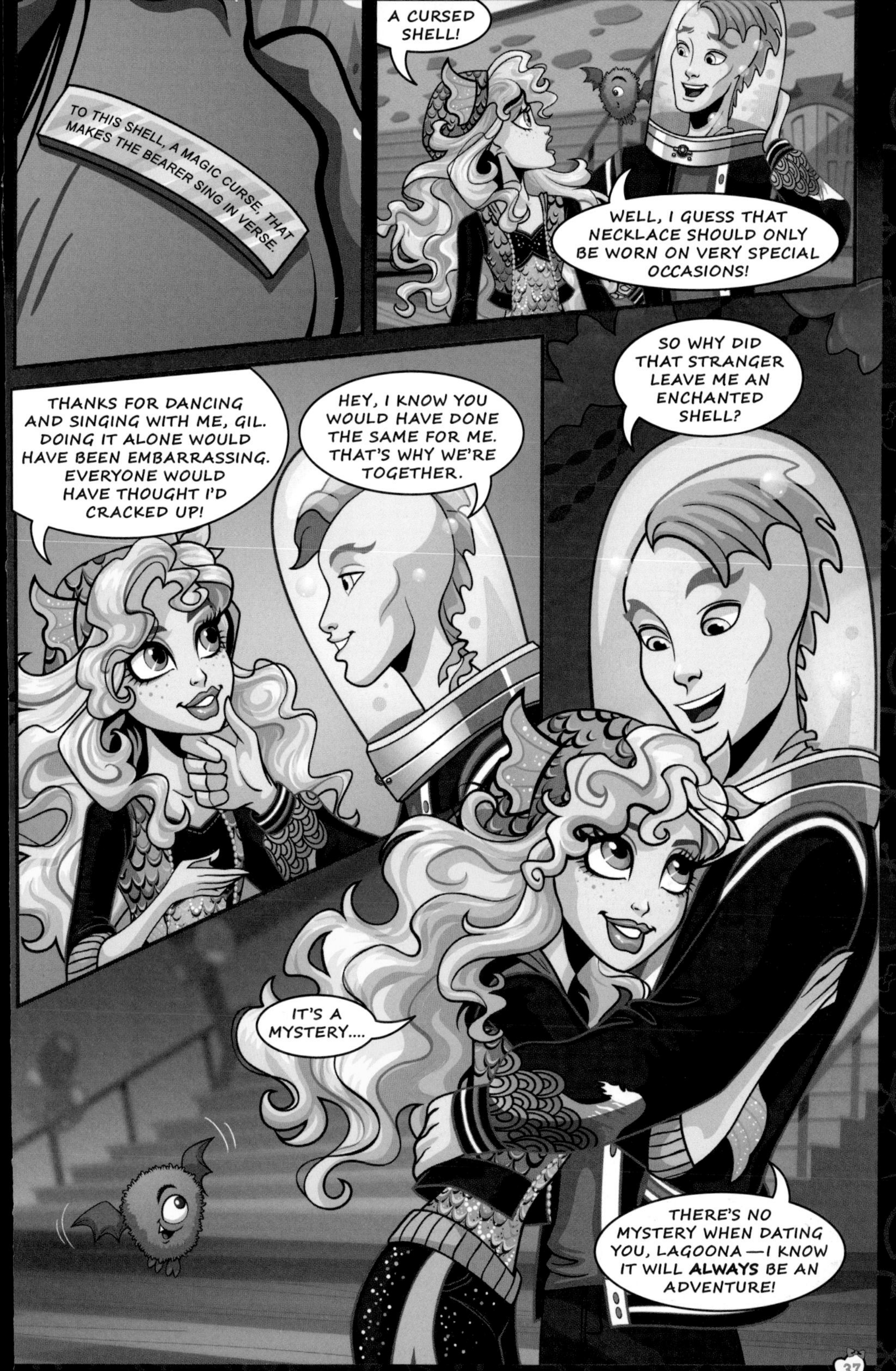
TO THIS SHELL, A MAGIC CURSE, THAT MAKES THE BEARER SING IN VERSE.
A CURSED SHELL!
WELL, I GUESS THAT NECKLACE SHOULD ONLY BE WORN ON VERY SPECIAL OCCASIONS!
THANKS FOR DANCING AND SINGING WITH ME, GIL. DOING IT ALONE WOULD HAVE BEEN EMBARRASSING. EVERYONE WOULD HAVE THOUGHT I'D CRACKED UP!
HEY, I KNOW YOU WOULD HAVE DONE THE SAME FOR ME. THAT'S WHY WE'RE TOGETHER.
SO WHY DID THAT STRANGER LEAVE ME AN ENCHANTED SHELL?
IT'S A MYSTERY....
THERE'S NO MYSTERY WHEN DATING YOU, LAGOONA—I KNOW IT WILL **ALWAYS** BE AN ADVENTURE!

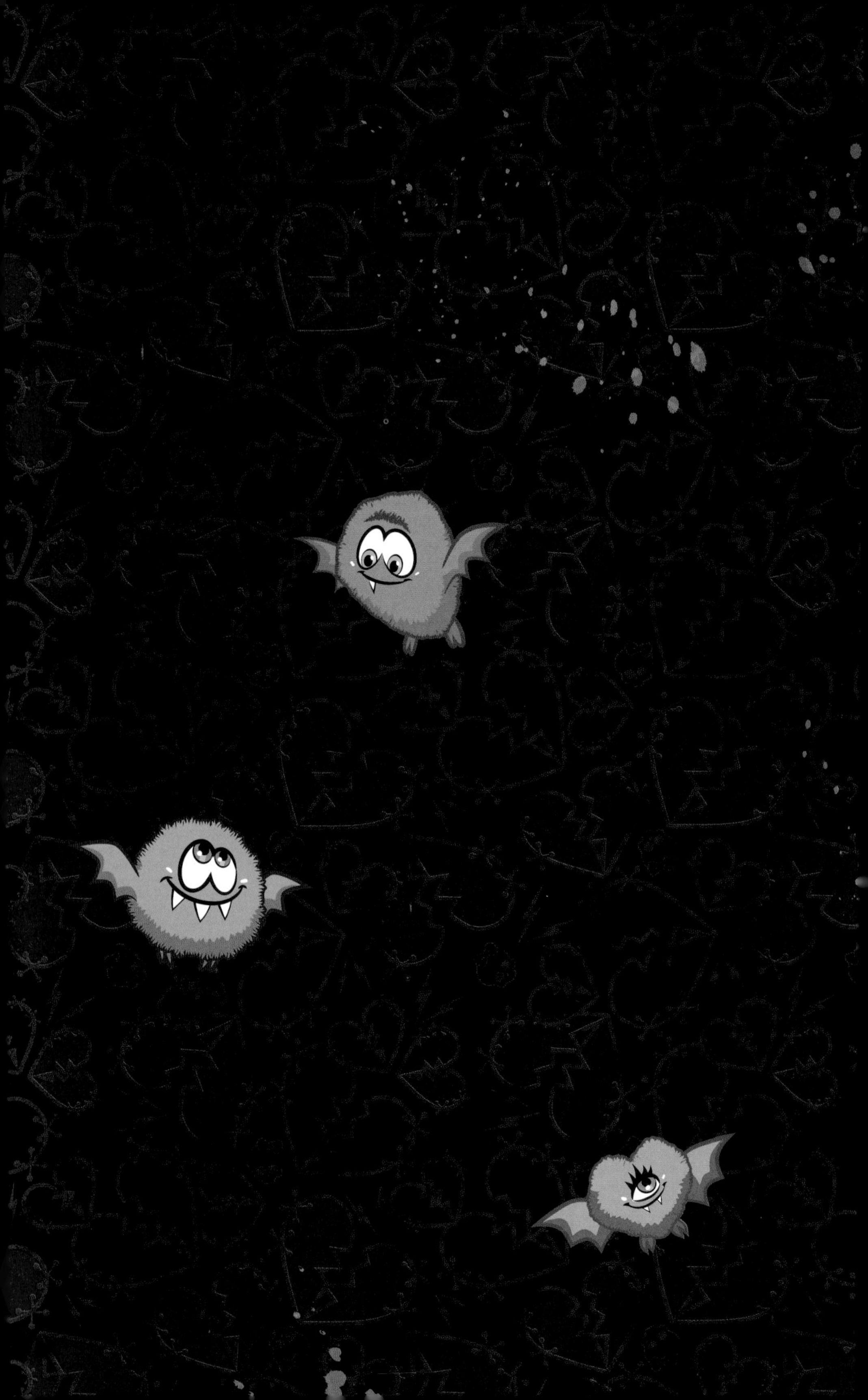

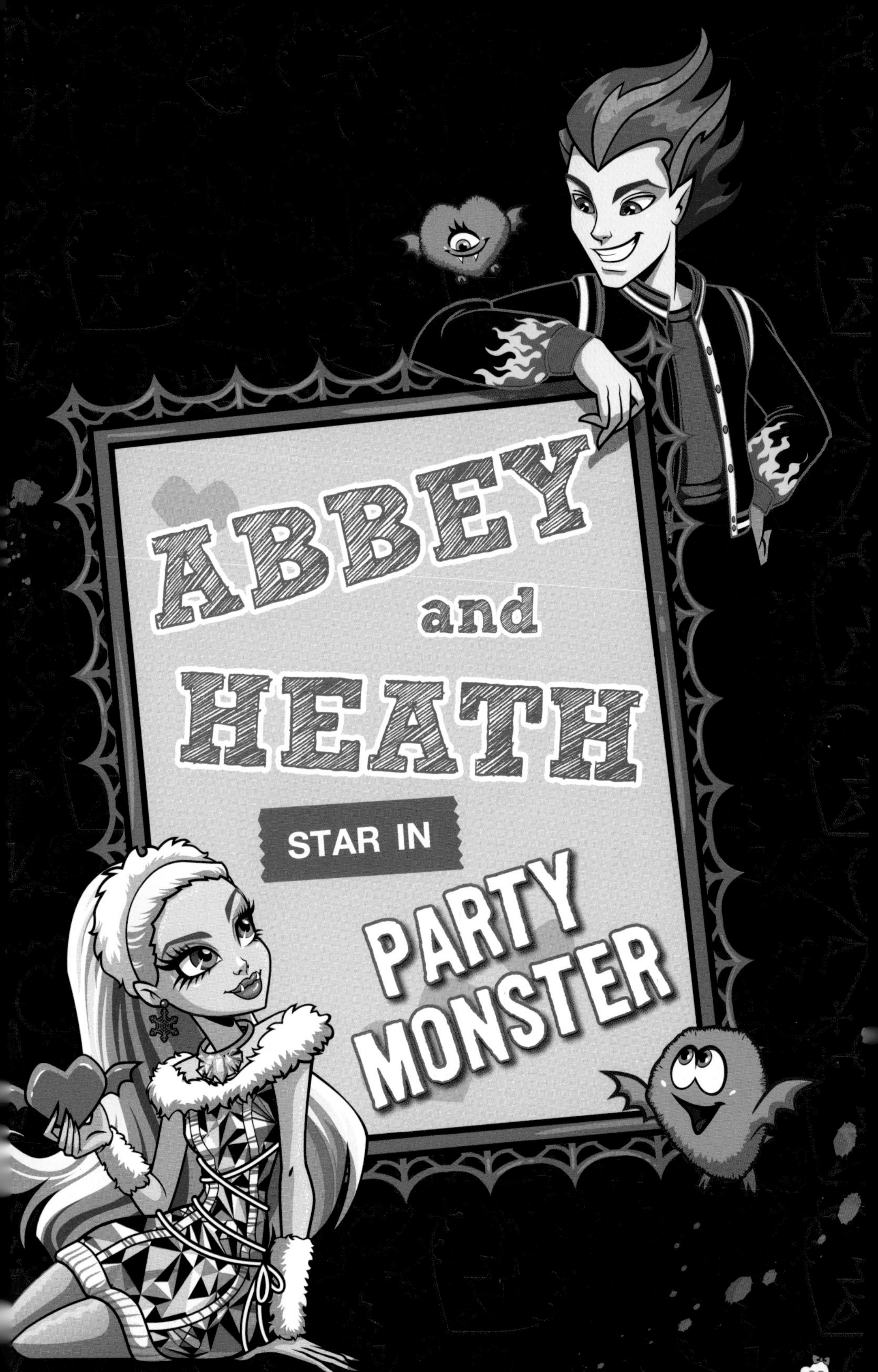
ABBEY
and
HEATH
STAR IN
PARTY
MONSTER

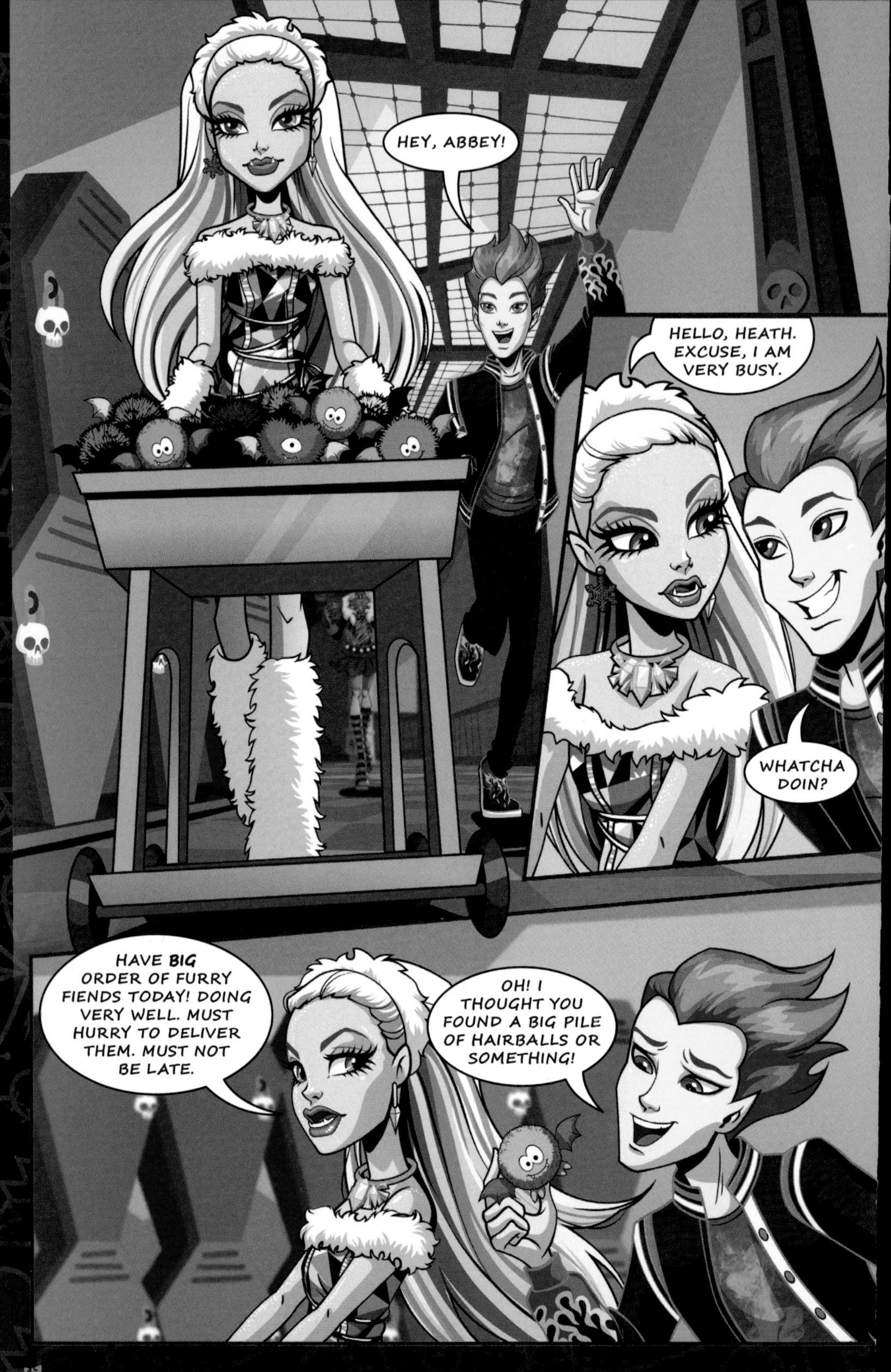
HEY, ABBEY!
HELLO, HEATH. EXCUSE, I AM VERY BUSY.
WHATCHA DOIN?
HAVE **BIG** ORDER OF FURRY FIENDS TODAY! DOING VERY WELL. MUST HURRY TO DELIVER THEM. MUST NOT BE LATE.
OH! I THOUGHT YOU FOUND A BIG PILE OF HAIRBALLS OR SOMETHING!

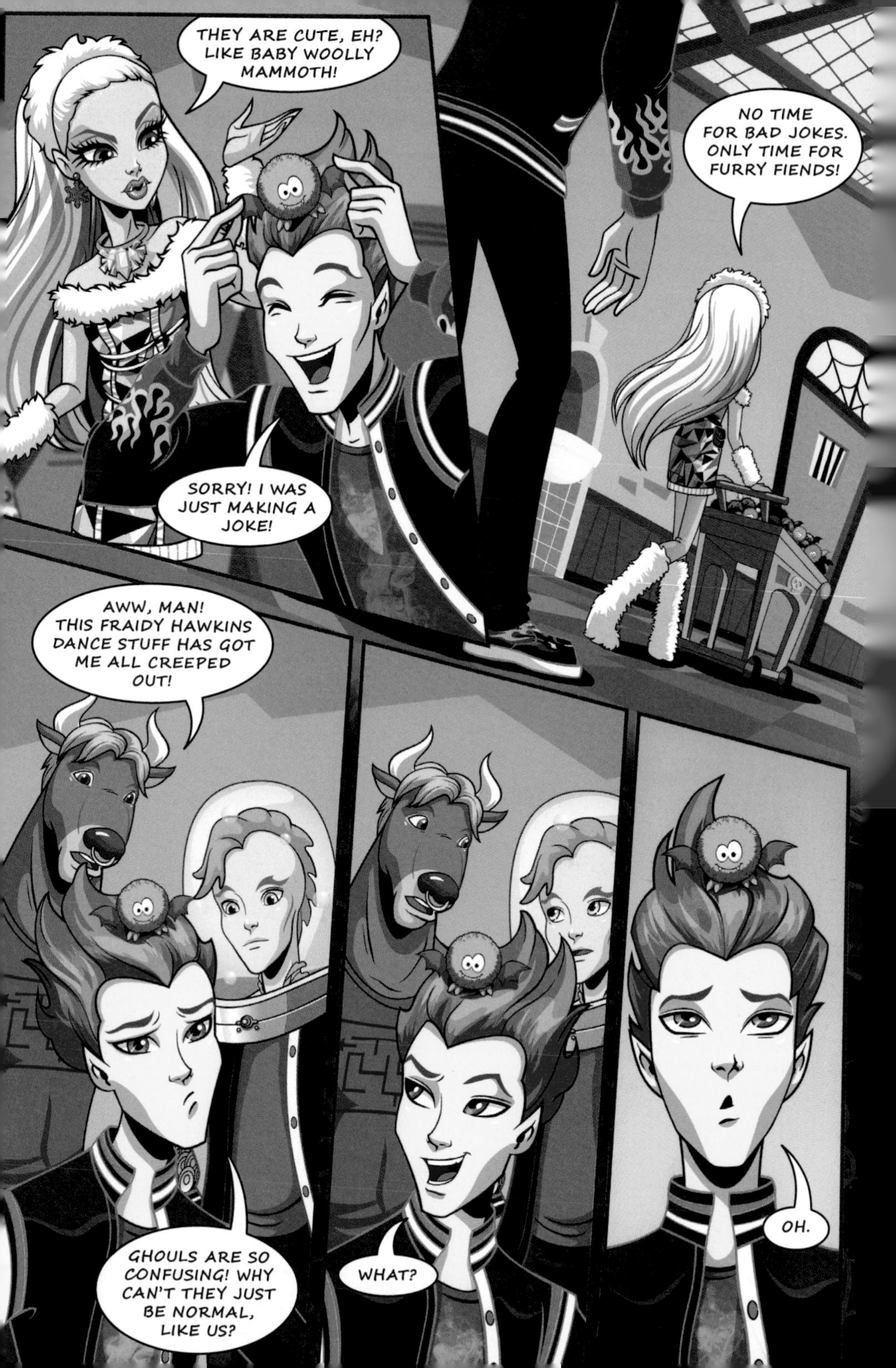
THEY ARE CUTE, EH? LIKE BABY WOOLLY MAMMOTH!
SORRY! I WAS JUST MAKING A JOKE!
NO TIME FOR BAD JOKES. ONLY TIME FOR FURRY FIENDS!
AWW, MAN! THIS FRAIDY HAWKINS DANCE STUFF HAS GOT ME ALL CREEPED OUT!
GHOULS ARE SO CONFUSING! WHY CAN'T THEY JUST BE NORMAL, LIKE US?
WHAT?
OH.

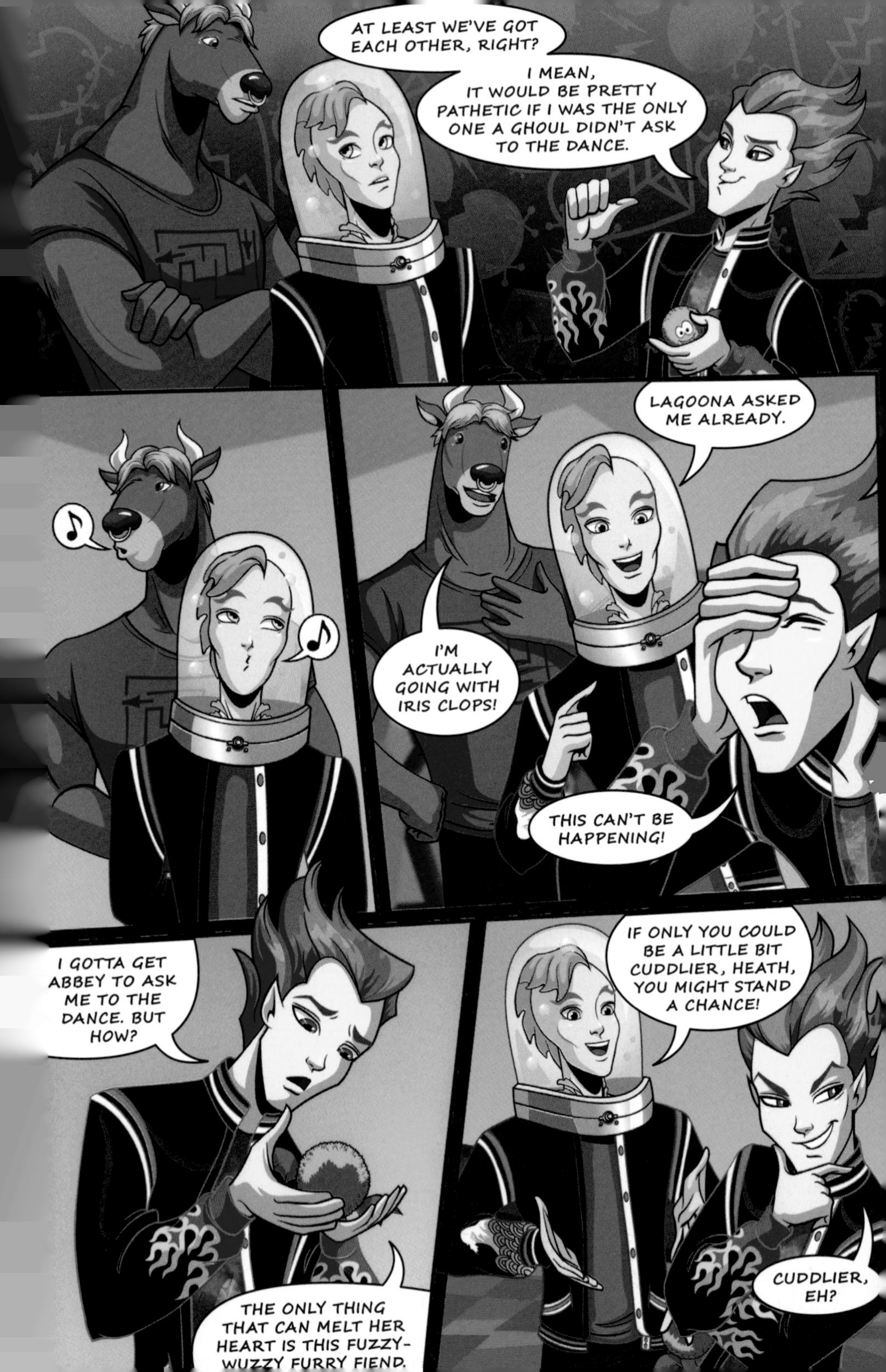
AT LEAST WE'VE GOT EACH OTHER, RIGHT?
I MEAN, IT WOULD BE PRETTY PATHETIC IF I WAS THE ONLY ONE A GHOUL DIDN'T ASK TO THE DANCE.
♪
♪
LAGOONA ASKED ME ALREADY.
I'M ACTUALLY GOING WITH IRIS CLOPS!
THIS CAN'T BE HAPPENING!
I GOTTA GET ABBEY TO ASK ME TO THE DANCE. BUT HOW?
THE ONLY THING THAT CAN MELT HER HEART IS THIS FUZZY-WUZZY FURRY FIEND.
IF ONLY YOU COULD BE A LITTLE BIT CUDDLIER, HEATH, YOU MIGHT STAND A CHANCE!
CUDDLIER, EH?

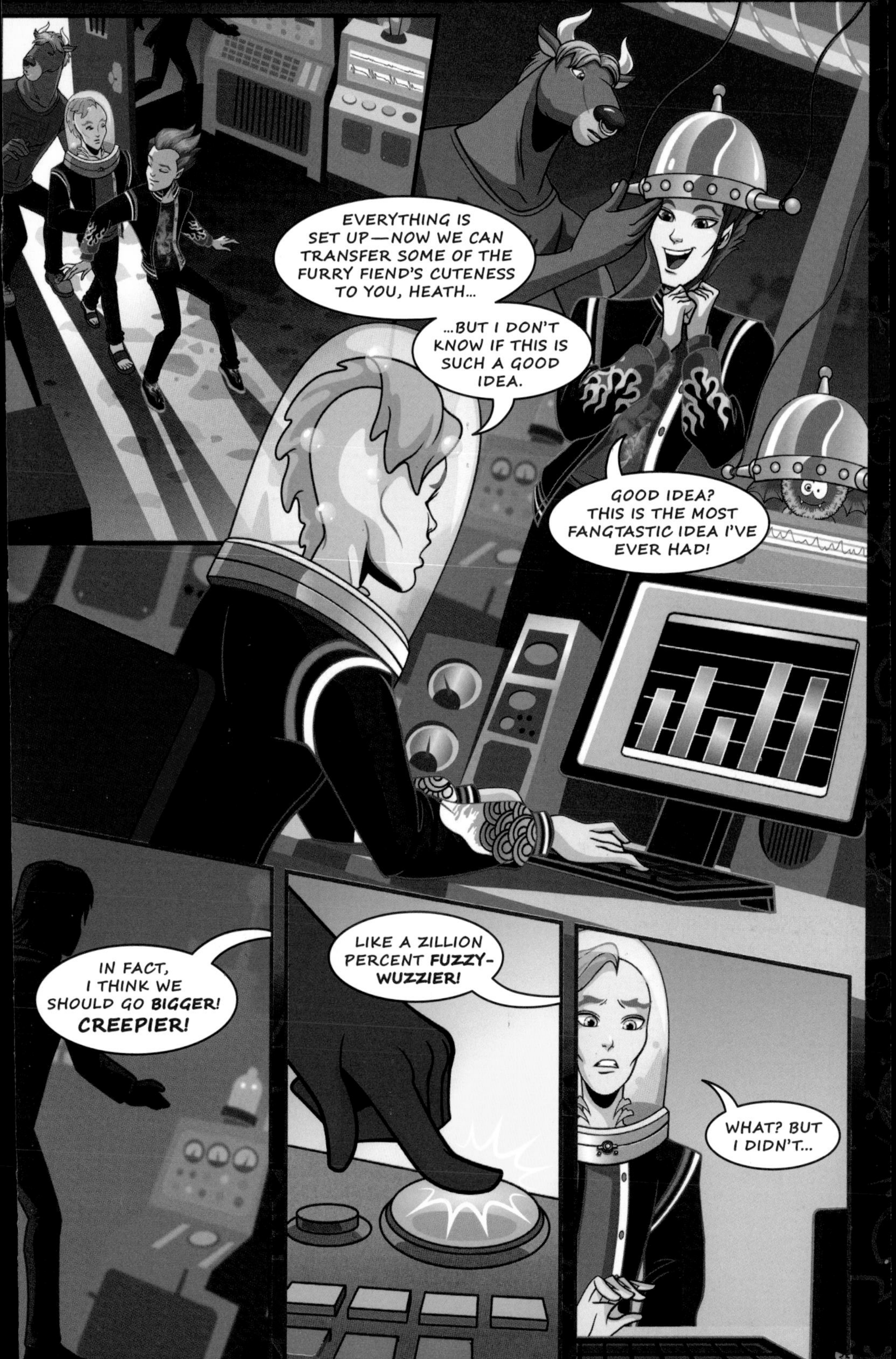
EVERYTHING IS SET UP—NOW WE CAN TRANSFER SOME OF THE FURRY FIEND'S CUTENESS TO YOU, HEATH...
...BUT I DON'T KNOW IF THIS IS SUCH A GOOD IDEA.
GOOD IDEA? THIS IS THE MOST FANGTASTIC IDEA I'VE EVER HAD!
IN FACT, I THINK WE SHOULD GO **BIGGER! CREEPIER!**
LIKE A ZILLION PERCENT **FUZZY-WUZZIER!**
WHAT? BUT I DIDN'T...

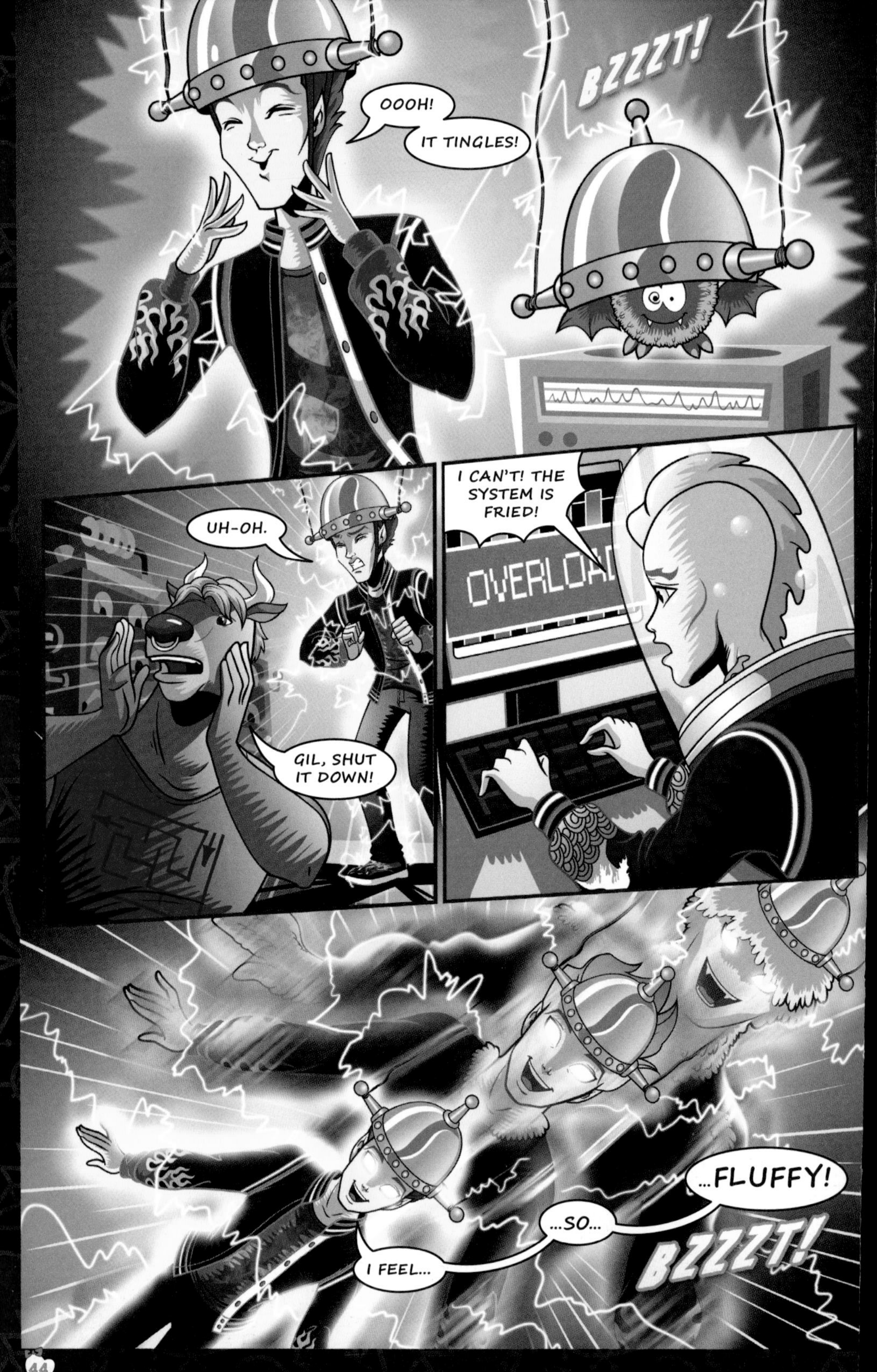
OOOH!
IT TINGLES!
BZZZZT!
UH-OH.
GIL, SHUT IT DOWN!
I CAN'T! THE SYSTEM IS FRIED!
OVERLOAD
I FEEL...
...SO...
...FLUFFY!
BZZZT!

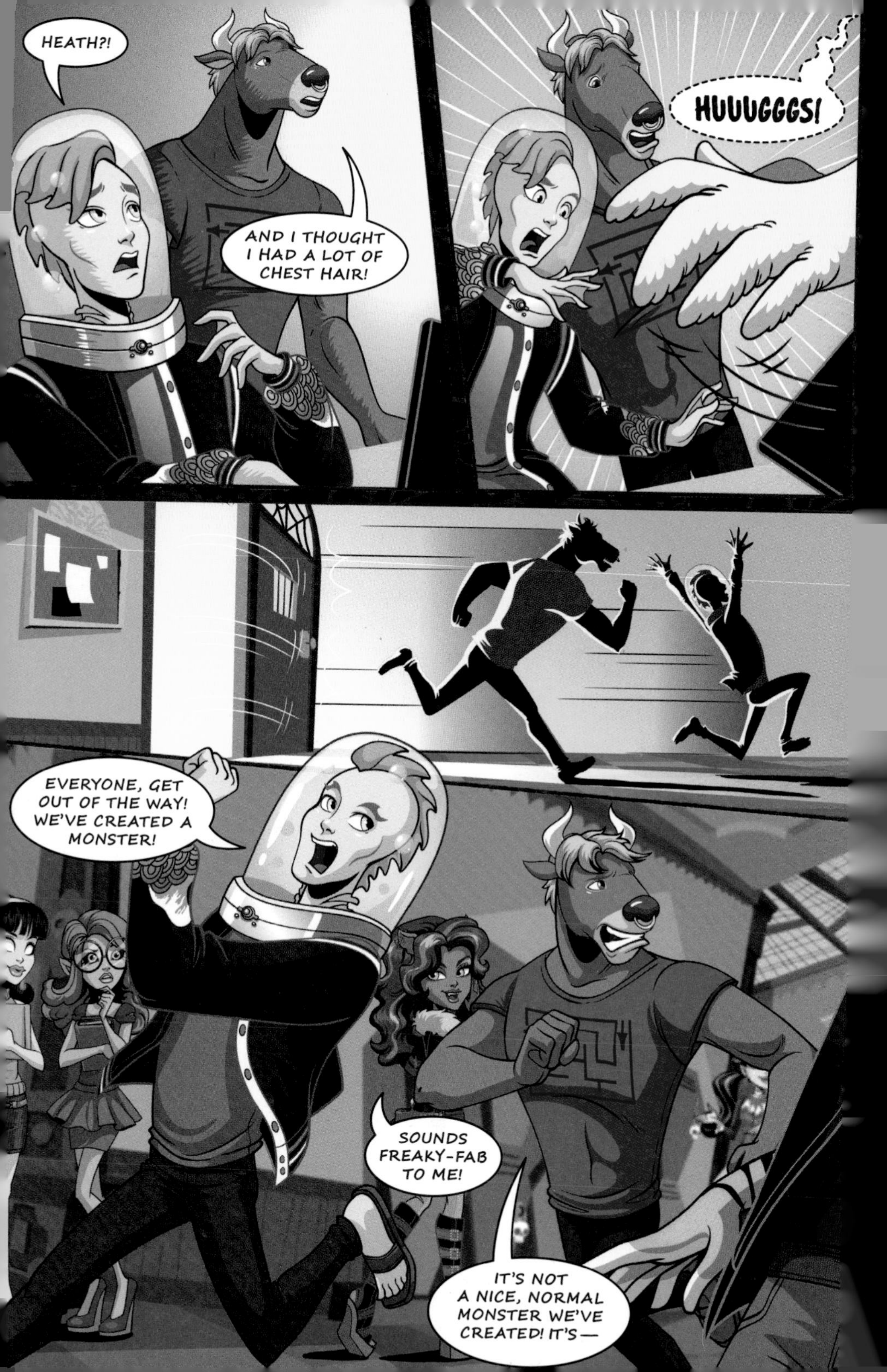
HEATH?!
AND I THOUGHT I HAD A LOT OF CHEST HAIR!
HUUUGGGS!
EVERYONE, GET OUT OF THE WAY! WE'VE CREATED A MONSTER!
SOUNDS FREAKY-FAB TO ME!
IT'S NOT A NICE, NORMAL MONSTER WE'VE CREATED! IT'S—

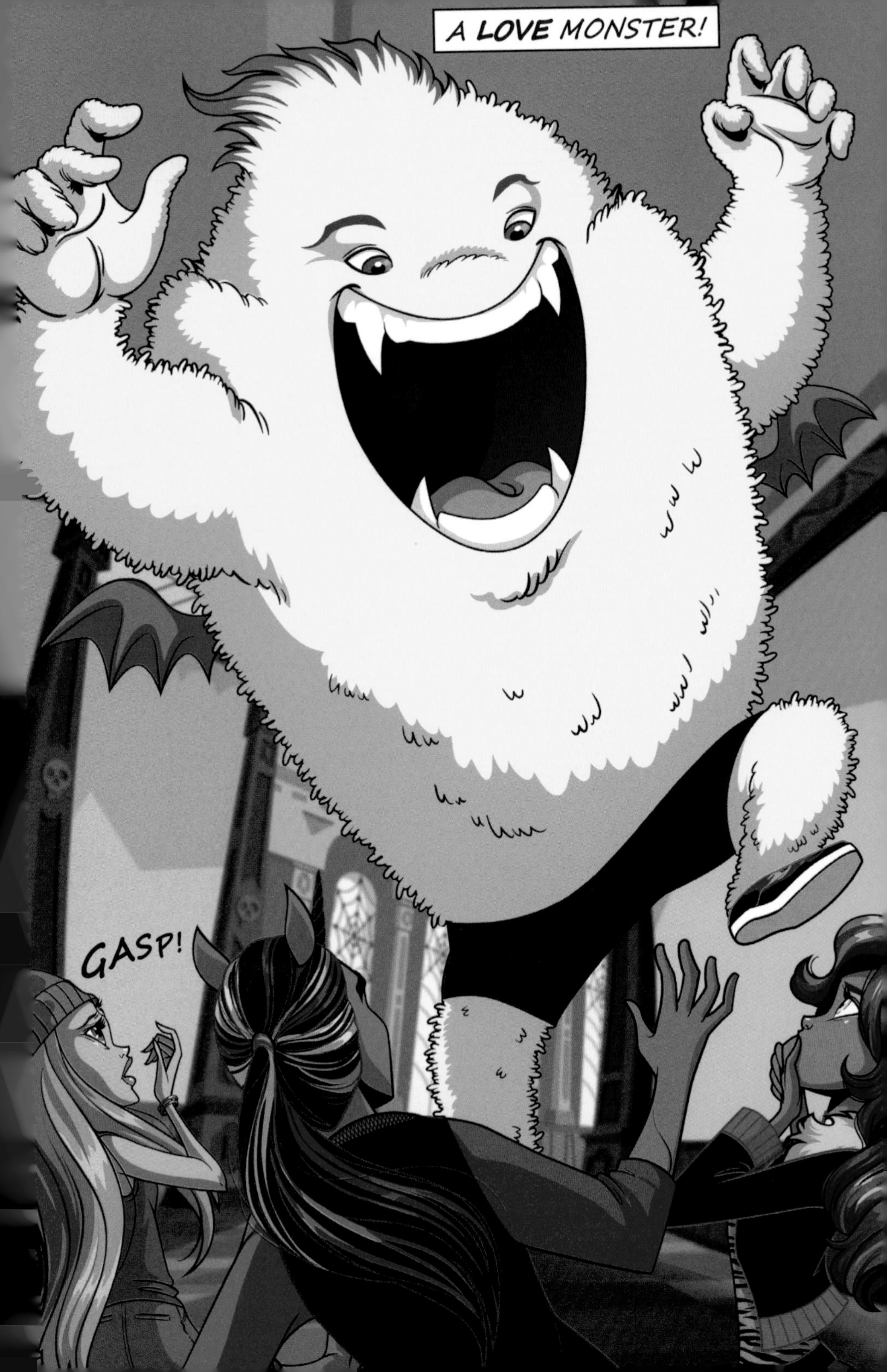
A LOVE MONSTER!
GASP!

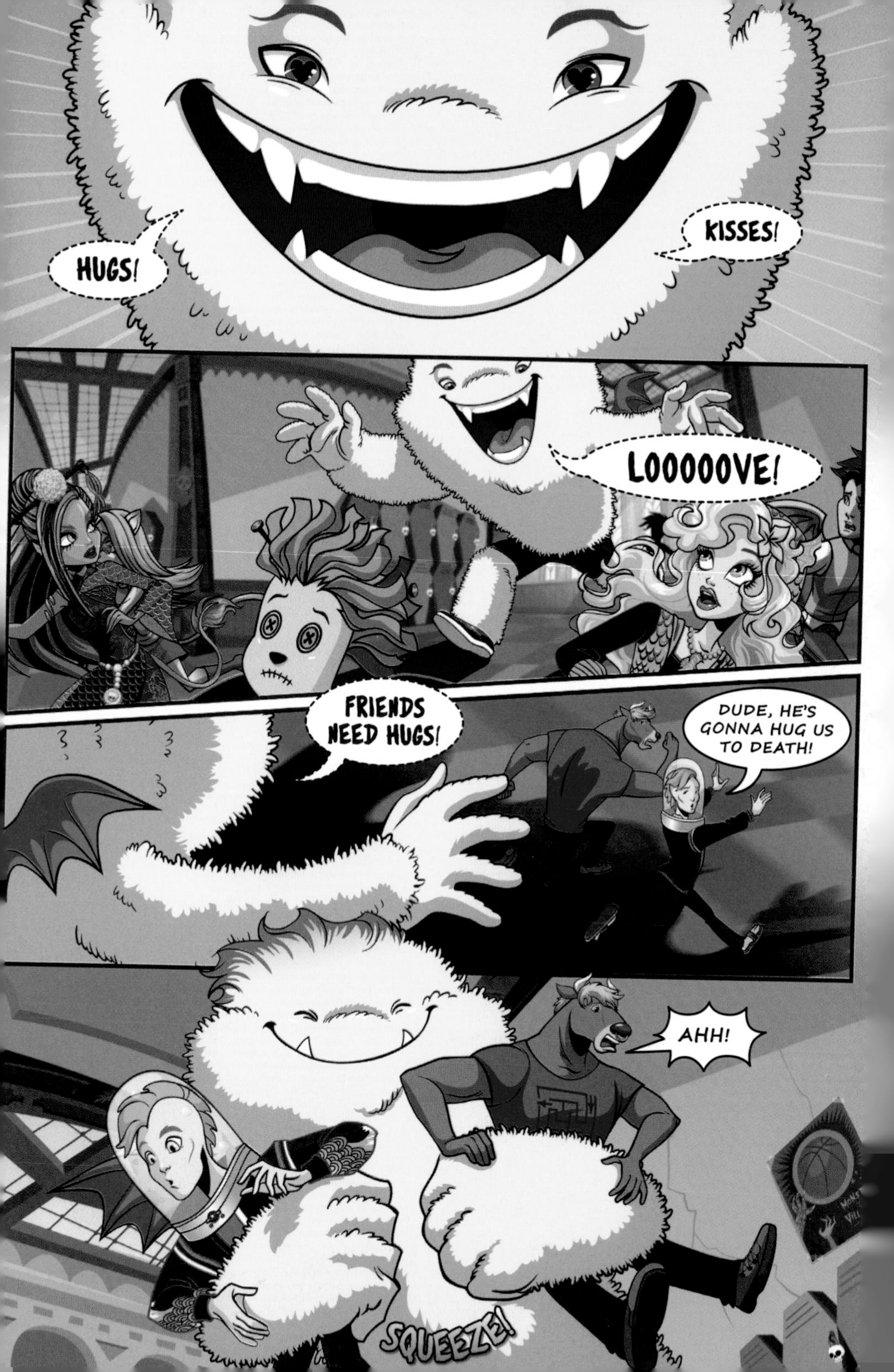
HUGS!
KISSES!
LOOOOOVE!
FRIENDS NEED HUGS!
DUDE, HE'S GONNA HUG US TO DEATH!
AHH!
SQUEEZE!

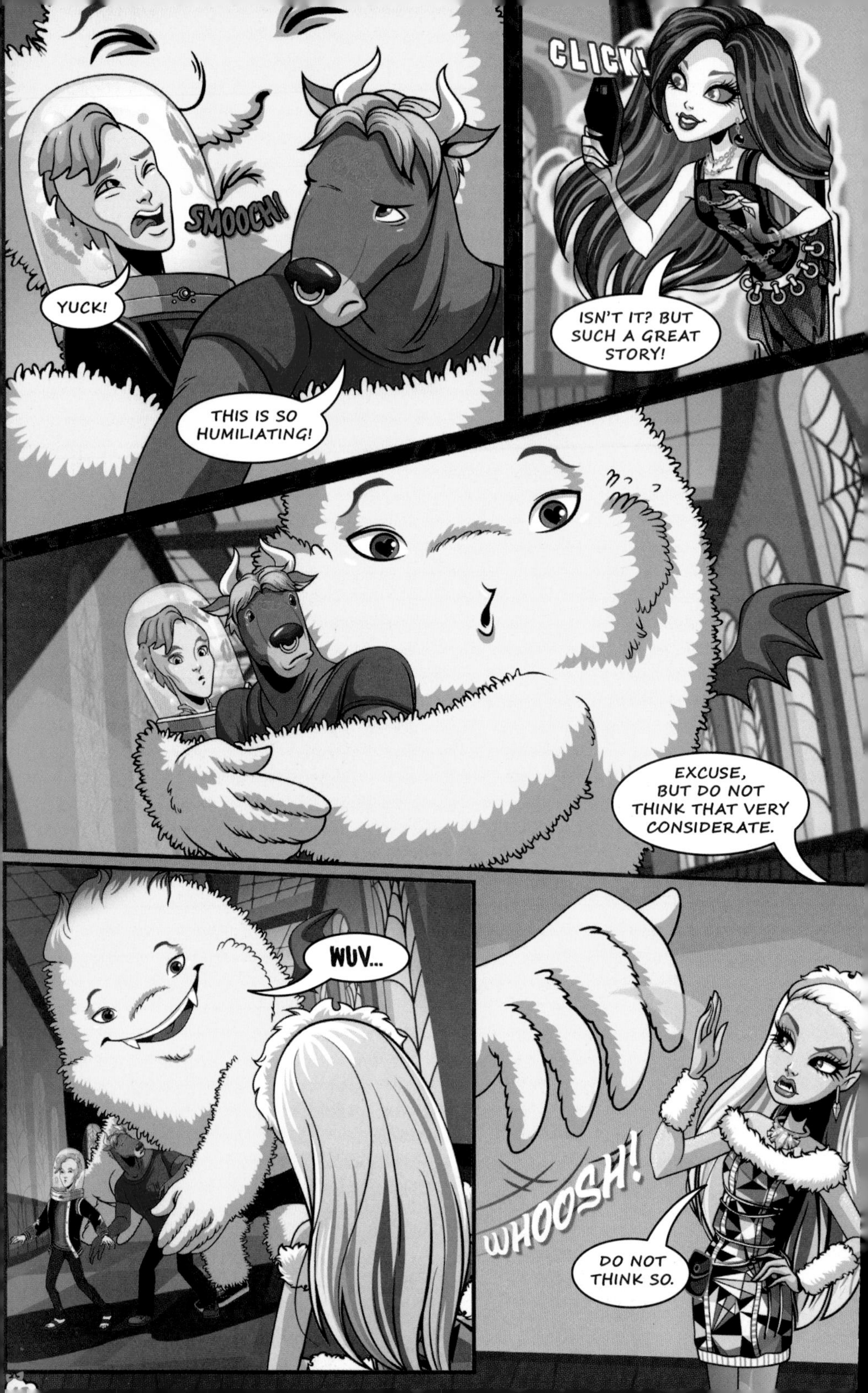
SMOOCH!
YUCK!
THIS IS SO HUMILIATING!
CLICK!
ISN'T IT? BUT SUCH A GREAT STORY!
EXCUSE, BUT DO NOT THINK THAT VERY CONSIDERATE.
WUV...
WHOOSH!
DO NOT THINK SO.

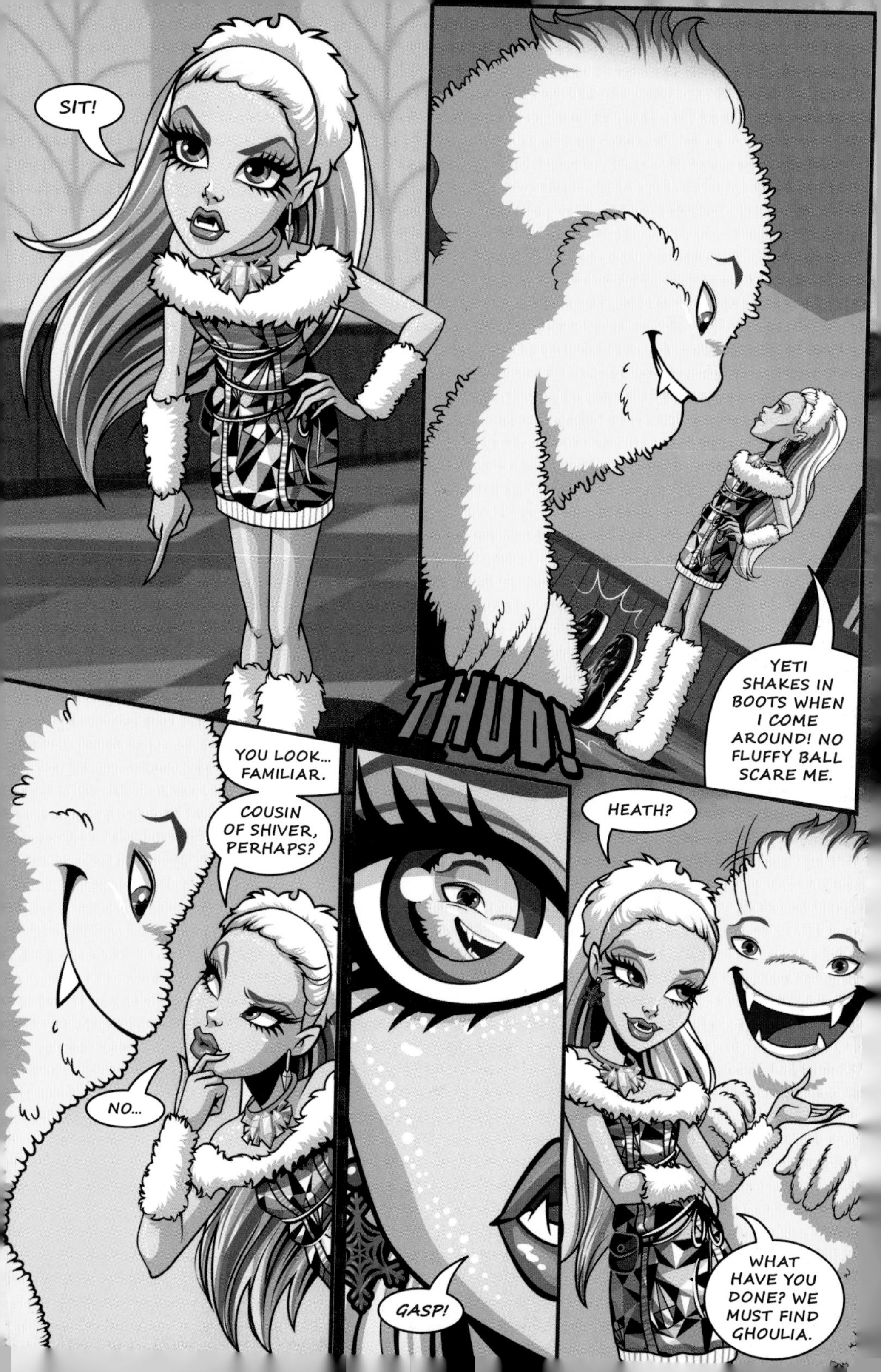
SIT!
YETI SHAKES IN BOOTS WHEN I COME AROUND! NO FLUFFY BALL SCARE ME.
THUD!
YOU LOOK... FAMILIAR.
COUSIN OF SHIVER, PERHAPS?
NO...
GASP!
HEATH?
WHAT HAVE YOU DONE? WE MUST FIND GHOULIA.

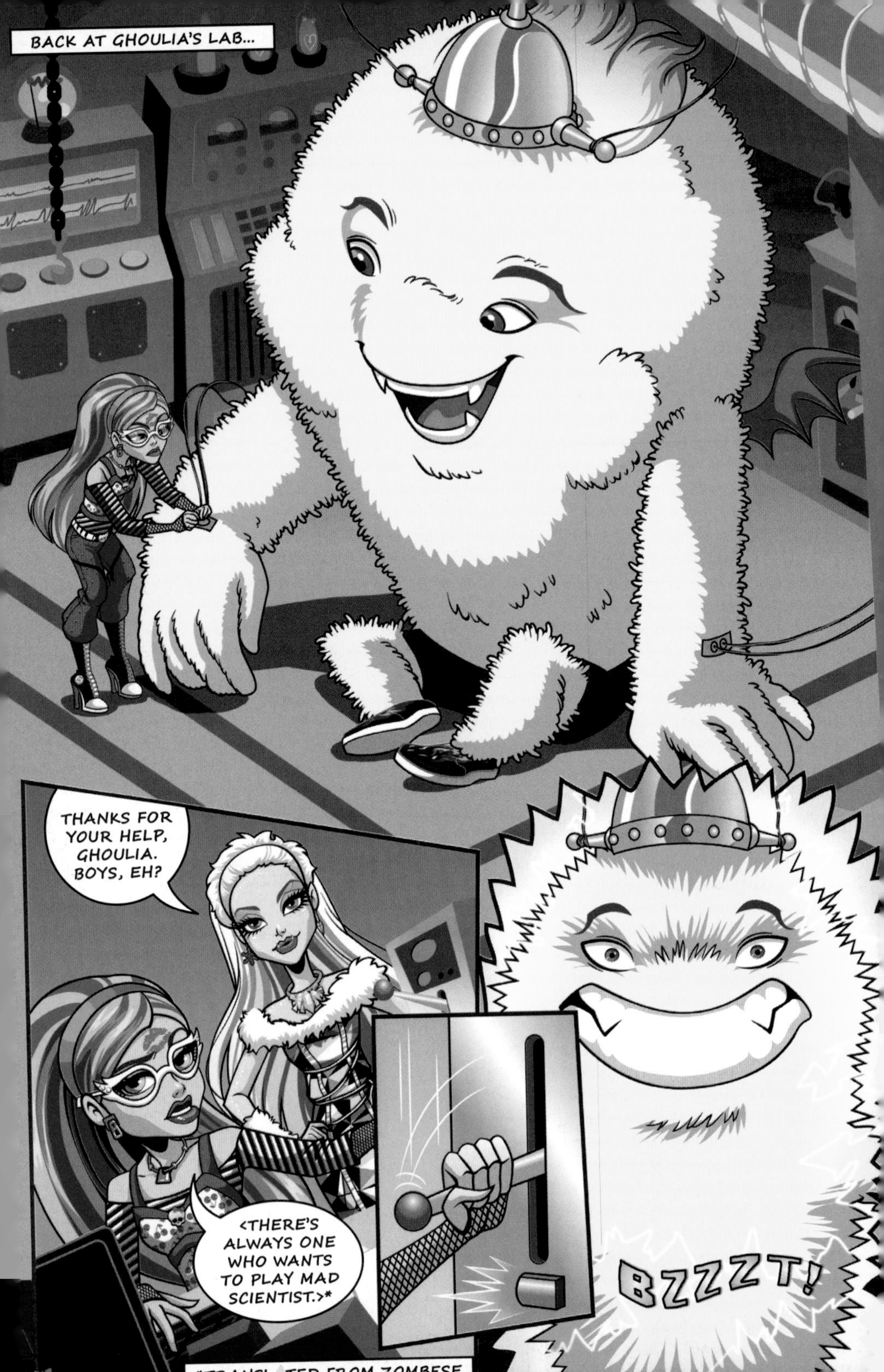
BACK AT GHOULIA'S LAB...
THANKS FOR YOUR HELP, GHOULIA. BOYS, EH?
<THERE'S ALWAYS ONE WHO WANTS TO PLAY MAD SCIENTIST.>*
BZZZT!

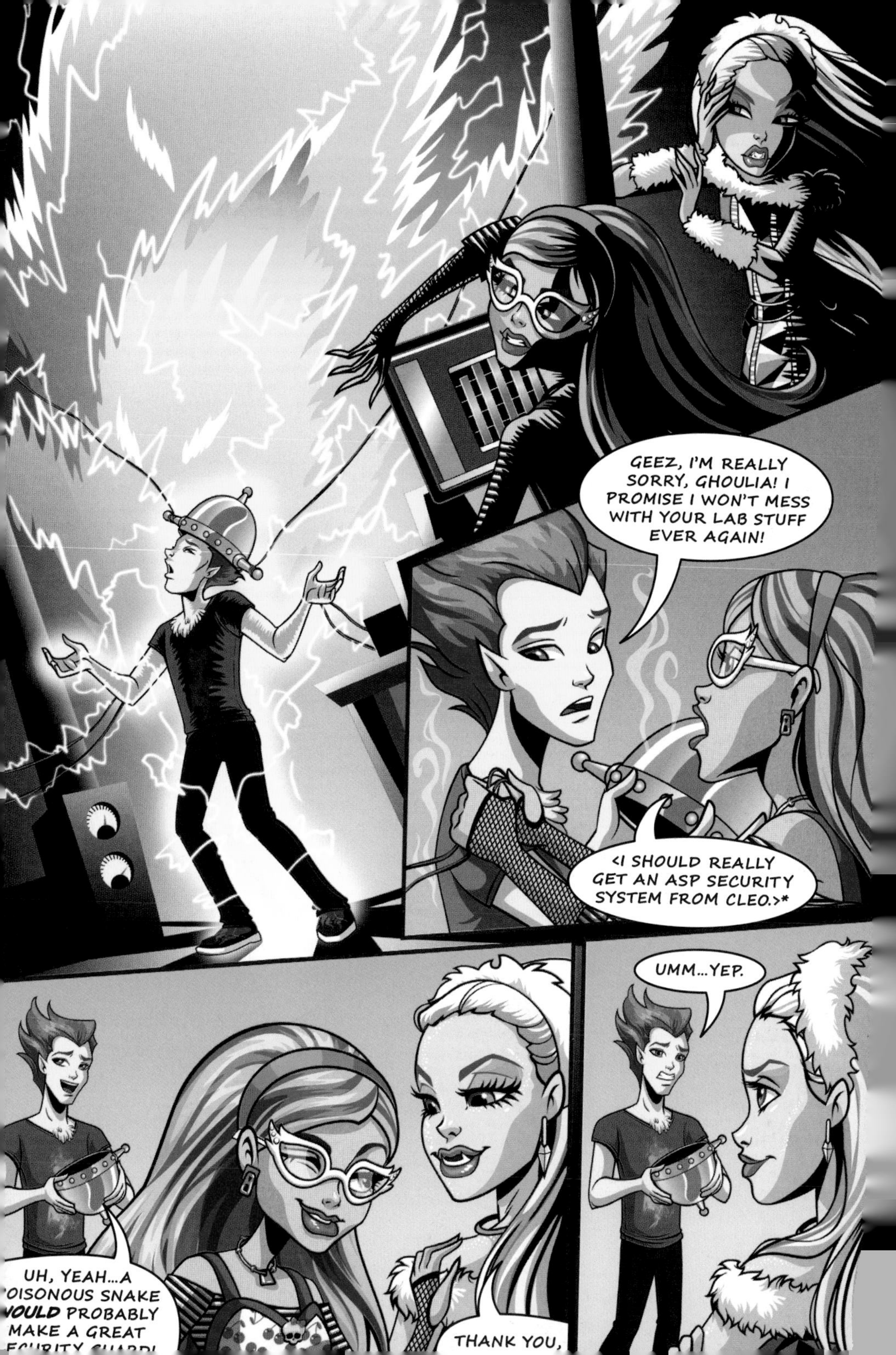
GEEZ, I'M REALLY SORRY, GHOULIA! I PROMISE I WON'T MESS WITH YOUR LAB STUFF EVER AGAIN!
<I SHOULD REALLY GET AN ASP SECURITY SYSTEM FROM CLEO.>*
UMM...YEP.
UH, YEAH...A POISONOUS SNAKE *WOULD* PROBABLY MAKE A GREAT
THANK YOU,

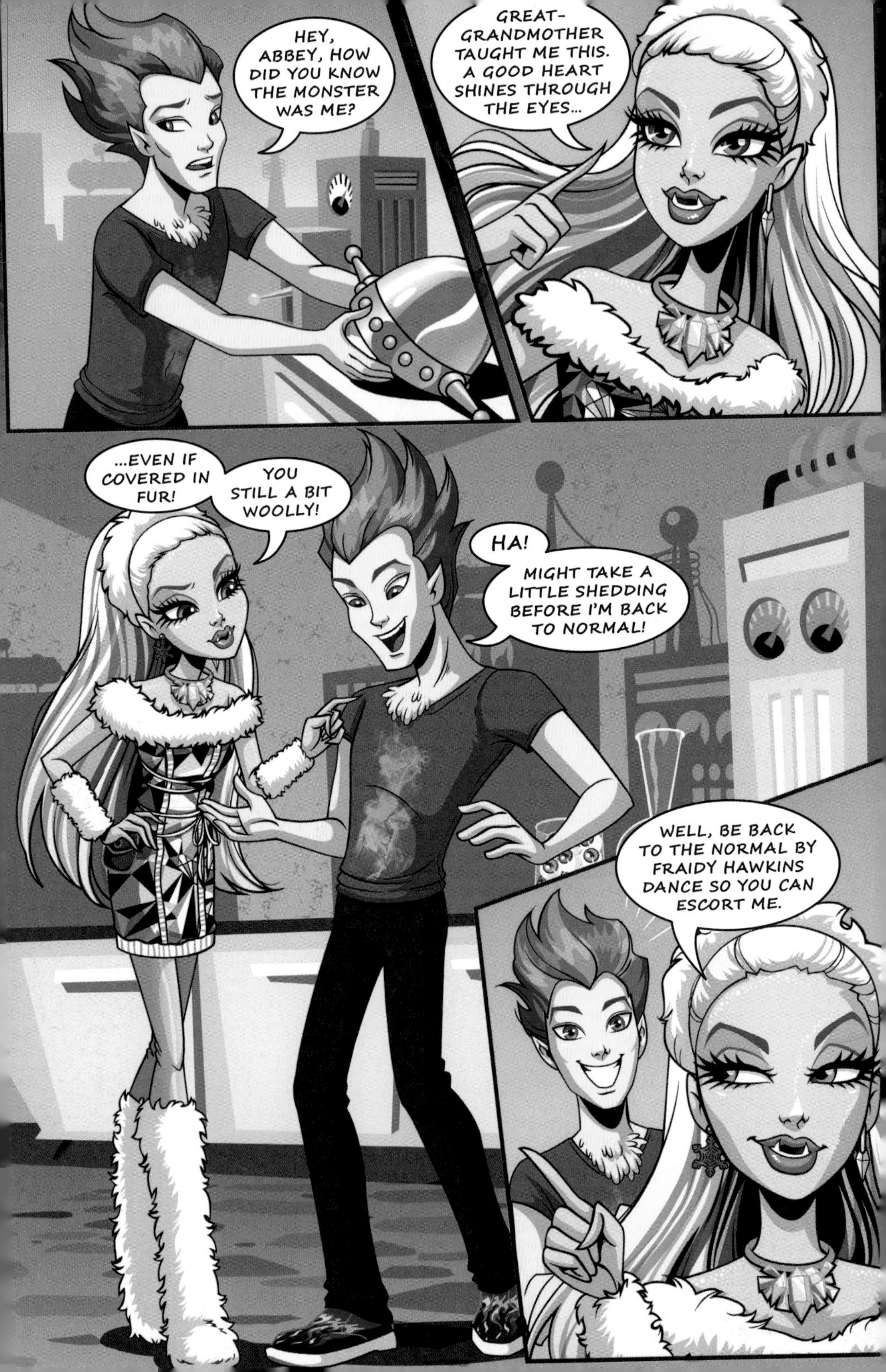
HEY, ABBEY, HOW DID YOU KNOW THE MONSTER WAS ME?
GREAT-GRANDMOTHER TAUGHT ME THIS. A GOOD HEART SHINES THROUGH THE EYES...
...EVEN IF COVERED IN FUR!
YOU STILL A BIT WOOLLY!
HA!
MIGHT TAKE A LITTLE SHEDDING BEFORE I'M BACK TO NORMAL!
WELL, BE BACK TO THE NORMAL BY FRAIDY HAWKINS DANCE SO YOU CAN ESCORT ME.

SCARAH
and
INVISI BILLY

STAR IN

SHOCK AND AWW!

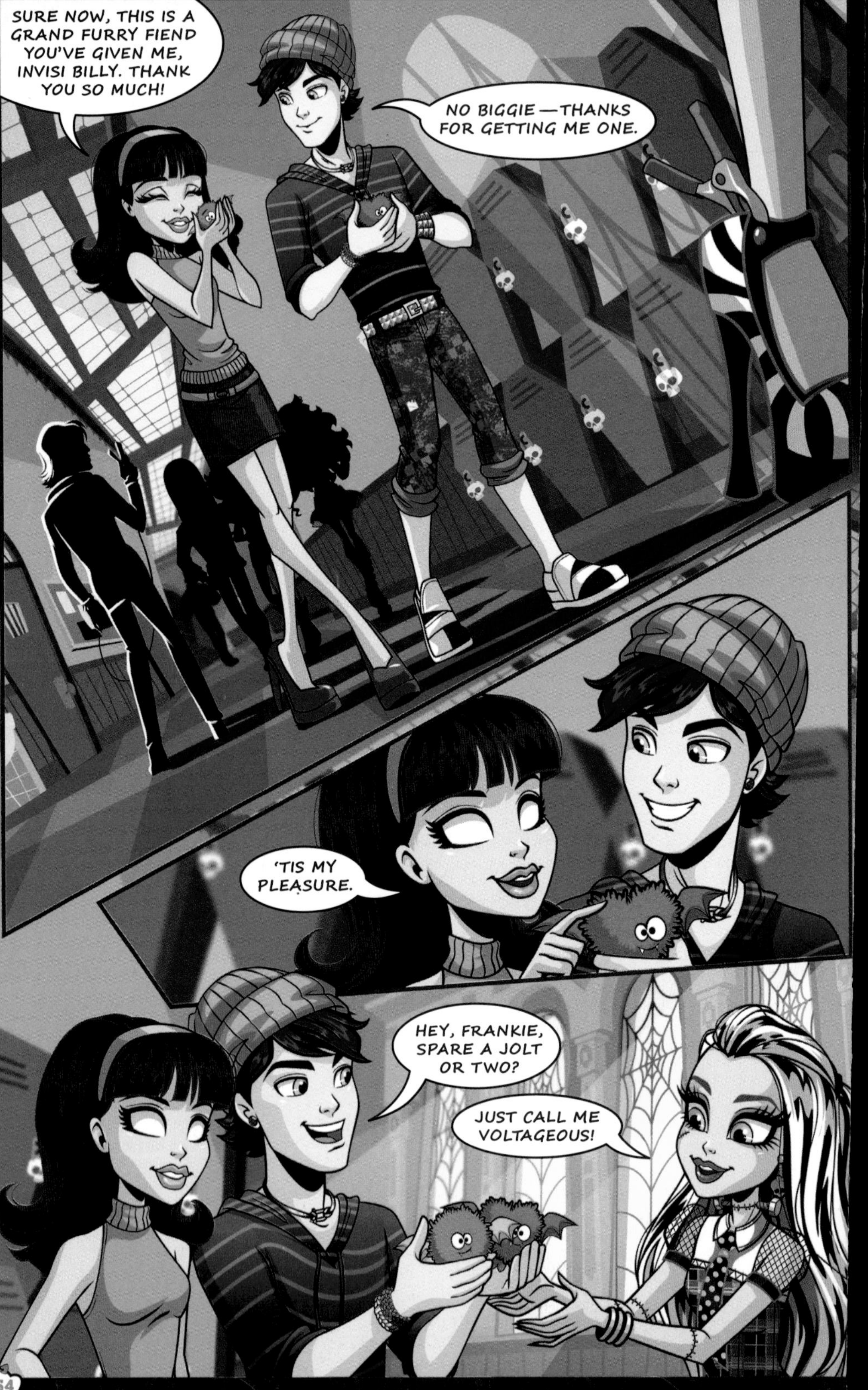
SURE NOW, THIS IS A GRAND FURRY FIEND YOU'VE GIVEN ME, INVISI BILLY. THANK YOU SO MUCH!
NO BIGGIE—THANKS FOR GETTING ME ONE.
'TIS MY PLEASURE.
HEY, FRANKIE, SPARE A JOLT OR TWO?
JUST CALL ME VOLTAGEOUS!

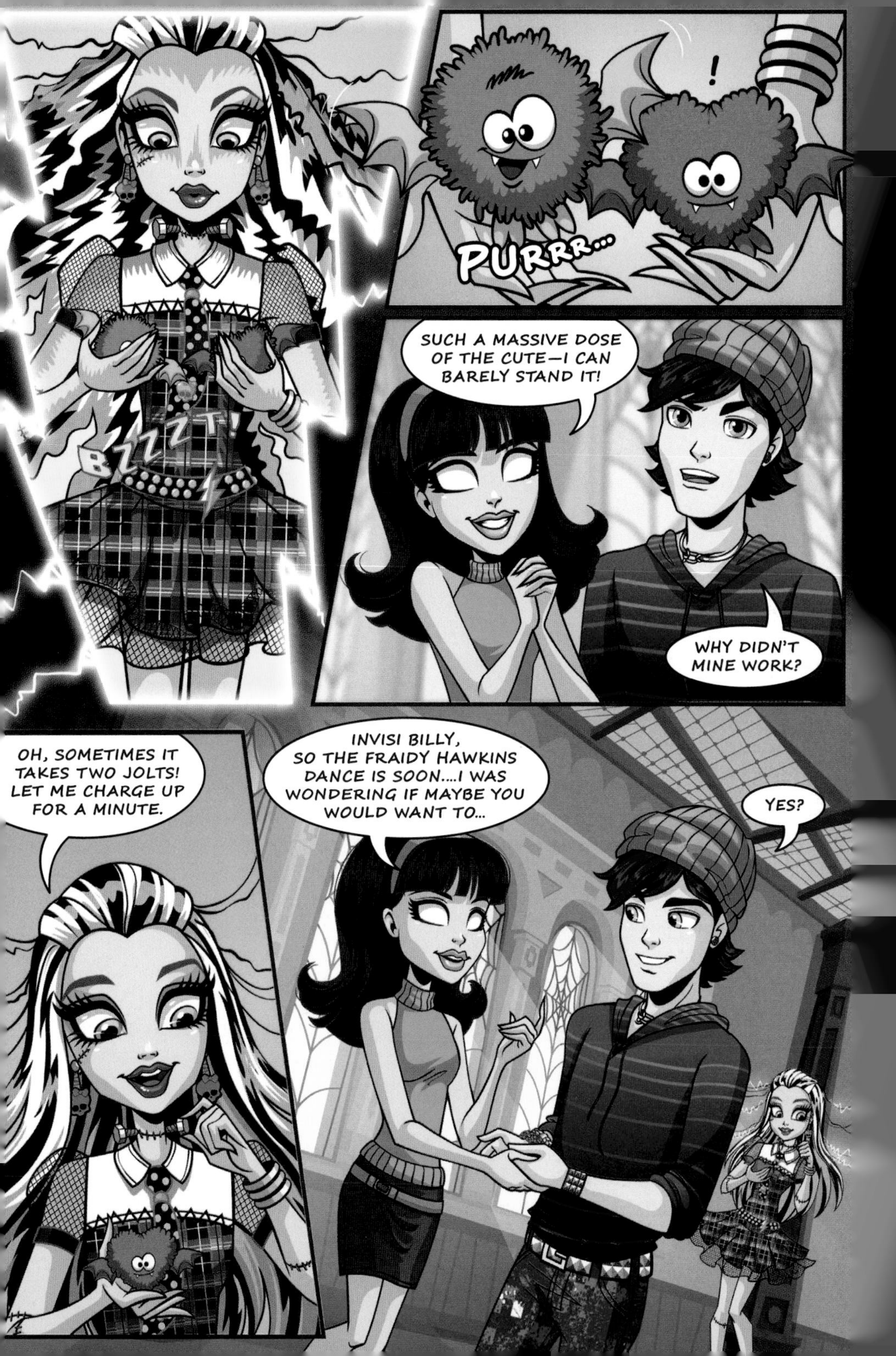
BZZZZT!
PURRR...
SUCH A MASSIVE DOSE OF THE CUTE—I CAN BARELY STAND IT!
WHY DIDN'T MINE WORK?
OH, SOMETIMES IT TAKES TWO JOLTS! LET ME CHARGE UP FOR A MINUTE.
INVISI BILLY, SO THE FRAIDY HAWKINS DANCE IS SOON....I WAS WONDERING IF MAYBE YOU WOULD WANT TO...
YES?

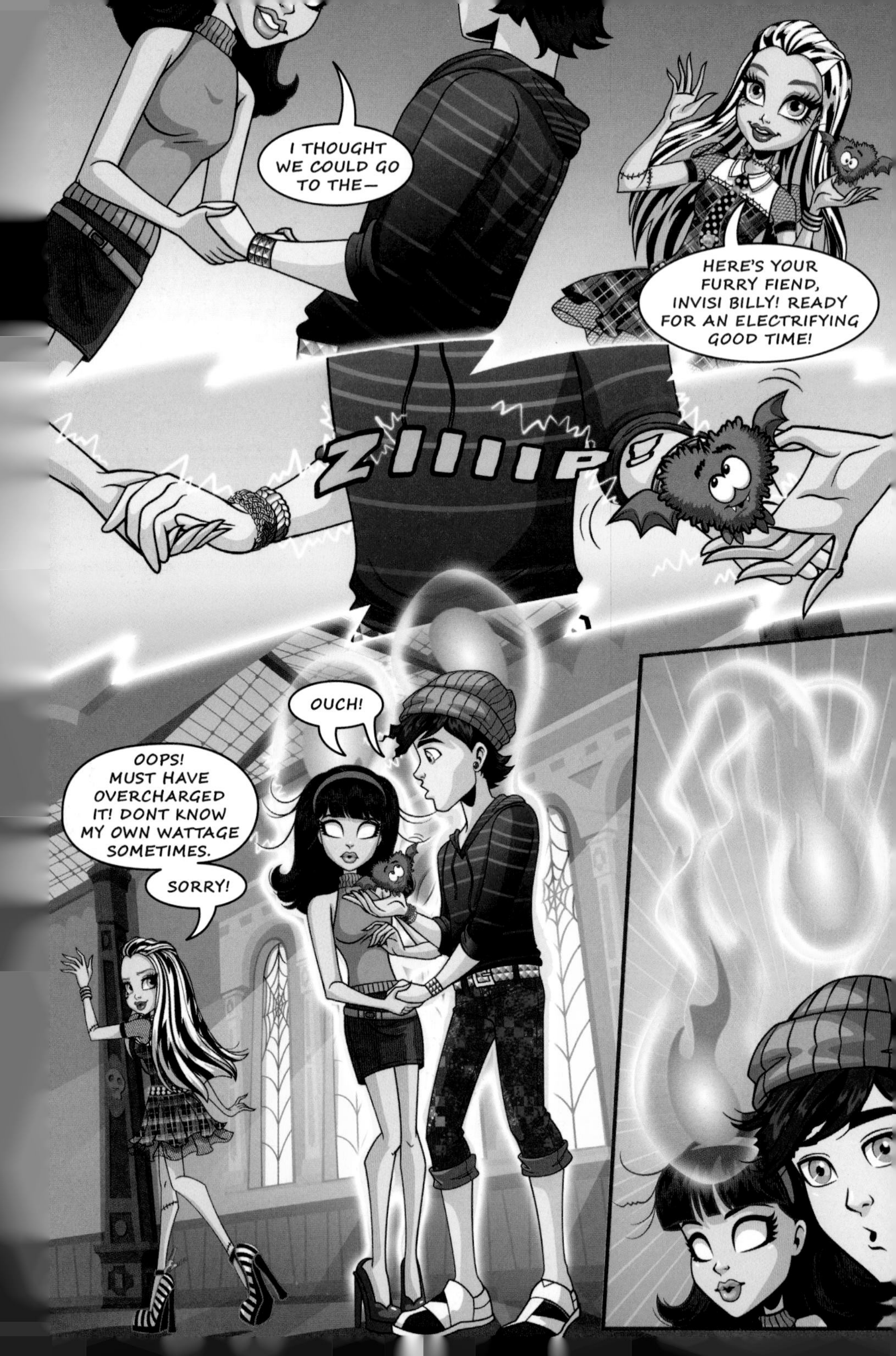
I THOUGHT WE COULD GO TO THE—
HERE'S YOUR FURRY FIEND, INVISI BILLY! READY FOR AN ELECTRIFYING GOOD TIME!
ZIIIIP
OUCH!
OOPS! MUST HAVE OVERCHARGED IT! DONT KNOW MY OWN WATTAGE SOMETIMES.
SORRY!

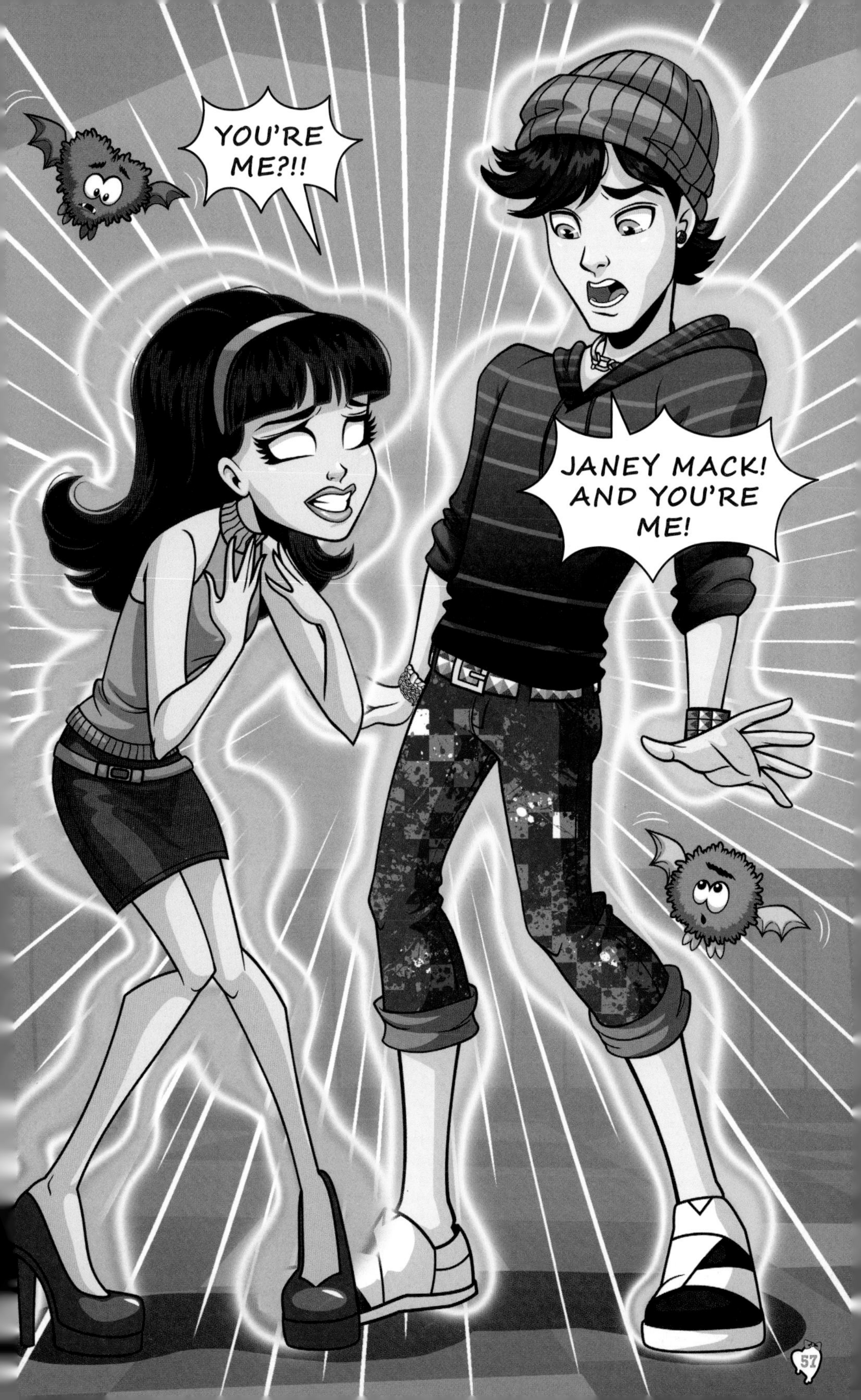
YOU'RE ME?!!
JANEY MACK! AND YOU'RE ME!

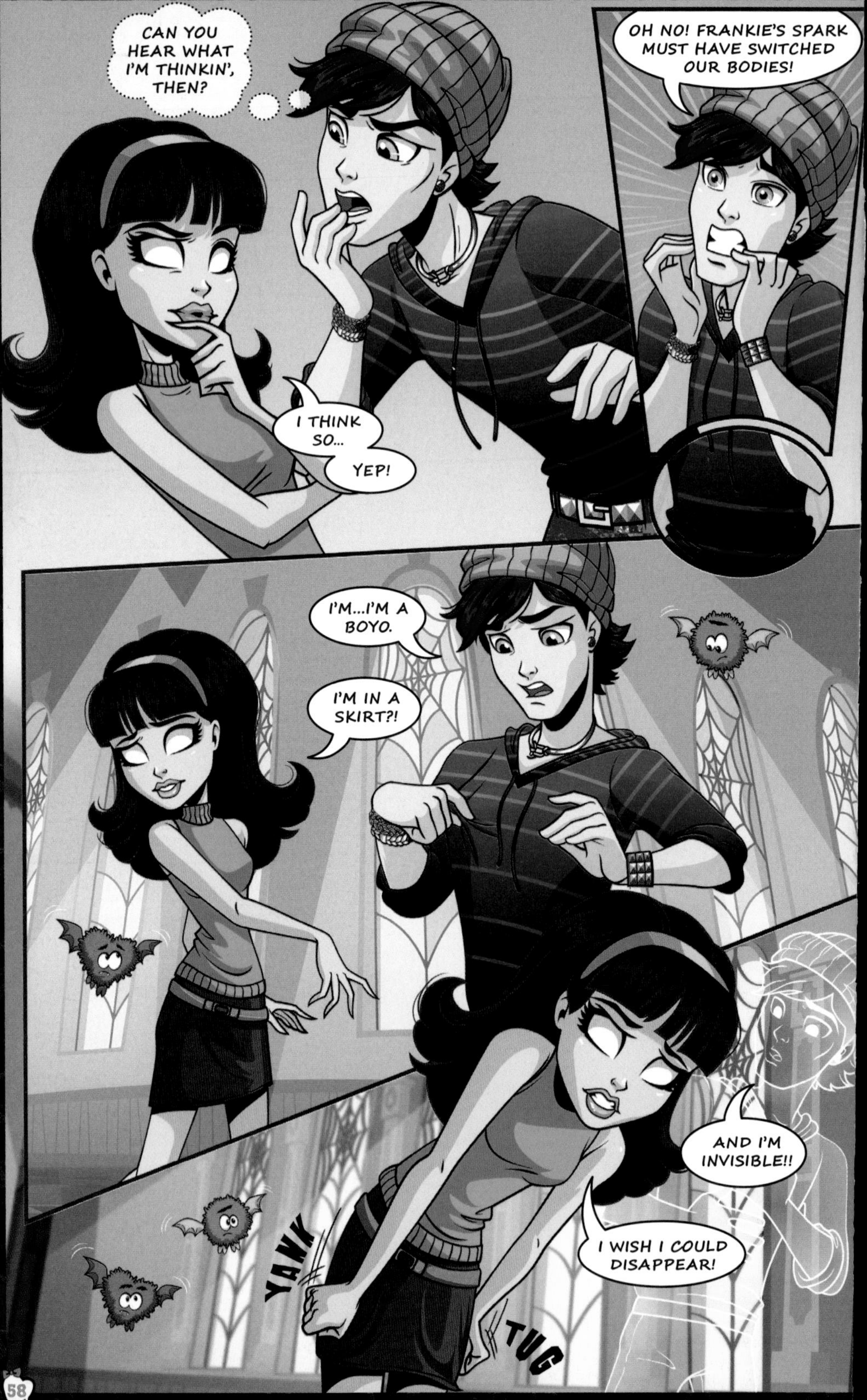
CAN YOU HEAR WHAT I'M THINKIN', THEN?
I THINK SO...
YEP!
OH NO! FRANKIE'S SPARK MUST HAVE SWITCHED OUR BODIES!
I'M...I'M A BOYO.
I'M IN A SKIRT?!
AND I'M INVISIBLE!!
I WISH I COULD DISAPPEAR!
YANK
TUG

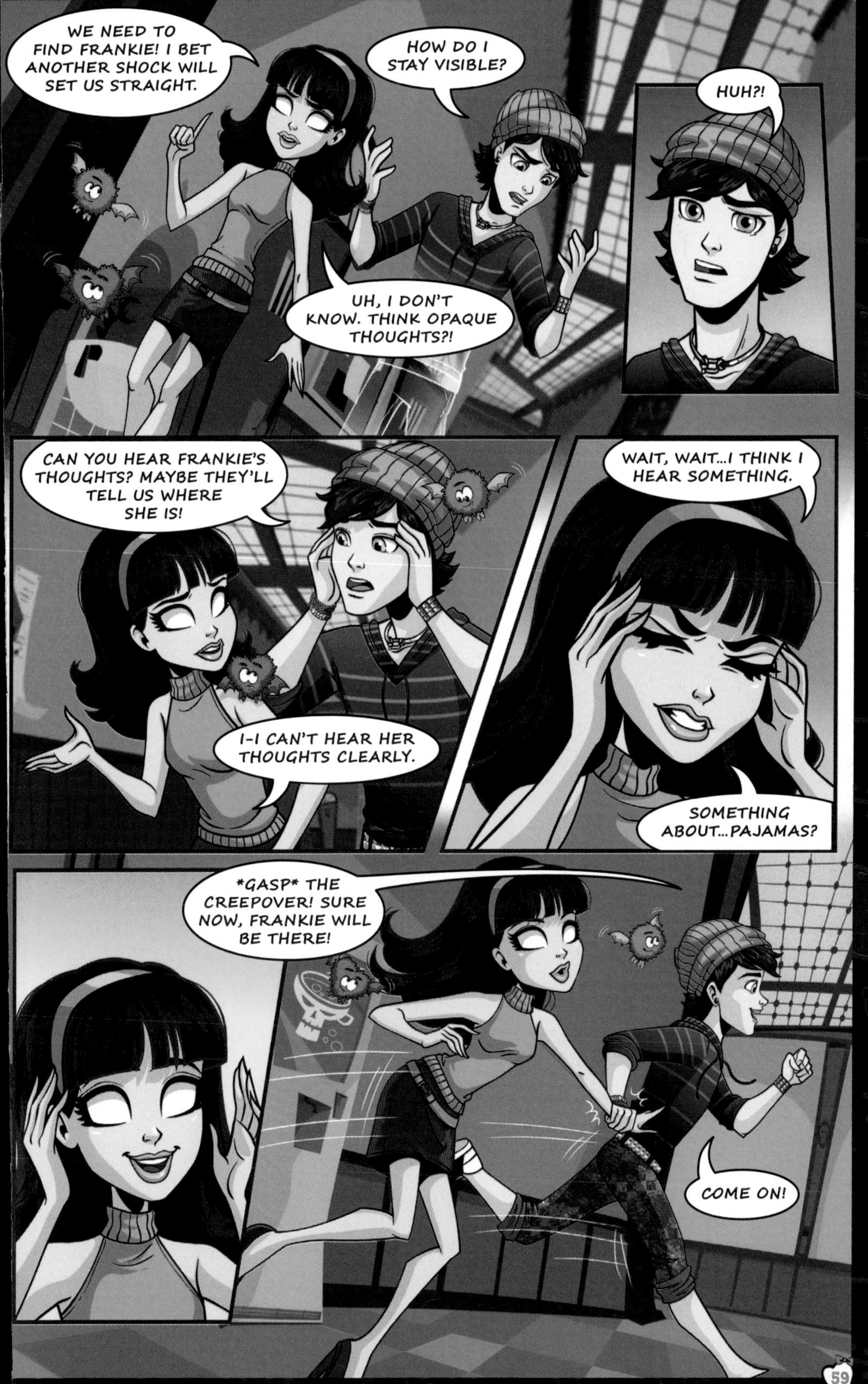
WE NEED TO FIND FRANKIE! I BET ANOTHER SHOCK WILL SET US STRAIGHT.
HOW DO I STAY VISIBLE?
UH, I DON'T KNOW. THINK OPAQUE THOUGHTS?!
HUH?!
CAN YOU HEAR FRANKIE'S THOUGHTS? MAYBE THEY'LL TELL US WHERE SHE IS!
I-I CAN'T HEAR HER THOUGHTS CLEARLY.
WAIT, WAIT...I THINK I HEAR SOMETHING.
SOMETHING ABOUT...PAJAMAS?
GASP THE CREEPOVER! SURE NOW, FRANKIE WILL BE THERE!
COME ON!

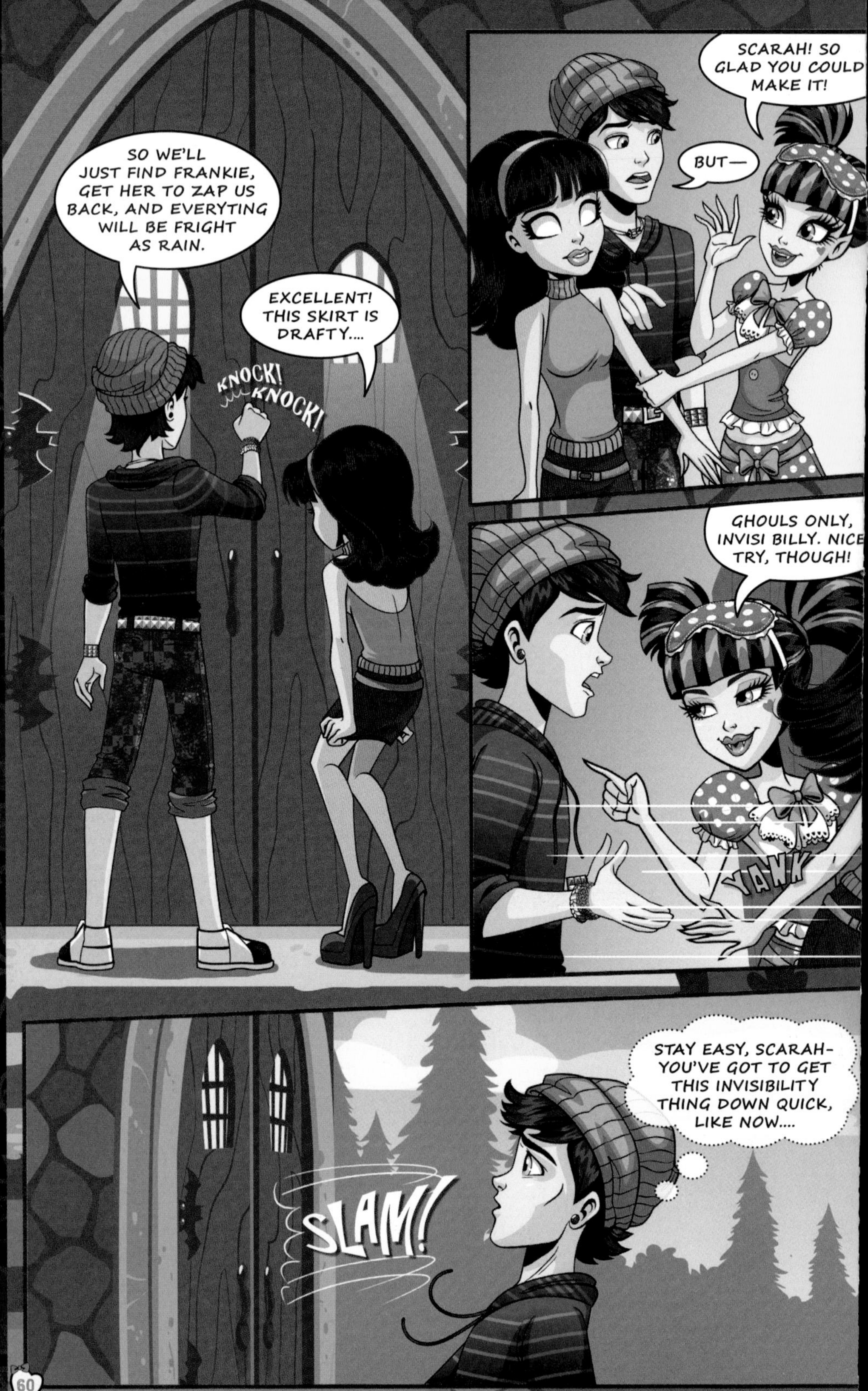

SO WE'LL JUST FIND FRANKIE, GET HER TO ZAP US BACK, AND EVERYTING WILL BE FRIGHT AS RAIN.
EXCELLENT! THIS SKIRT IS DRAFTY....
KNOCK! KNOCK!
SCARAH! SO GLAD YOU COULD MAKE IT!
BUT—
GHOULS ONLY, INVISI BILLY. NICE TRY, THOUGH!
YANK
SLAM!
STAY EASY, SCARAH- YOU'VE GOT TO GET THIS INVISIBILITY THING DOWN QUICK, LIKE NOW....

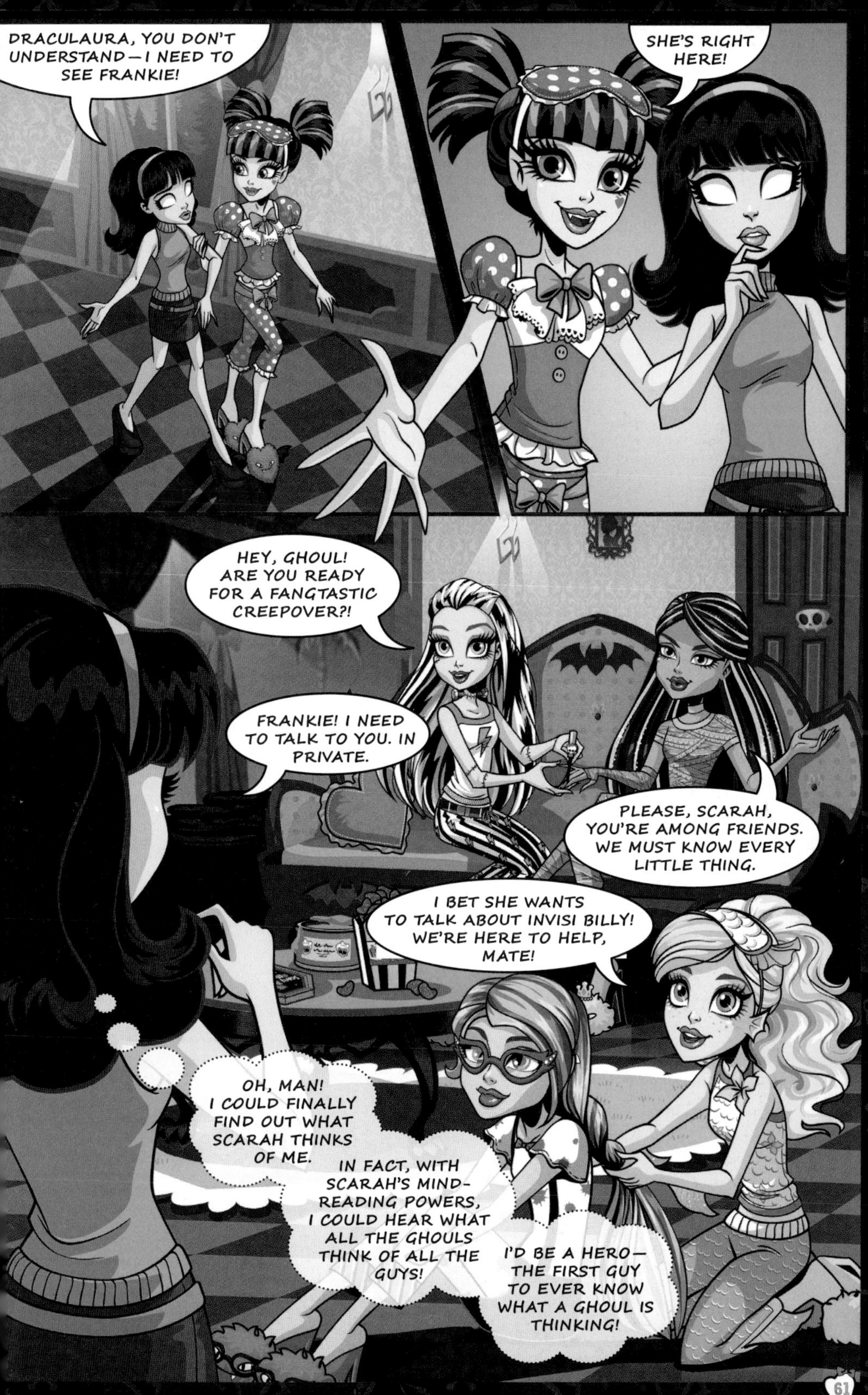

DRACULAURA, YOU DON'T UNDERSTAND—I NEED TO SEE FRANKIE!
SHE'S RIGHT HERE!
HEY, GHOUL! ARE YOU READY FOR A FANGTASTIC CREEPOVER?!
FRANKIE! I NEED TO TALK TO YOU. IN PRIVATE.
PLEASE, SCARAH, YOU'RE AMONG FRIENDS. WE MUST KNOW EVERY LITTLE THING.
I BET SHE WANTS TO TALK ABOUT INVISI BILLY! WE'RE HERE TO HELP, MATE!
OH, MAN! I COULD FINALLY FIND OUT WHAT SCARAH THINKS OF ME.
IN FACT, WITH SCARAH'S MIND-READING POWERS, I COULD HEAR WHAT ALL THE GHOULS THINK OF ALL THE GUYS!
I'D BE A HERO—THE FIRST GUY TO EVER KNOW WHAT A GHOUL IS THINKING!

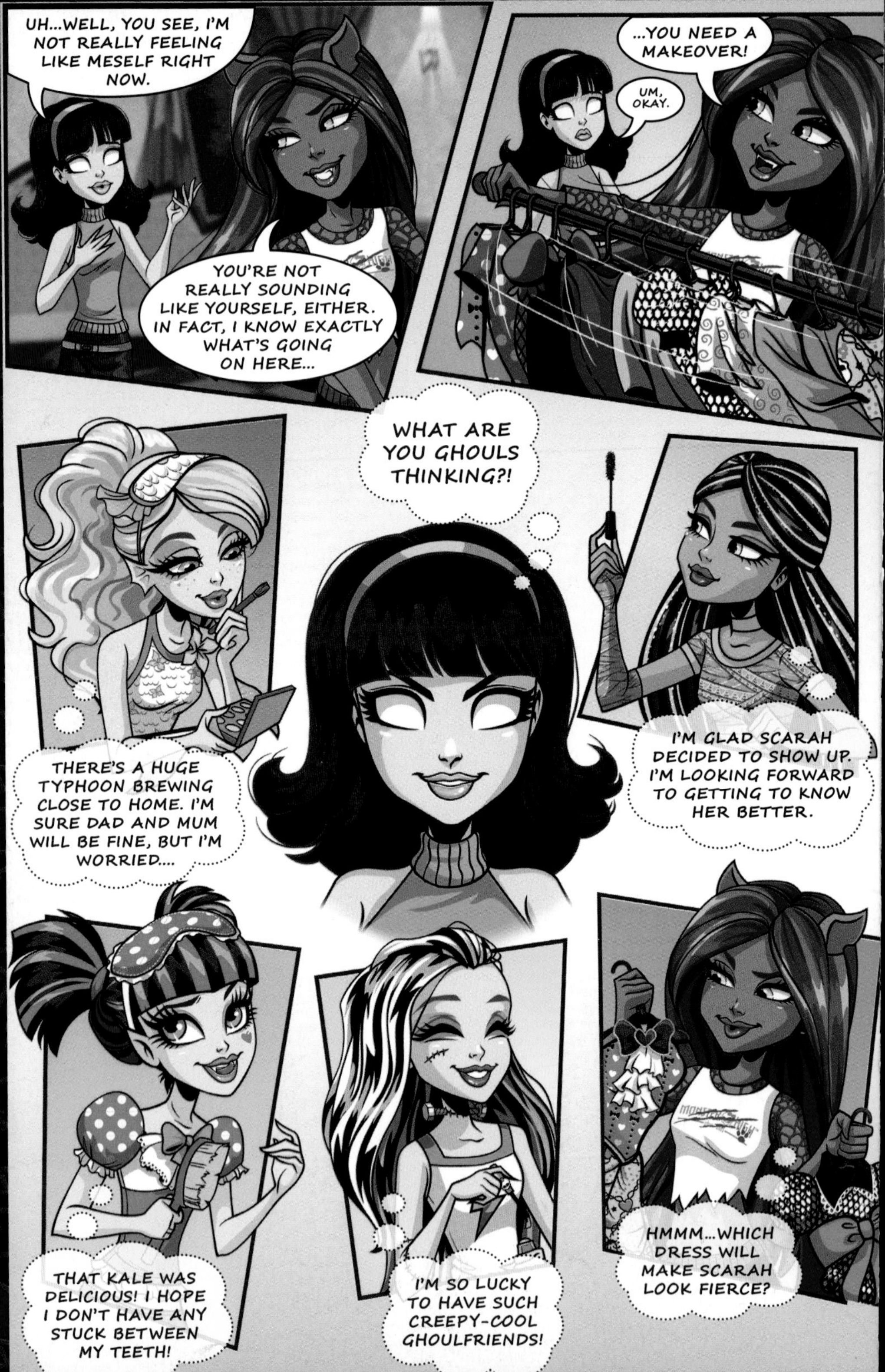
UH...WELL, YOU SEE, I'M NOT REALLY FEELING LIKE MESELF RIGHT NOW.
YOU'RE NOT REALLY SOUNDING LIKE YOURSELF, EITHER. IN FACT, I KNOW EXACTLY WHAT'S GOING ON HERE...
...YOU NEED A MAKEOVER!
UM, OKAY.
WHAT ARE YOU GHOULS THINKING?!
THERE'S A HUGE TYPHOON BREWING CLOSE TO HOME. I'M SURE DAD AND MUM WILL BE FINE, BUT I'M WORRIED...
I'M GLAD SCARAH DECIDED TO SHOW UP. I'M LOOKING FORWARD TO GETTING TO KNOW HER BETTER.
THAT KALE WAS DELICIOUS! I HOPE I DON'T HAVE ANY STUCK BETWEEN MY TEETH!
I'M SO LUCKY TO HAVE SUCH CREEPY-COOL GHOULFRIENDS!
HMMM...WHICH DRESS WILL MAKE SCARAH LOOK FIERCE?

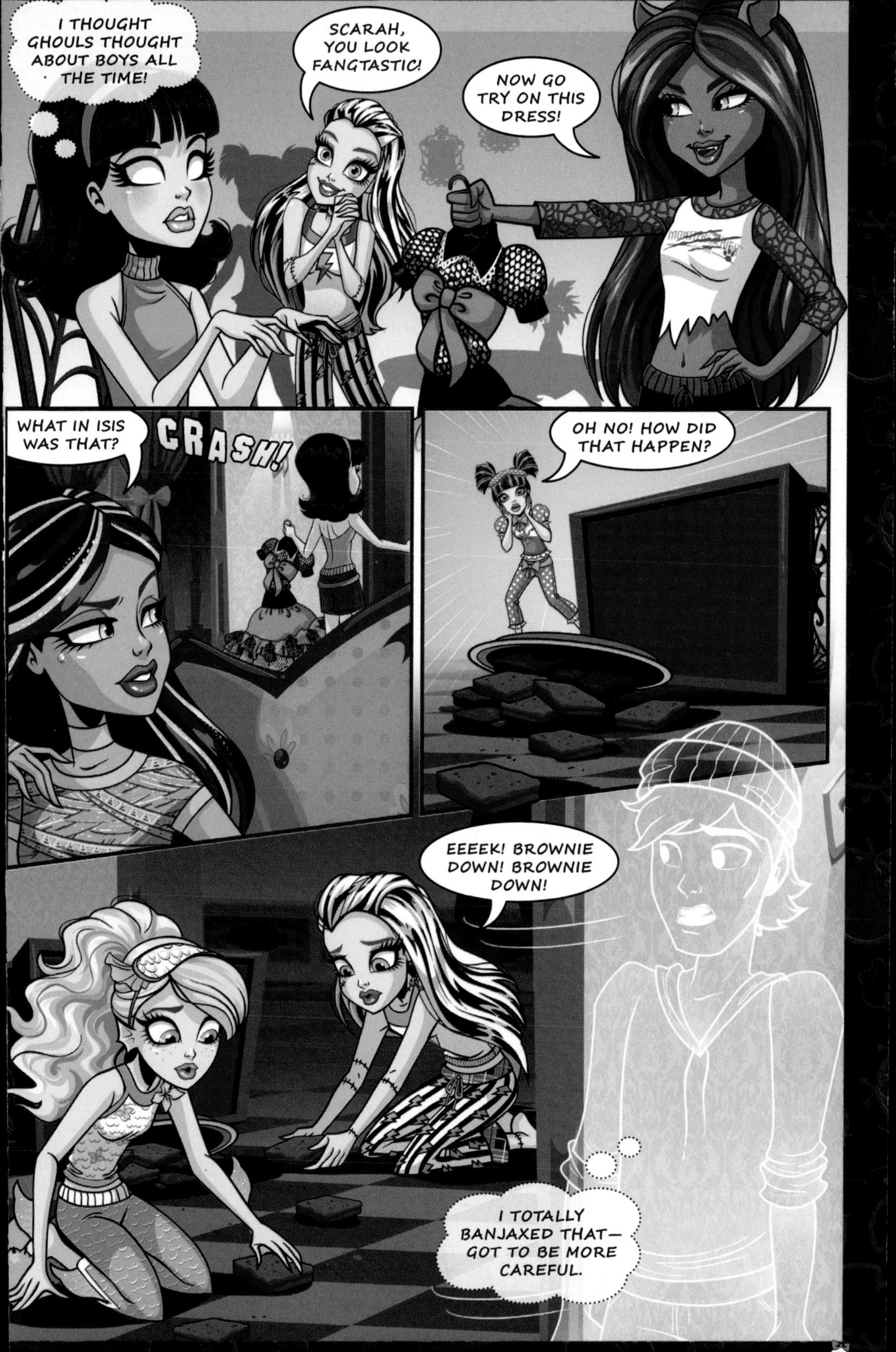
I THOUGHT GHOULS THOUGHT ABOUT BOYS ALL THE TIME!
SCARAH, YOU LOOK FANGTASTIC!
NOW GO TRY ON THIS DRESS!
WHAT IN ISIS WAS THAT?
CRASH!
OH NO! HOW DID THAT HAPPEN?
EEEEK! BROWNIE DOWN! BROWNIE DOWN!
I TOTALLY BANJAXED THAT— GOT TO BE MORE CAREFUL.

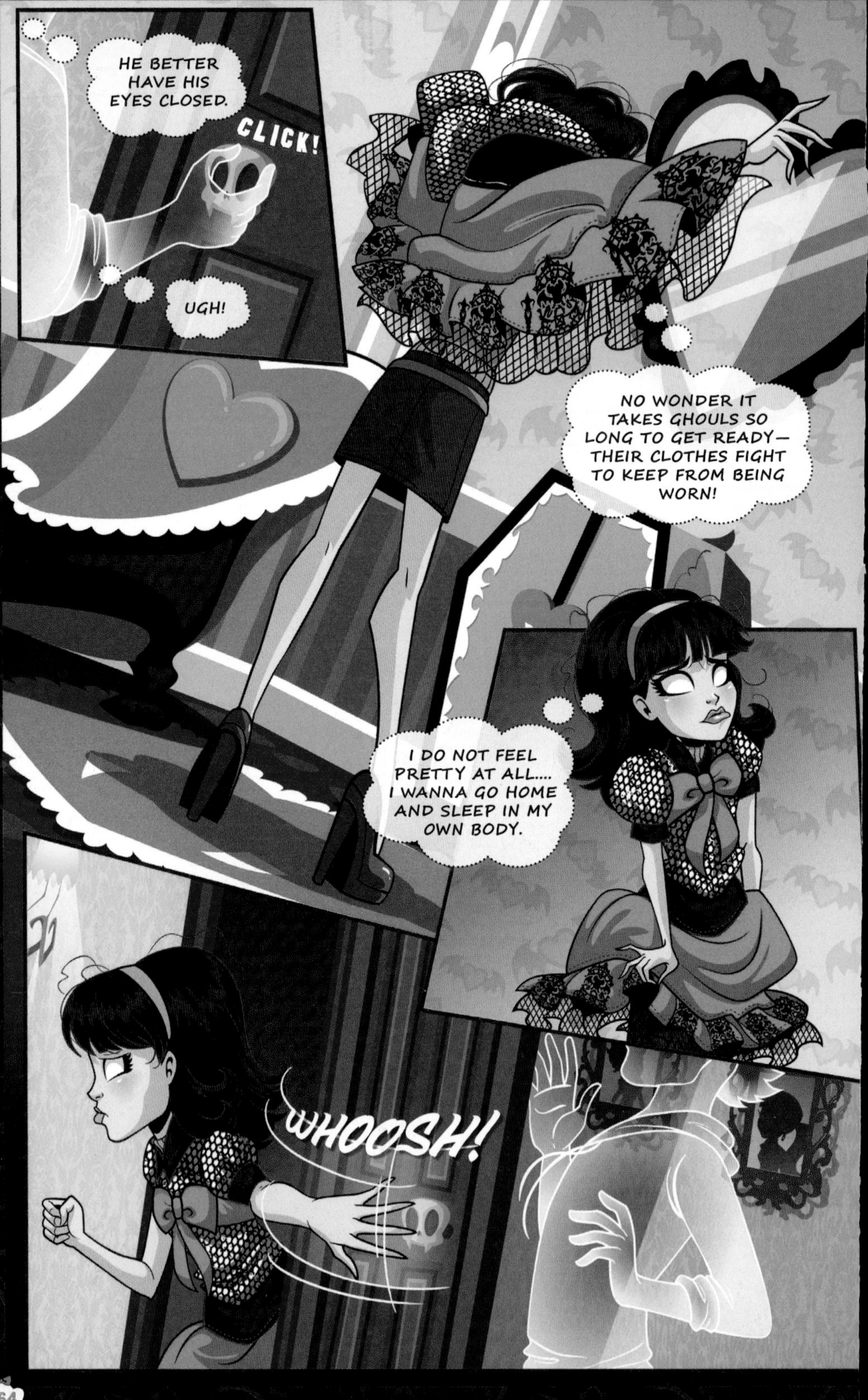
HE BETTER HAVE HIS EYES CLOSED.
CLICK!
UGH!
NO WONDER IT TAKES GHOULS SO LONG TO GET READY—THEIR CLOTHES FIGHT TO KEEP FROM BEING WORN!
I DO NOT FEEL PRETTY AT ALL.... I WANNA GO HOME AND SLEEP IN MY OWN BODY.
WHOOSH!

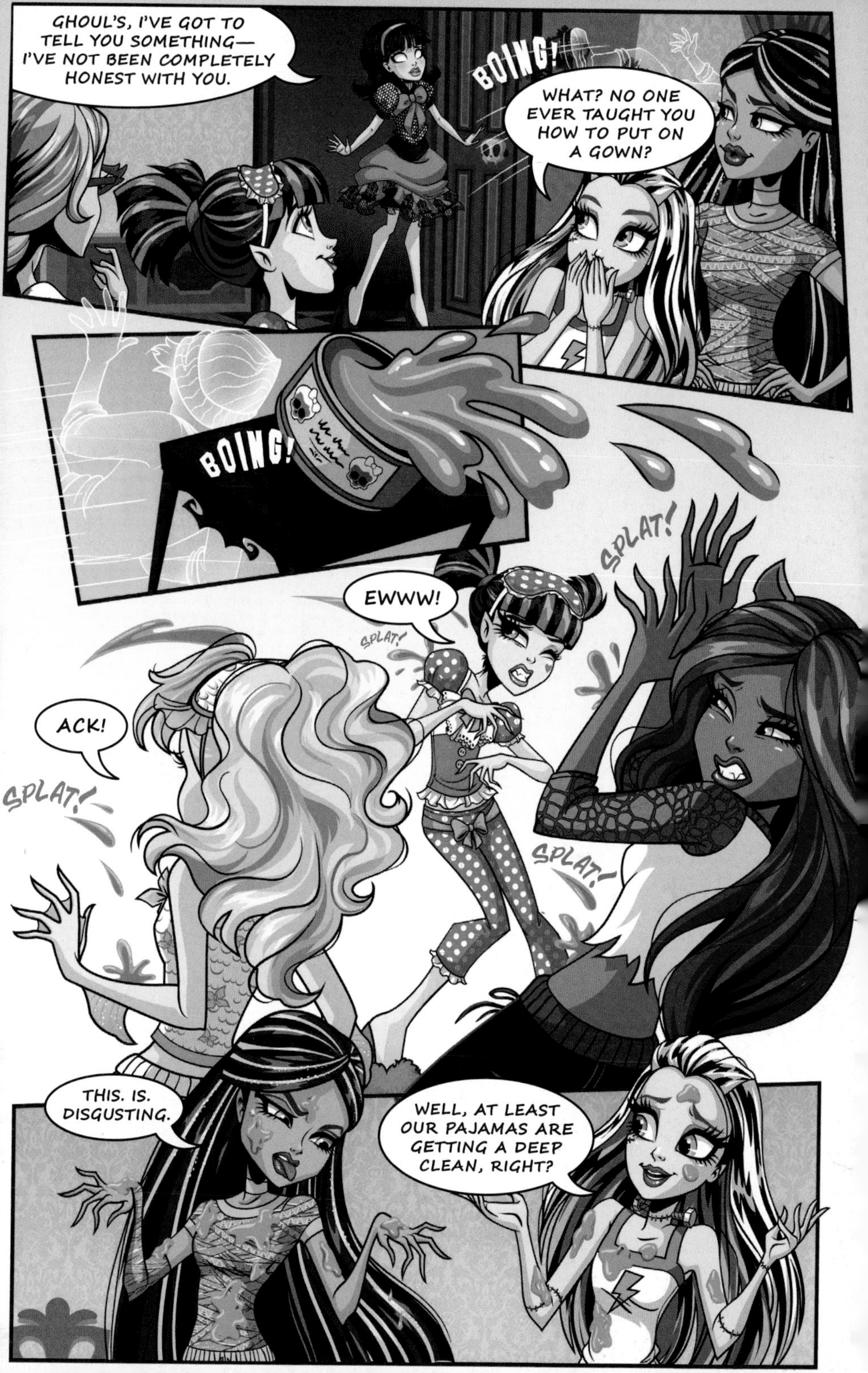
GHOUL'S, I'VE GOT TO TELL YOU SOMETHING— I'VE NOT BEEN COMPLETELY HONEST WITH YOU.
BOING!
WHAT? NO ONE EVER TAUGHT YOU HOW TO PUT ON A GOWN?
BOING!
SPLAT!
EWWW!
SPLAT!
ACK!
SPLAT!
SPLAT!
THIS. IS. DISGUSTING.
WELL, AT LEAST OUR PAJAMAS ARE GETTING A DEEP CLEAN, RIGHT?

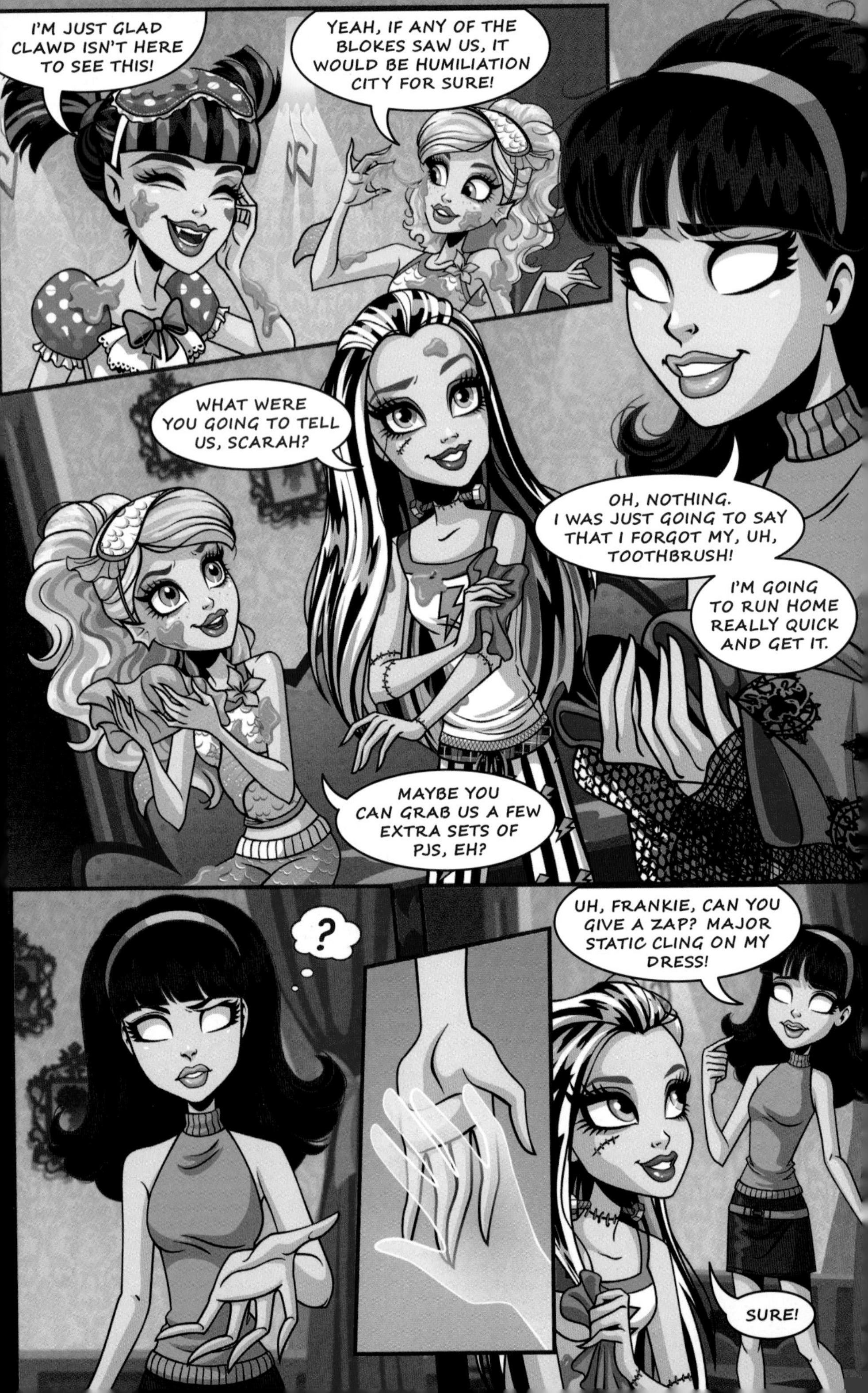
I'M JUST GLAD CLAWD ISN'T HERE TO SEE THIS!
YEAH, IF ANY OF THE BLOKES SAW US, IT WOULD BE HUMILIATION CITY FOR SURE!
WHAT WERE YOU GOING TO TELL US, SCARAH?
OH, NOTHING. I WAS JUST GOING TO SAY THAT I FORGOT MY, UH, TOOTHBRUSH!
I'M GOING TO RUN HOME REALLY QUICK AND GET IT.
MAYBE YOU CAN GRAB US A FEW EXTRA SETS OF PJS, EH?
?
UH, FRANKIE, CAN YOU GIVE A ZAP? MAJOR STATIC CLING ON MY DRESS!
SURE!

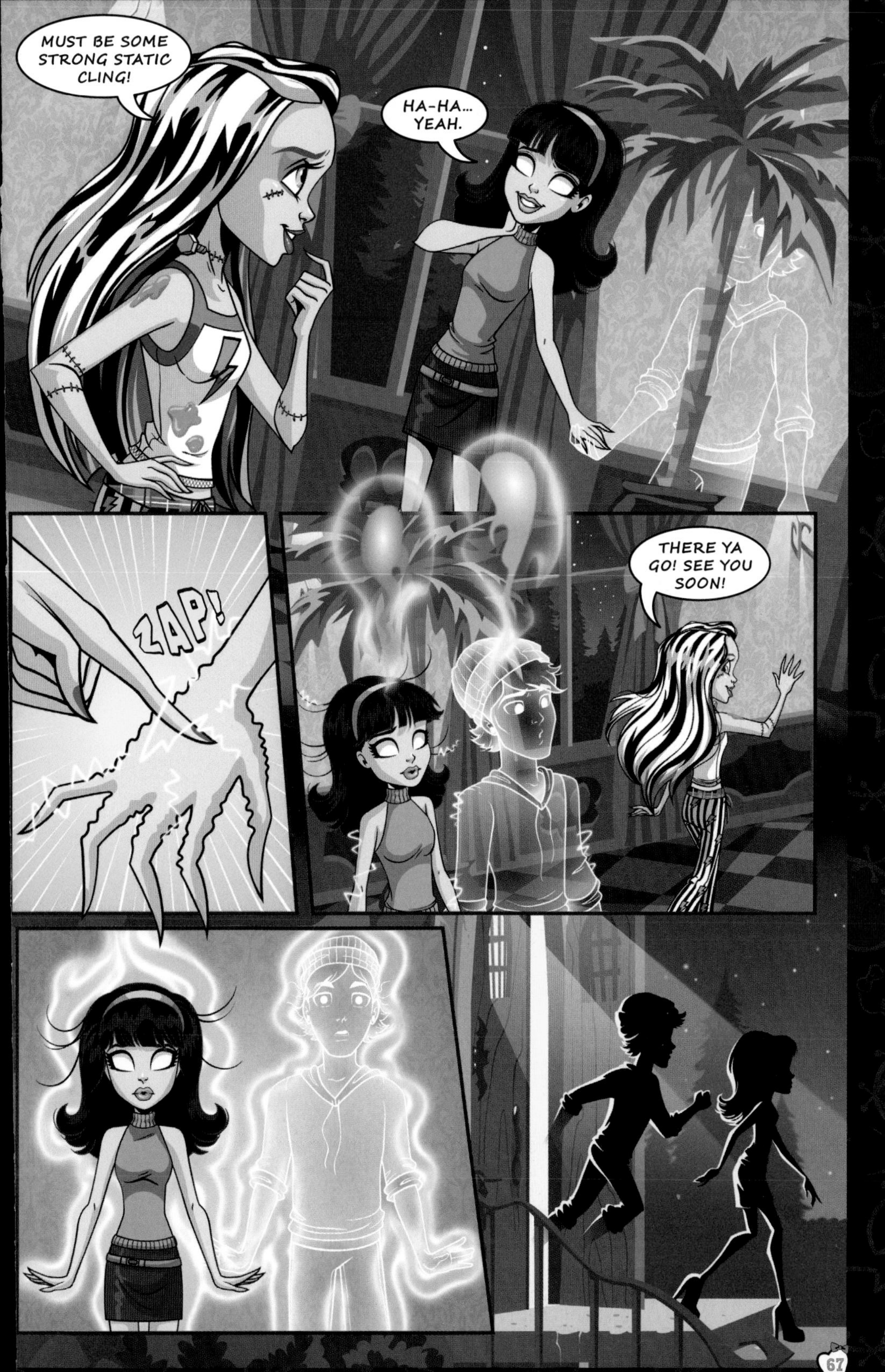

MUST BE SOME STRONG STATIC CLING!
HA-HA... YEAH.
ZAP!
THERE YA GO! SEE YOU SOON!

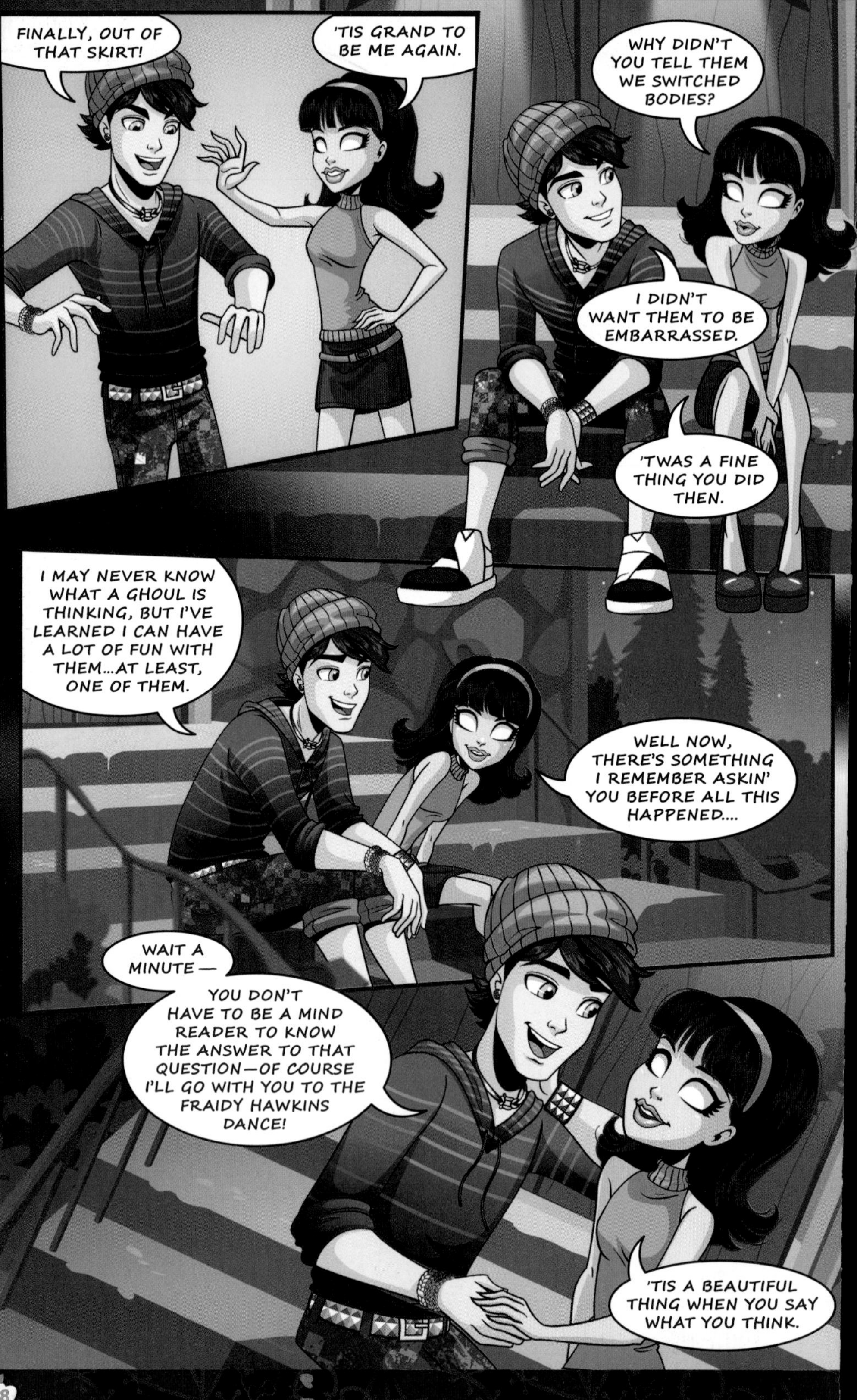
FINALLY, OUT OF THAT SKIRT!
'TIS GRAND TO BE ME AGAIN.
WHY DIDN'T YOU TELL THEM WE SWITCHED BODIES?
I DIDN'T WANT THEM TO BE EMBARRASSED.
'TWAS A FINE THING YOU DID THEN.
I MAY NEVER KNOW WHAT A GHOUL IS THINKING, BUT I'VE LEARNED I CAN HAVE A LOT OF FUN WITH THEM...AT LEAST, ONE OF THEM.
WELL NOW, THERE'S SOMETHING I REMEMBER ASKIN' YOU BEFORE ALL THIS HAPPENED....
WAIT A MINUTE—
YOU DON'T HAVE TO BE A MIND READER TO KNOW THE ANSWER TO THAT QUESTION—OF COURSE I'LL GO WITH YOU TO THE FRAIDY HAWKINS DANCE!
'TIS A BEAUTIFUL THING WHEN YOU SAY WHAT YOU THINK.

CLEO and DEUCE

STAR IN

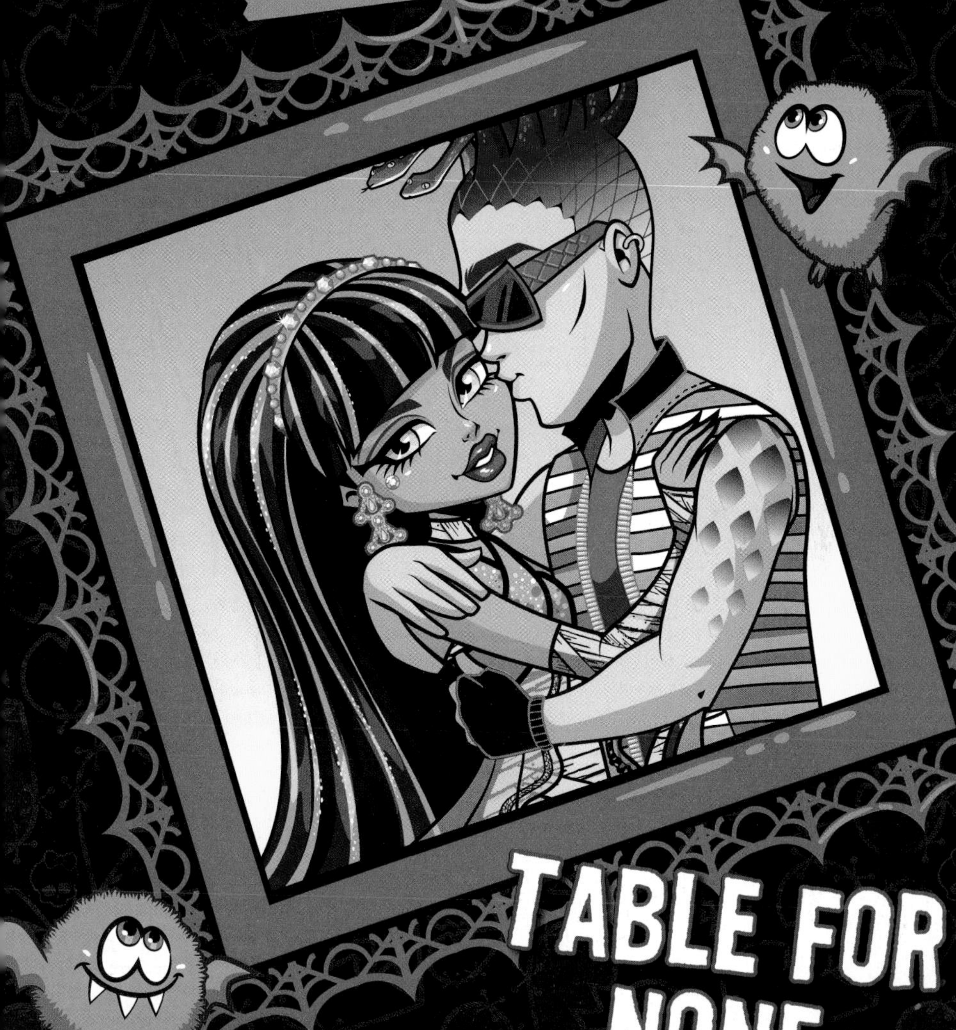

TABLE FOR NONE

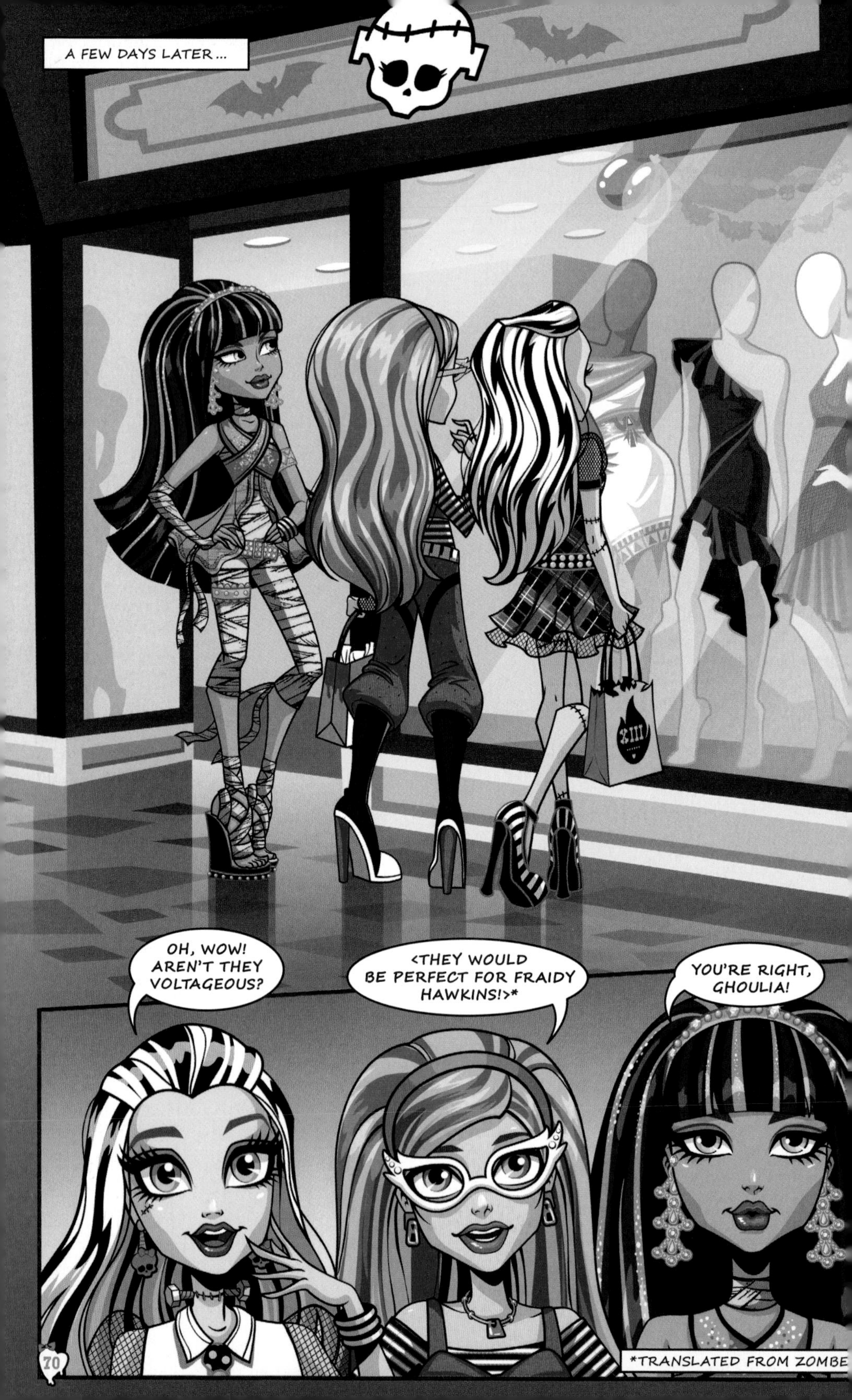
A FEW DAYS LATER...
OH, WOW! AREN'T THEY VOLTAGEOUS?
<THEY WOULD BE PERFECT FOR FRAIDY HAWKINS!>*
YOU'RE RIGHT, GHOULIA!
*TRANSLATED FROM ZOMBE

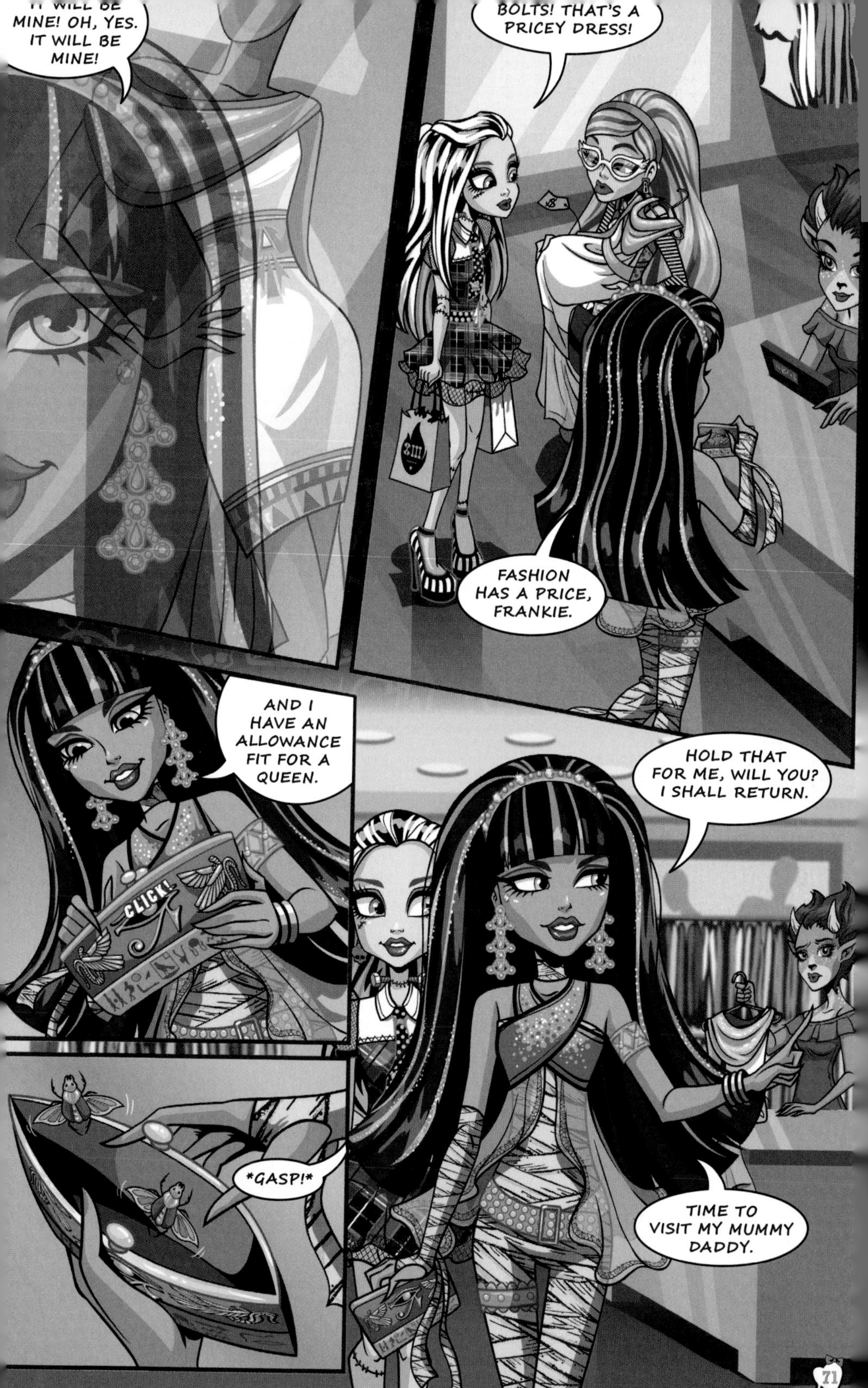
MINE! OH, YES. IT WILL BE MINE!
BOLTS! THAT'S A PRICEY DRESS!
FASHION HAS A PRICE, FRANKIE.
AND I HAVE AN ALLOWANCE FIT FOR A QUEEN.
CLICK!
GASP!
HOLD THAT FOR ME, WILL YOU? I SHALL RETURN.
TIME TO VISIT MY MUMMY DADDY.

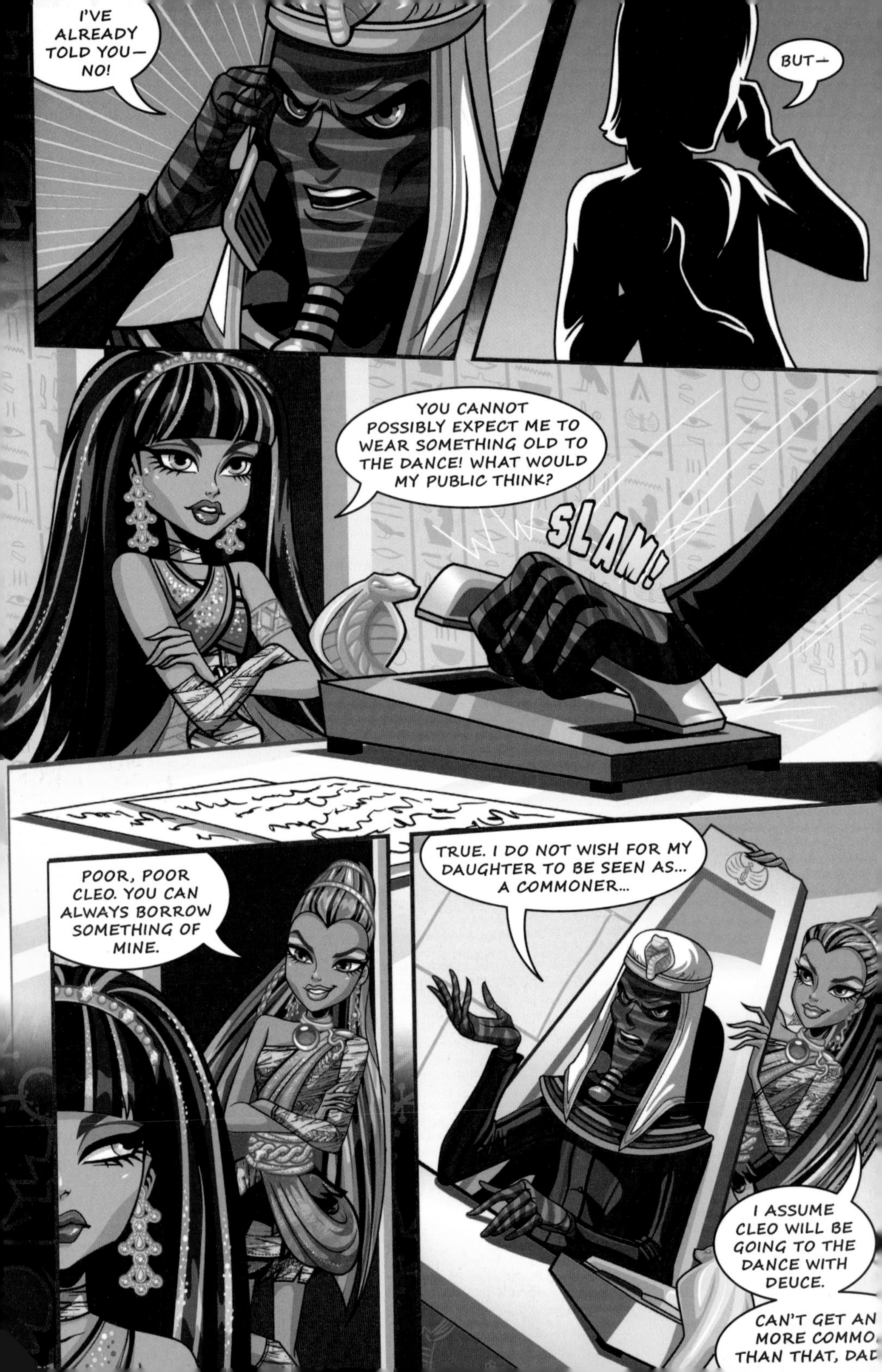
I'VE ALREADY TOLD YOU— NO!
BUT—
YOU CANNOT POSSIBLY EXPECT ME TO WEAR SOMETHING OLD TO THE DANCE! WHAT WOULD MY PUBLIC THINK?
SLAM!
POOR, POOR CLEO. YOU CAN ALWAYS BORROW SOMETHING OF MINE.
TRUE. I DO NOT WISH FOR MY DAUGHTER TO BE SEEN AS... A COMMONER...
I ASSUME CLEO WILL BE GOING TO THE DANCE WITH DEUCE.
CAN'T GET AN MORE COMMO THAN THAT, DAD

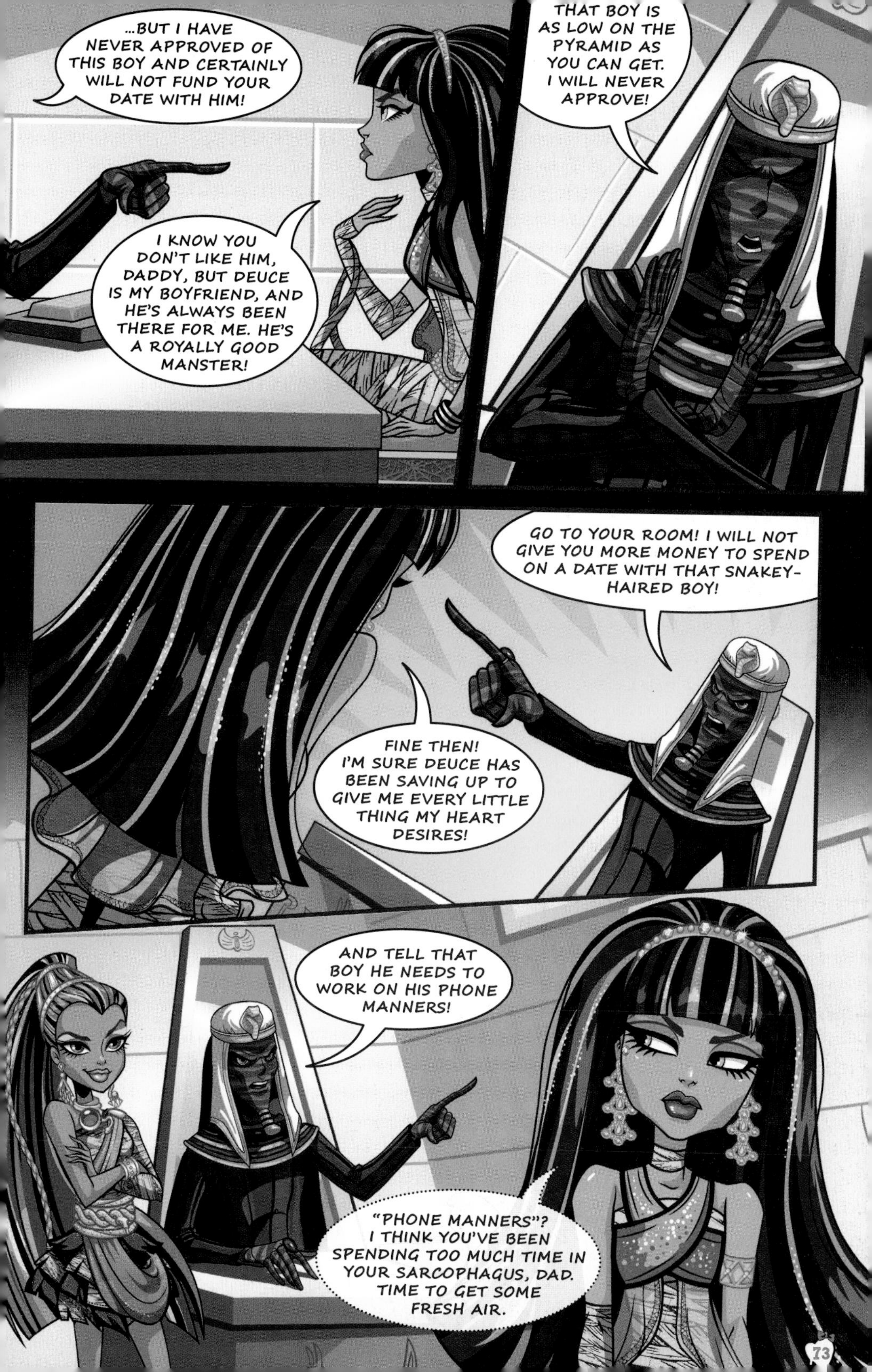
...BUT I HAVE NEVER APPROVED OF THIS BOY AND CERTAINLY WILL NOT FUND YOUR DATE WITH HIM!
I KNOW YOU DON'T LIKE HIM, DADDY, BUT DEUCE IS MY BOYFRIEND, AND HE'S ALWAYS BEEN THERE FOR ME. HE'S A ROYALLY GOOD MANSTER!
THAT BOY IS AS LOW ON THE PYRAMID AS YOU CAN GET. I WILL NEVER APPROVE!
GO TO YOUR ROOM! I WILL NOT GIVE YOU MORE MONEY TO SPEND ON A DATE WITH THAT SNAKEY-HAIRED BOY!
FINE THEN! I'M SURE DEUCE HAS BEEN SAVING UP TO GIVE ME EVERY LITTLE THING MY HEART DESIRES!
AND TELL THAT BOY HE NEEDS TO WORK ON HIS PHONE MANNERS!
"PHONE MANNERS"? I THINK YOU'VE BEEN SPENDING TOO MUCH TIME IN YOUR SARCOPHAGUS, DAD. TIME TO GET SOME FRESH AIR.

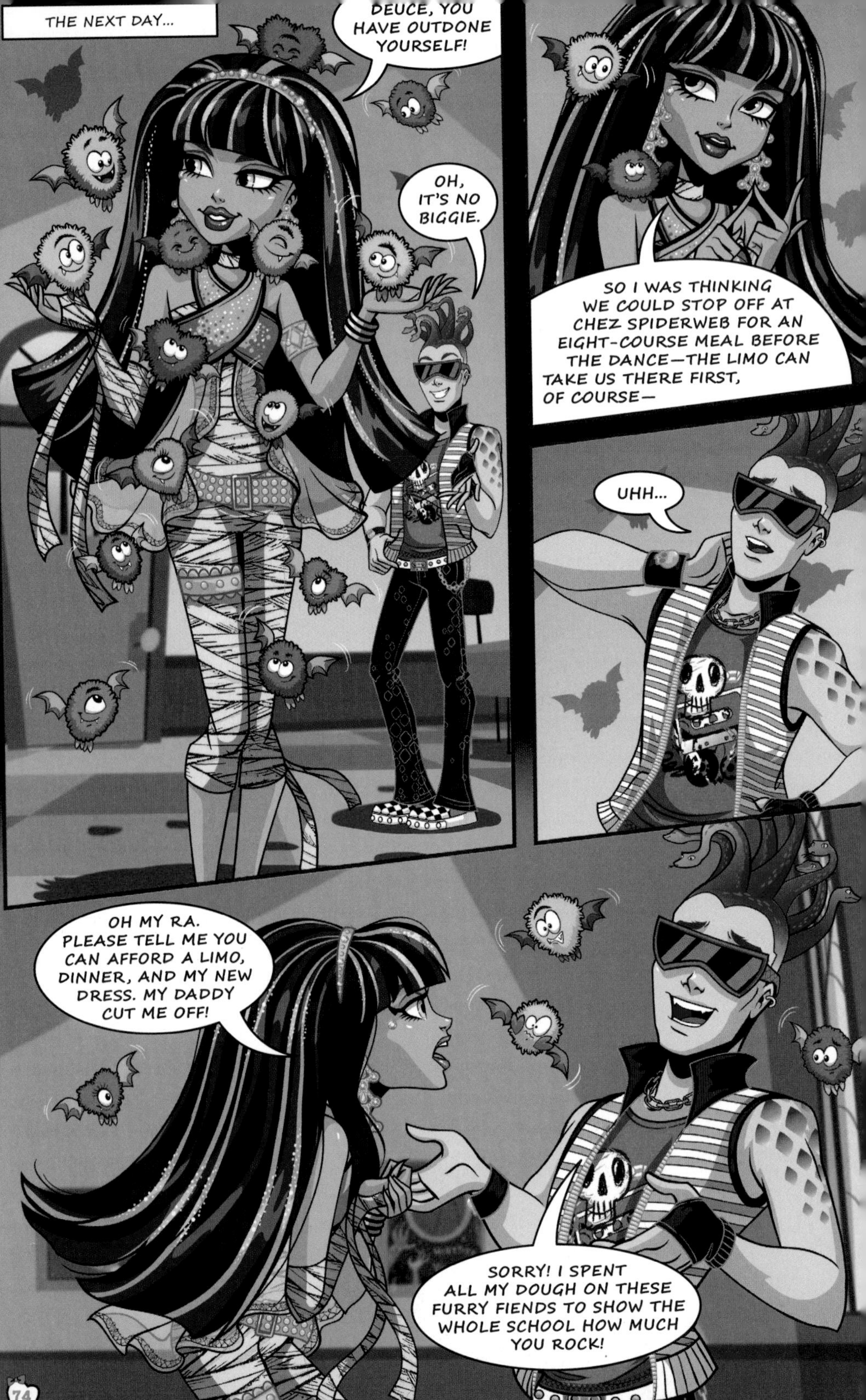
THE NEXT DAY...
DEUCE, YOU HAVE OUTDONE YOURSELF!
OH, IT'S NO BIGGIE.
SO I WAS THINKING WE COULD STOP OFF AT CHEZ SPIDERWEB FOR AN EIGHT-COURSE MEAL BEFORE THE DANCE—THE LIMO CAN TAKE US THERE FIRST, OF COURSE—
UHH...
OH MY RA. PLEASE TELL ME YOU CAN AFFORD A LIMO, DINNER, AND MY NEW DRESS. MY DADDY CUT ME OFF!
SORRY! I SPENT ALL MY DOUGH ON THESE FURRY FIENDS TO SHOW THE WHOLE SCHOOL HOW MUCH YOU ROCK!

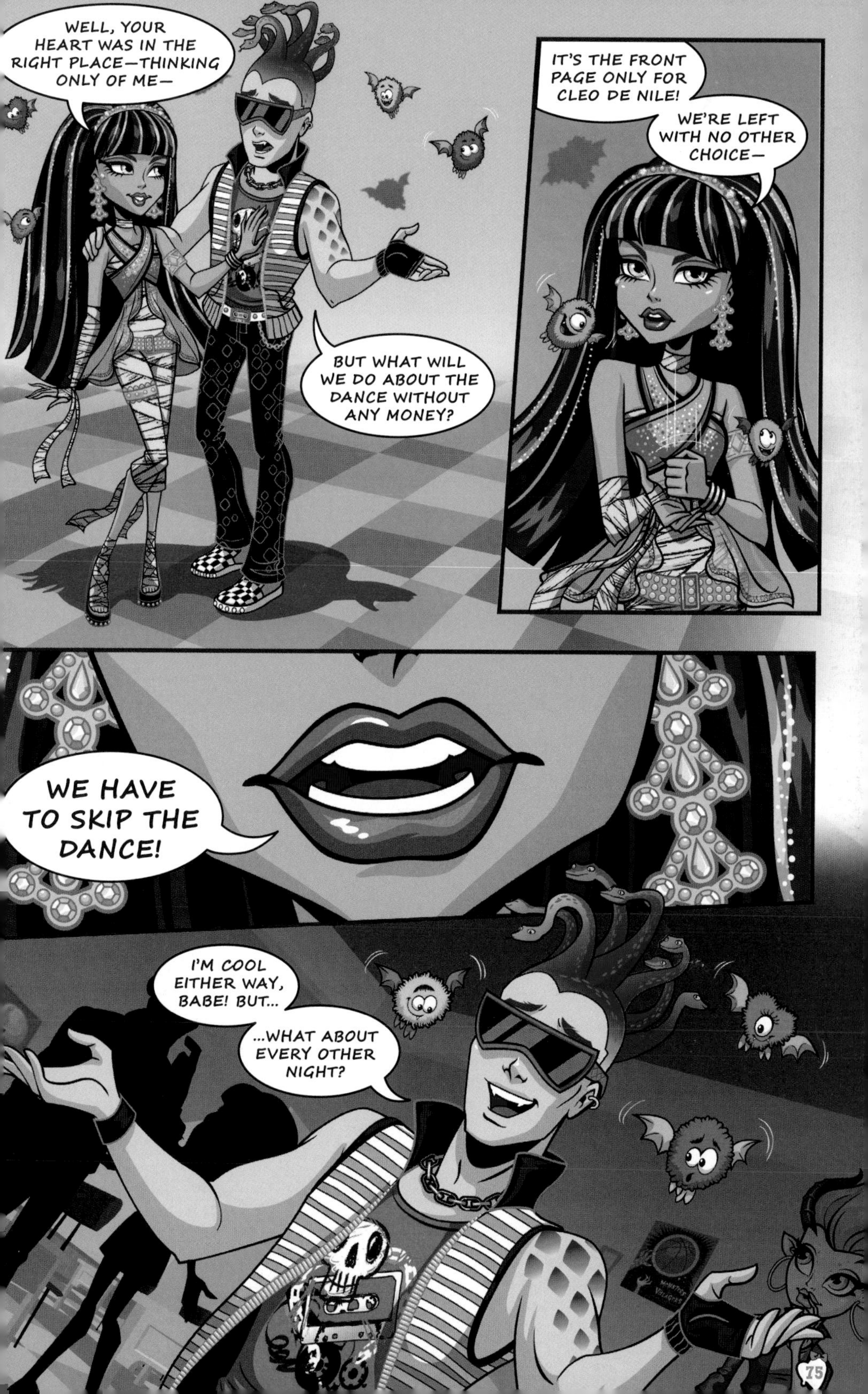
WELL, YOUR HEART WAS IN THE RIGHT PLACE—THINKING ONLY OF ME—
BUT WHAT WILL WE DO ABOUT THE DANCE WITHOUT ANY MONEY?
IT'S THE FRONT PAGE ONLY FOR CLEO DE NILE!
WE'RE LEFT WITH NO OTHER CHOICE—
WE HAVE TO SKIP THE DANCE!
I'M COOL EITHER WAY, BABE! BUT...
...WHAT ABOUT EVERY OTHER NIGHT?

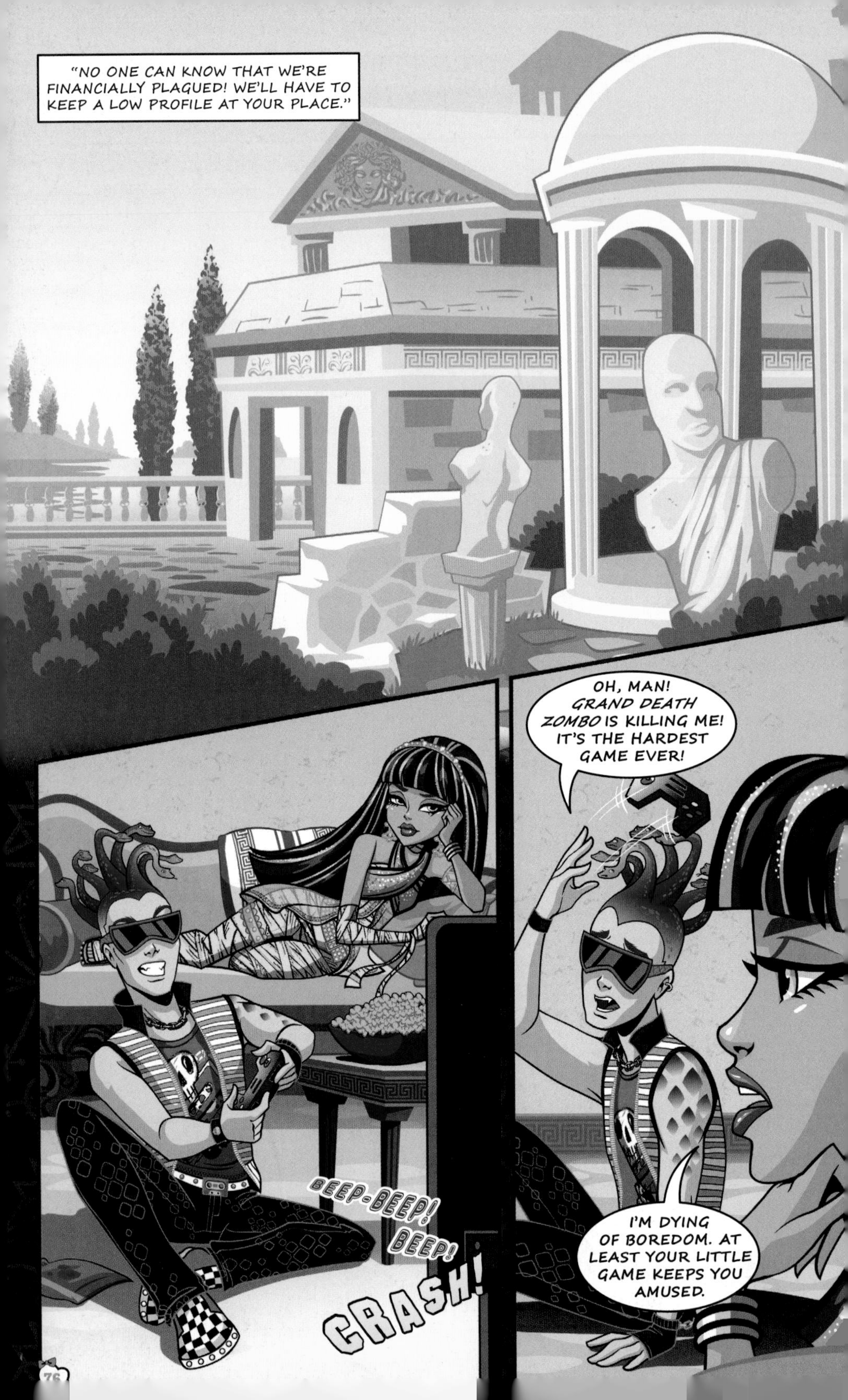
"NO ONE CAN KNOW THAT WE'RE FINANCIALLY PLAGUED! WE'LL HAVE TO KEEP A LOW PROFILE AT YOUR PLACE."
BEEP-BEEP!
BEEP!
CRASH!
OH, MAN! *GRAND DEATH ZOMBO* IS KILLING ME! IT'S THE HARDEST GAME EVER!
I'M DYING OF BOREDOM. AT LEAST YOUR LITTLE GAME KEEPS YOU AMUSED.

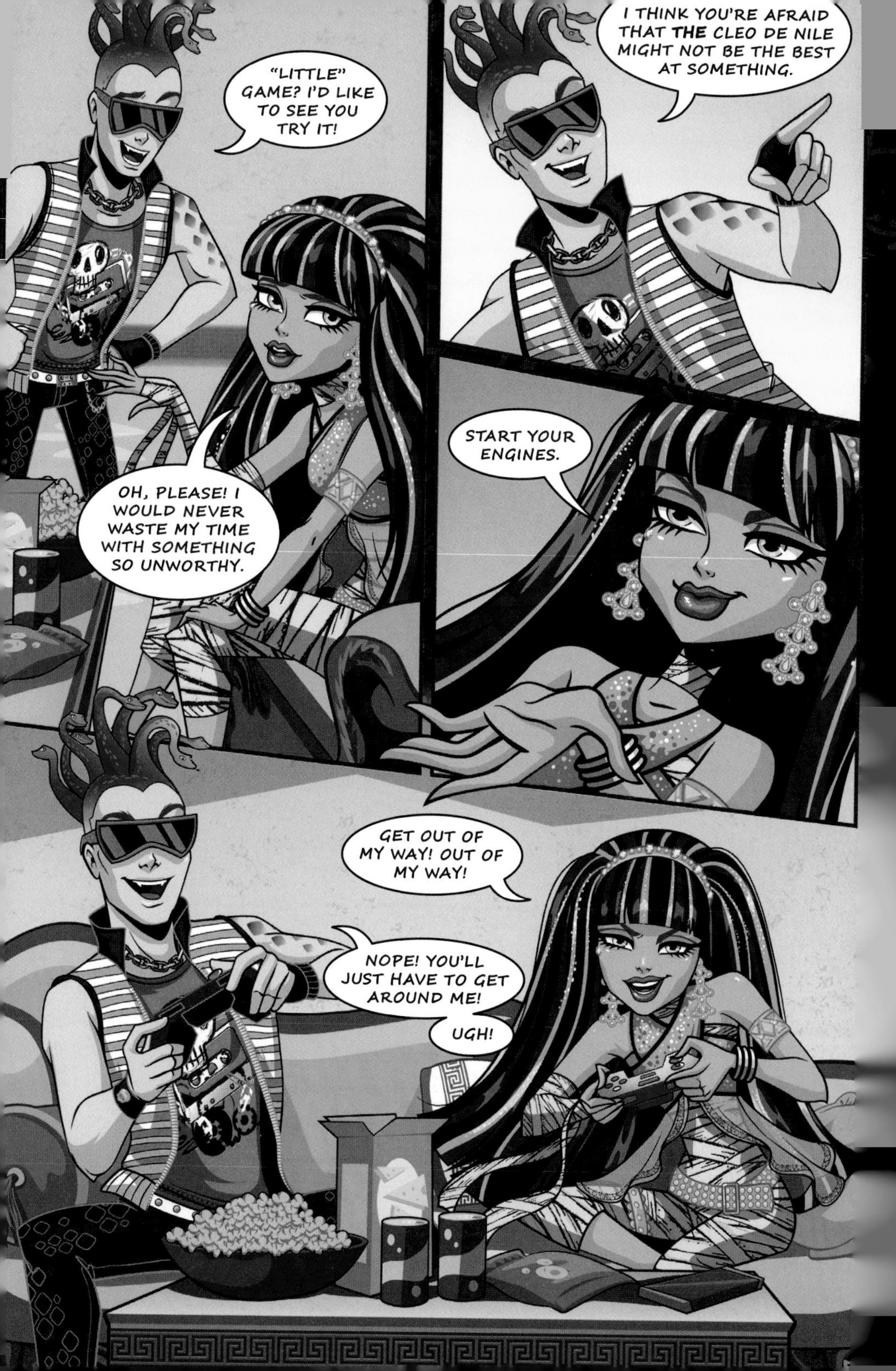
"LITTLE" GAME? I'D LIKE TO SEE YOU TRY IT!
OH, PLEASE! I WOULD NEVER WASTE MY TIME WITH SOMETHING SO UNWORTHY.
I THINK YOU'RE AFRAID THAT **THE** CLEO DE NILE MIGHT NOT BE THE BEST AT SOMETHING.
START YOUR ENGINES.
GET OUT OF MY WAY! OUT OF MY WAY!
NOPE! YOU'LL JUST HAVE TO GET AROUND ME!
UGH!

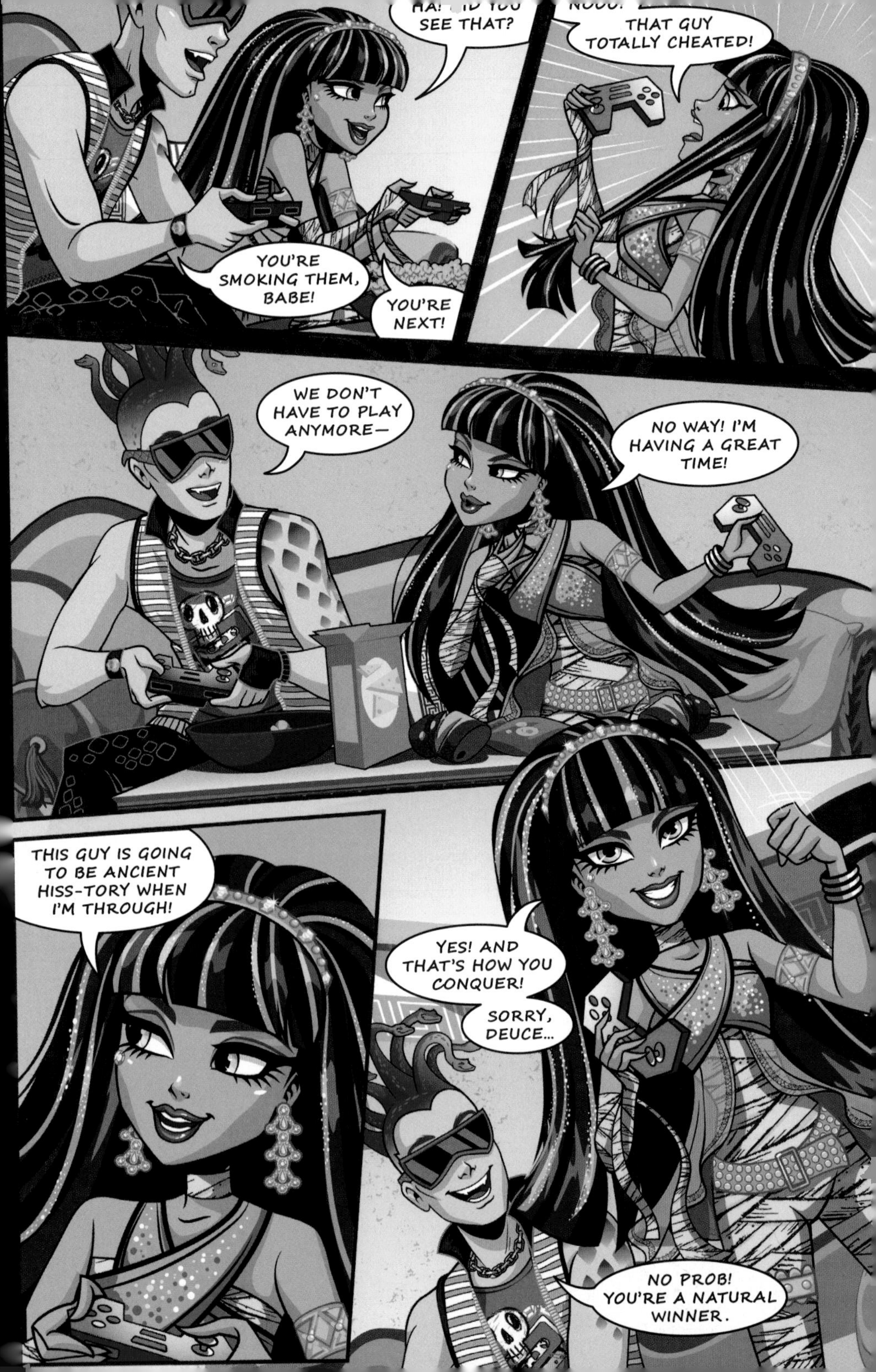
HA!
SEE THAT?
YOU'RE SMOKING THEM, BABE!
YOU'RE NEXT!
THAT GUY TOTALLY CHEATED!
WE DON'T HAVE TO PLAY ANYMORE—
NO WAY! I'M HAVING A GREAT TIME!
THIS GUY IS GOING TO BE ANCIENT HISS-TORY WHEN I'M THROUGH!
YES! AND THAT'S HOW YOU CONQUER!
SORRY, DEUCE...
NO PROB! YOU'RE A NATURAL WINNER.

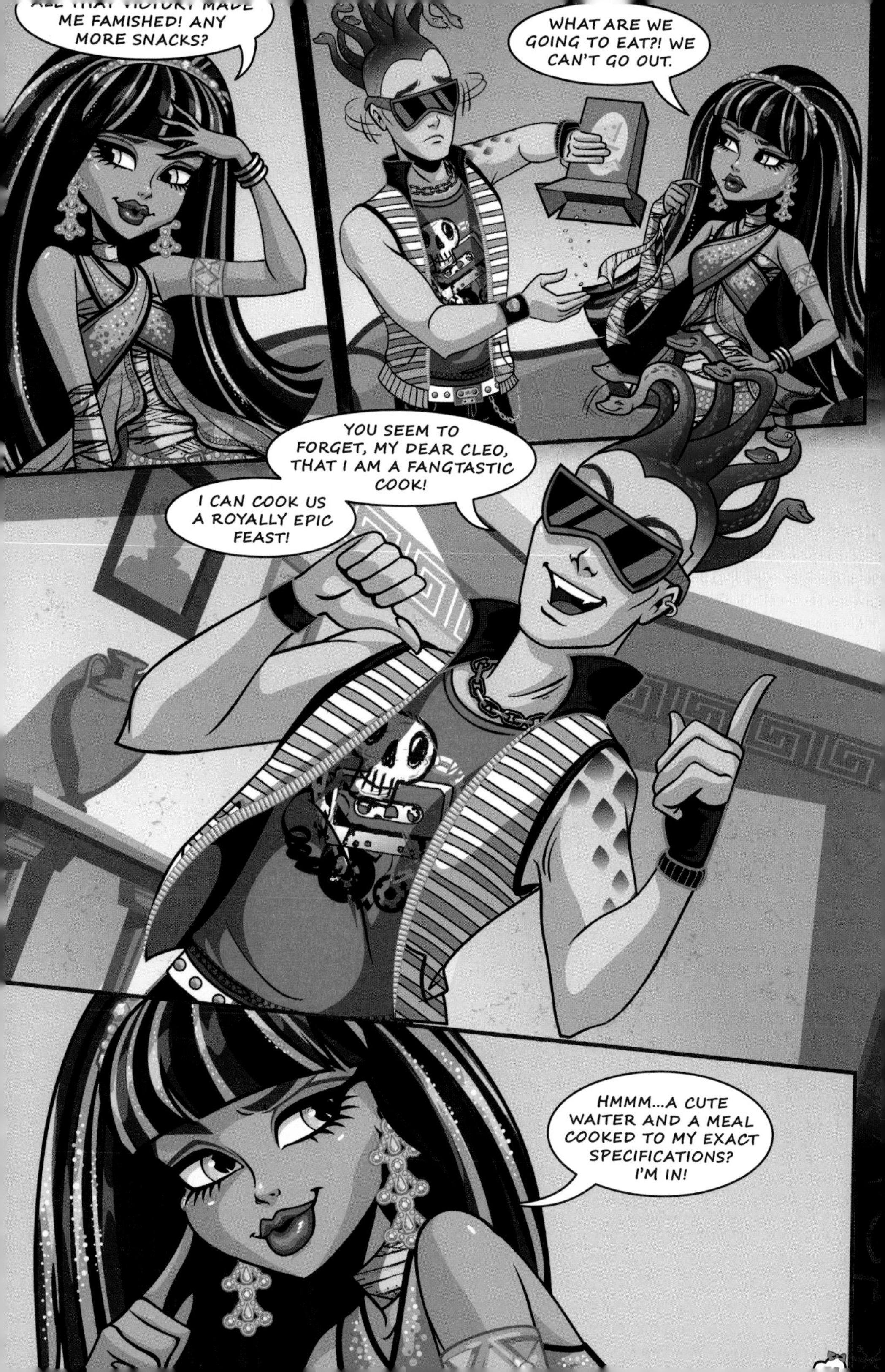
ME FAMISHED! ANY MORE SNACKS?
WHAT ARE WE GOING TO EAT?! WE CAN'T GO OUT.
YOU SEEM TO FORGET, MY DEAR CLEO, THAT I AM A FANGTASTIC COOK!
I CAN COOK US A ROYALLY EPIC FEAST!
HMMM...A CUTE WAITER AND A MEAL COOKED TO MY EXACT SPECIFICATIONS? I'M IN!

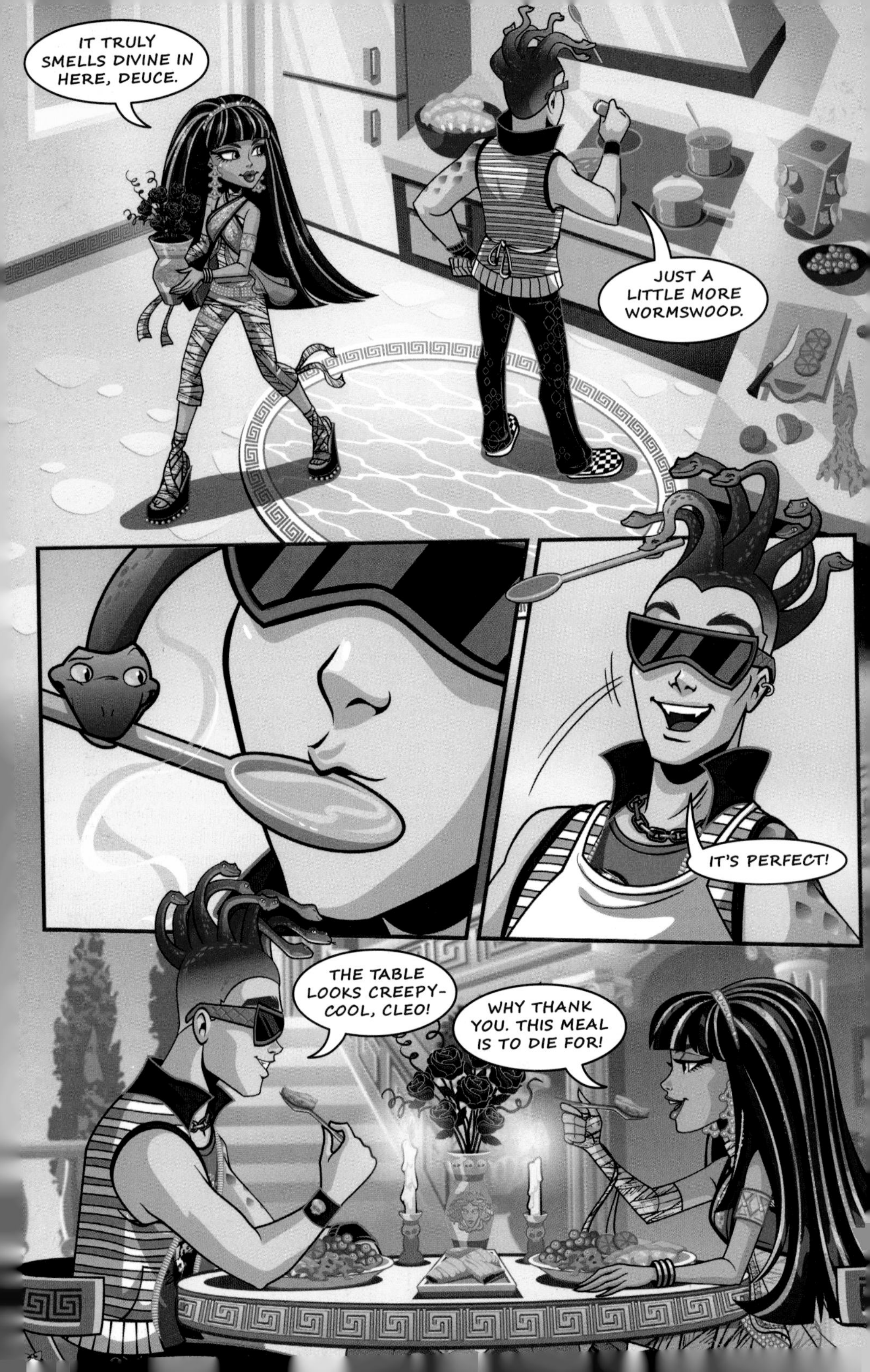
IT TRULY SMELLS DIVINE IN HERE, DEUCE.
JUST A LITTLE MORE WORMSWOOD.
IT'S PERFECT!
THE TABLE LOOKS CREEPY-COOL, CLEO!
WHY THANK YOU. THIS MEAL IS TO DIE FOR!

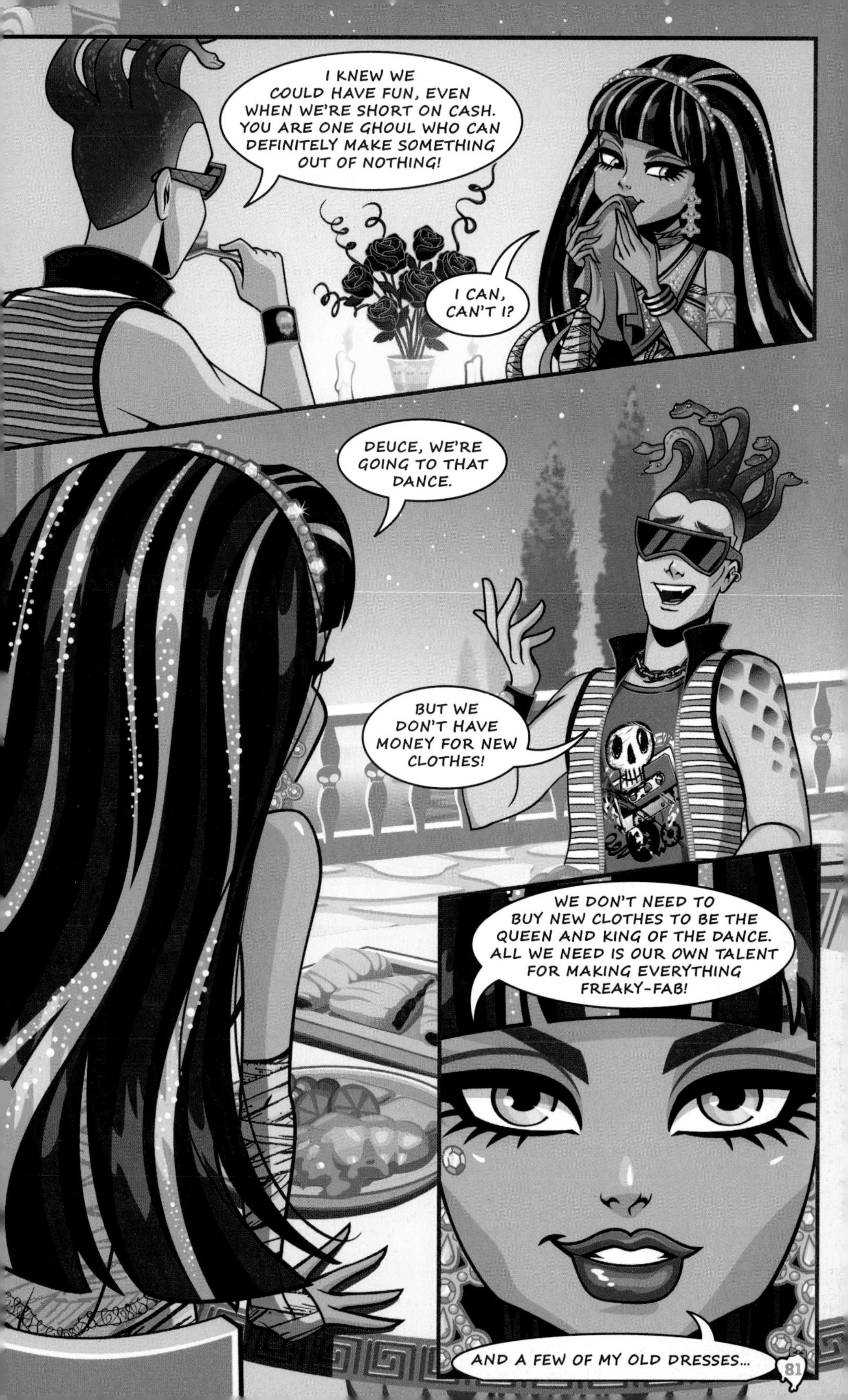
I KNEW WE COULD HAVE FUN, EVEN WHEN WE'RE SHORT ON CASH. YOU ARE ONE GHOUL WHO CAN DEFINITELY MAKE SOMETHING OUT OF NOTHING!
I CAN, CAN'T I?
DEUCE, WE'RE GOING TO THAT DANCE.
BUT WE DON'T HAVE MONEY FOR NEW CLOTHES!
WE DON'T NEED TO BUY NEW CLOTHES TO BE THE QUEEN AND KING OF THE DANCE. ALL WE NEED IS OUR OWN TALENT FOR MAKING EVERYTHING FREAKY-FAB!
AND A FEW OF MY OLD DRESSES...

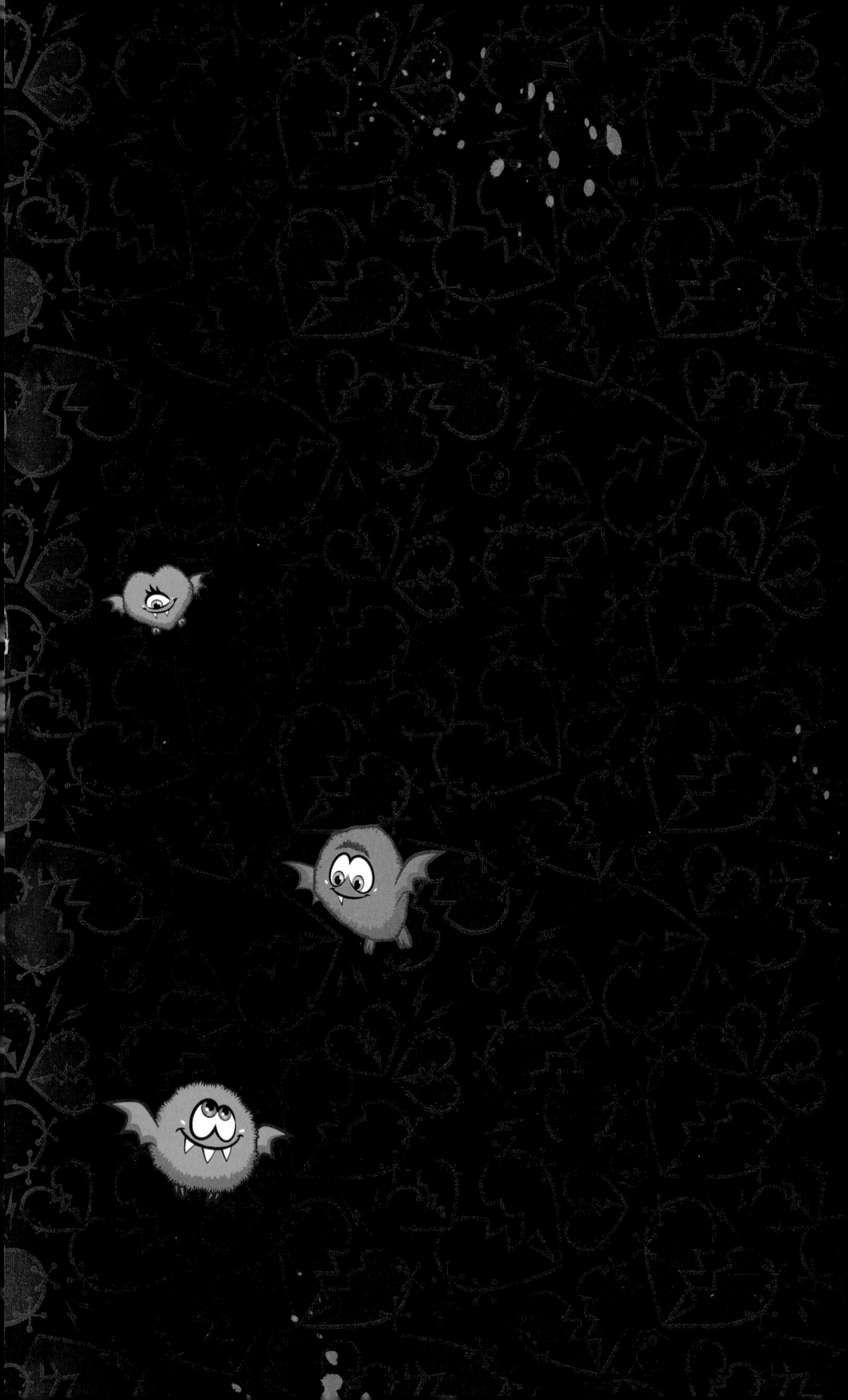

DRACULAURA and CLAWD

STAR IN

SHADOW OF A DOUBT

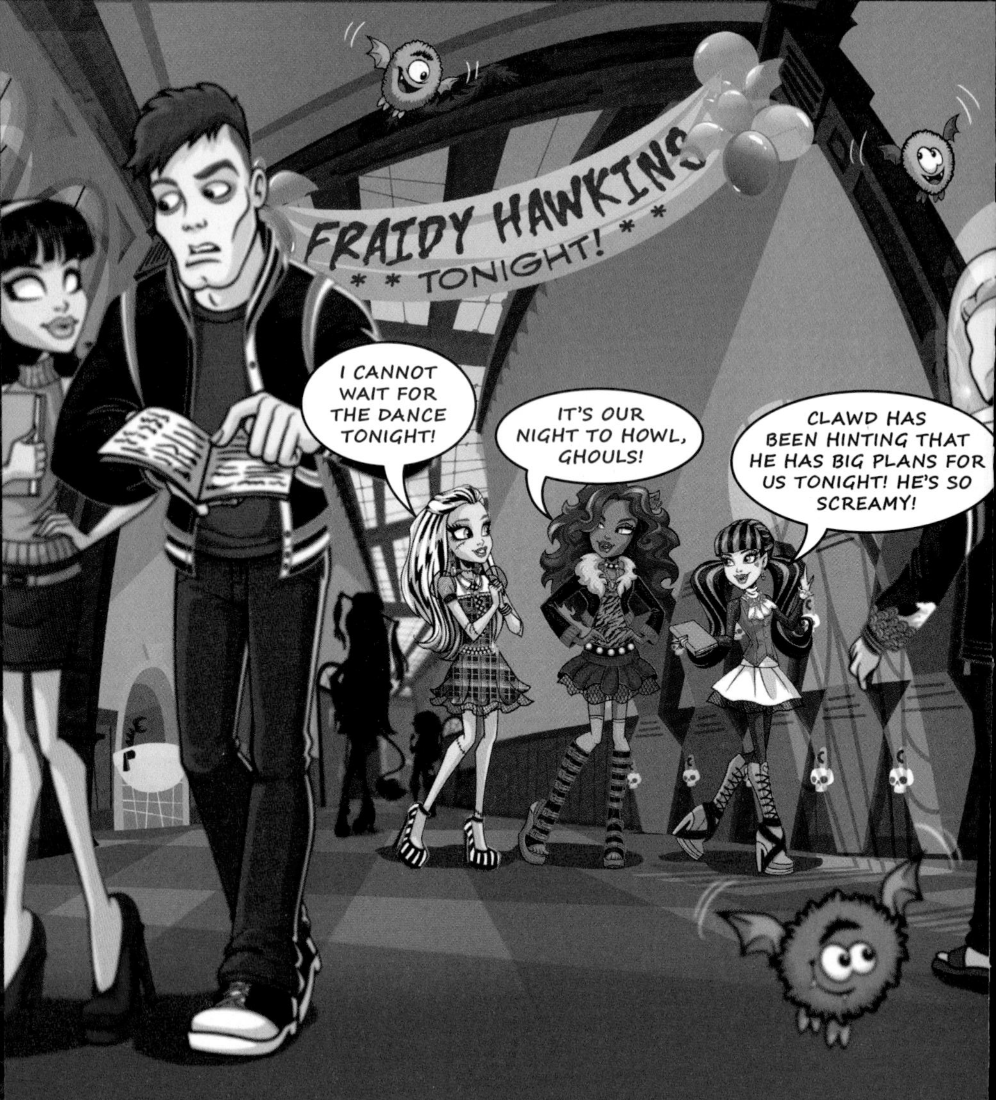
FRAIDY HAWKINS
* * TONIGHT! * *
I CANNOT WAIT FOR THE DANCE TONIGHT!
IT'S OUR NIGHT TO HOWL, GHOULS!
CLAWD HAS BEEN HINTING THAT HE HAS BIG PLANS FOR US TONIGHT! HE'S SO SCREAMY!

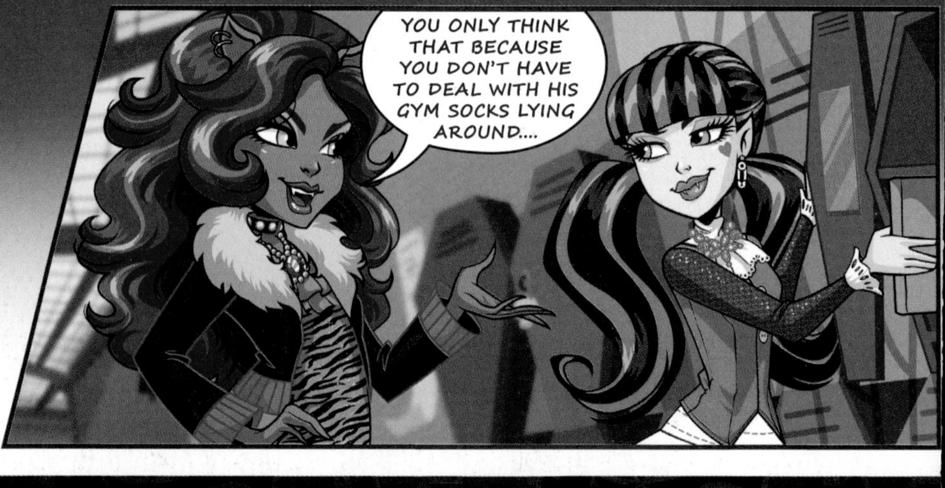
YOU ONLY THINK THAT BECAUSE YOU DON'T HAVE TO DEAL WITH HIS GYM SOCKS LYING AROUND....

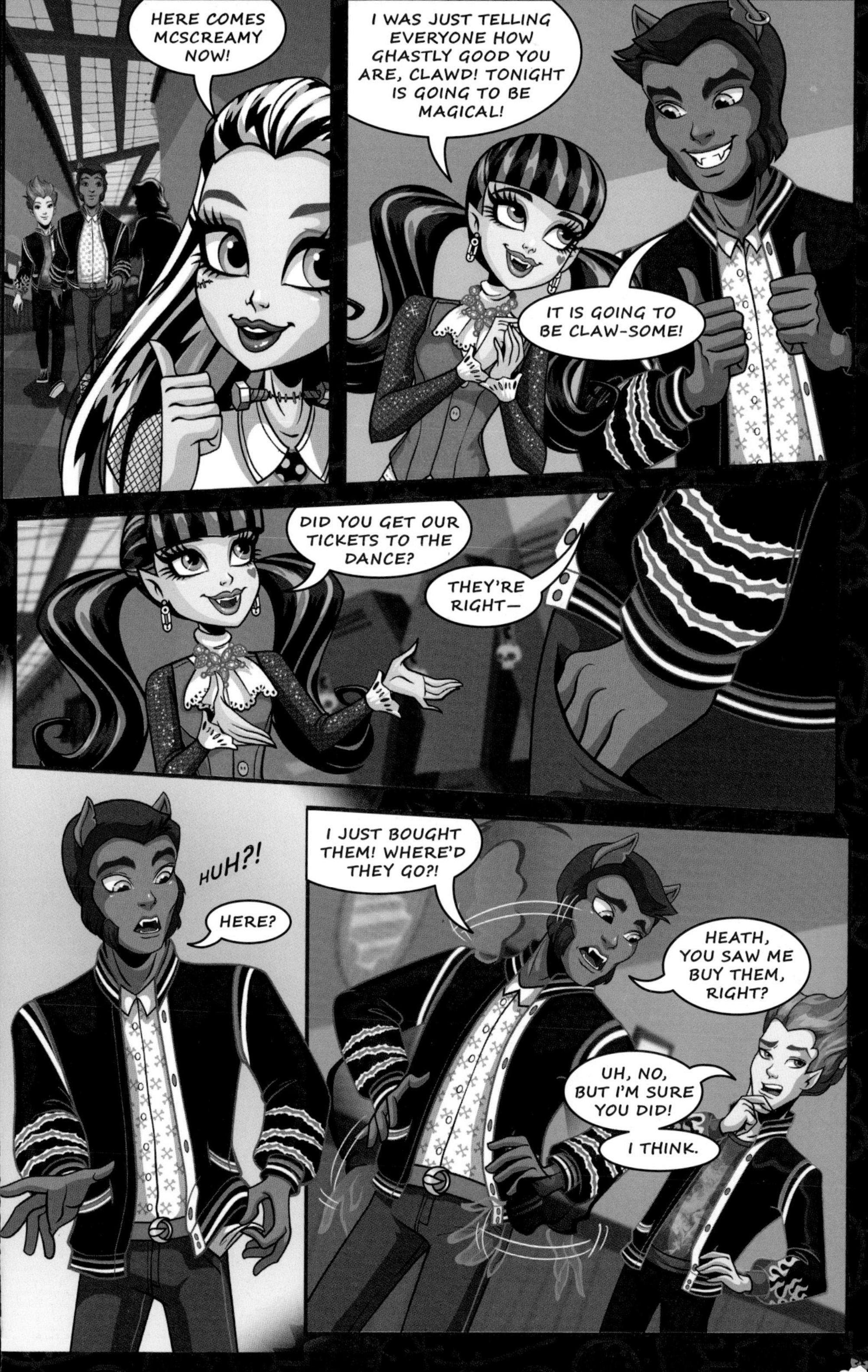
HERE COMES MCSCREAMY NOW!
I WAS JUST TELLING EVERYONE HOW GHASTLY GOOD YOU ARE, CLAWD! TONIGHT IS GOING TO BE MAGICAL!
IT IS GOING TO BE CLAW-SOME!
DID YOU GET OUR TICKETS TO THE DANCE?
THEY'RE RIGHT—
HUH?!
HERE?
I JUST BOUGHT THEM! WHERE'D THEY GO?!
HEATH, YOU SAW ME BUY THEM, RIGHT?
UH, NO, BUT I'M SURE YOU DID!
I THINK.

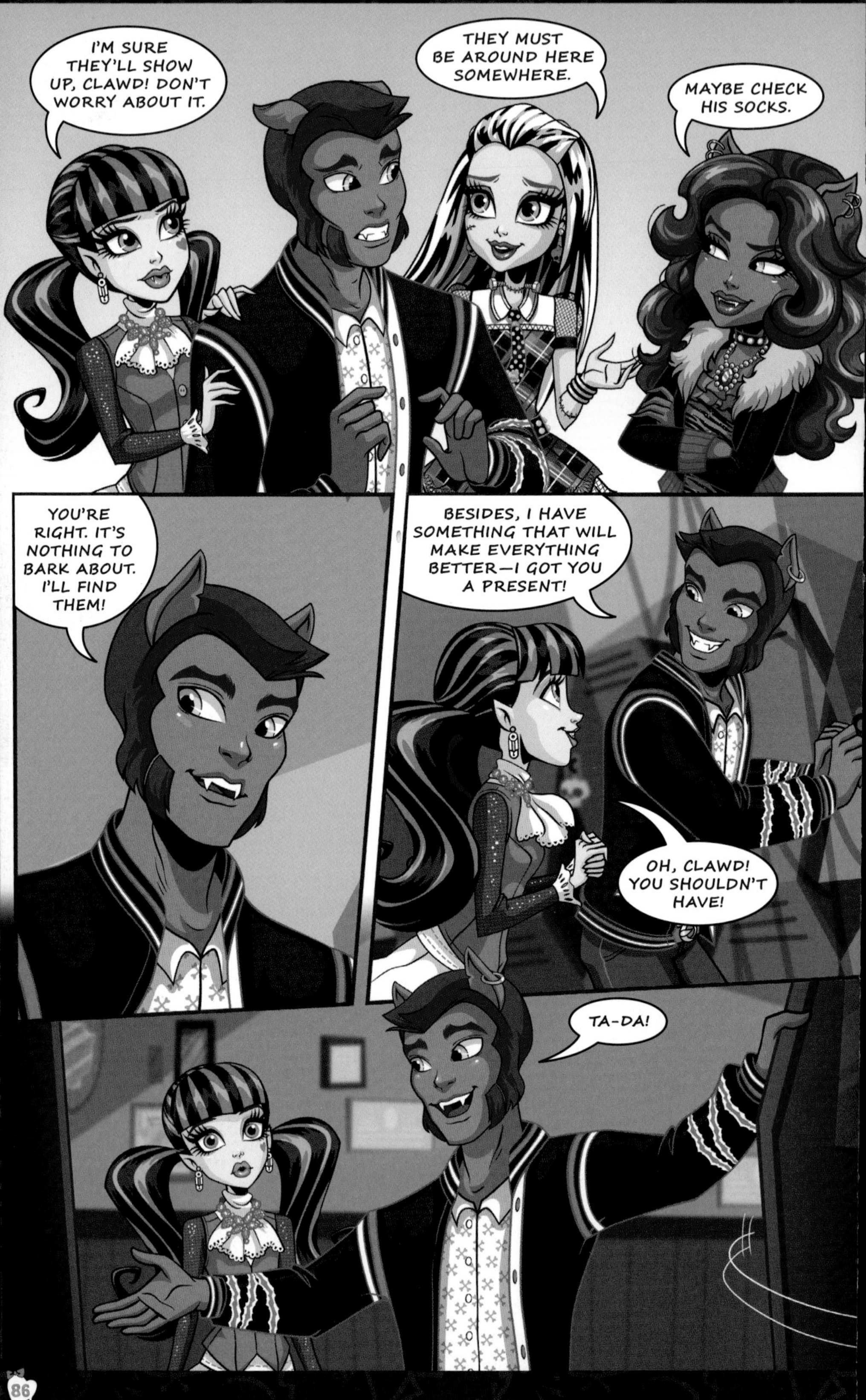
I'M SURE THEY'LL SHOW UP, CLAWD! DON'T WORRY ABOUT IT.
THEY MUST BE AROUND HERE SOMEWHERE.
MAYBE CHECK HIS SOCKS.
YOU'RE RIGHT. IT'S NOTHING TO BARK ABOUT. I'LL FIND THEM!
BESIDES, I HAVE SOMETHING THAT WILL MAKE EVERYTHING BETTER—I GOT YOU A PRESENT!
OH, CLAWD! YOU SHOULDN'T HAVE!
TA-DA!

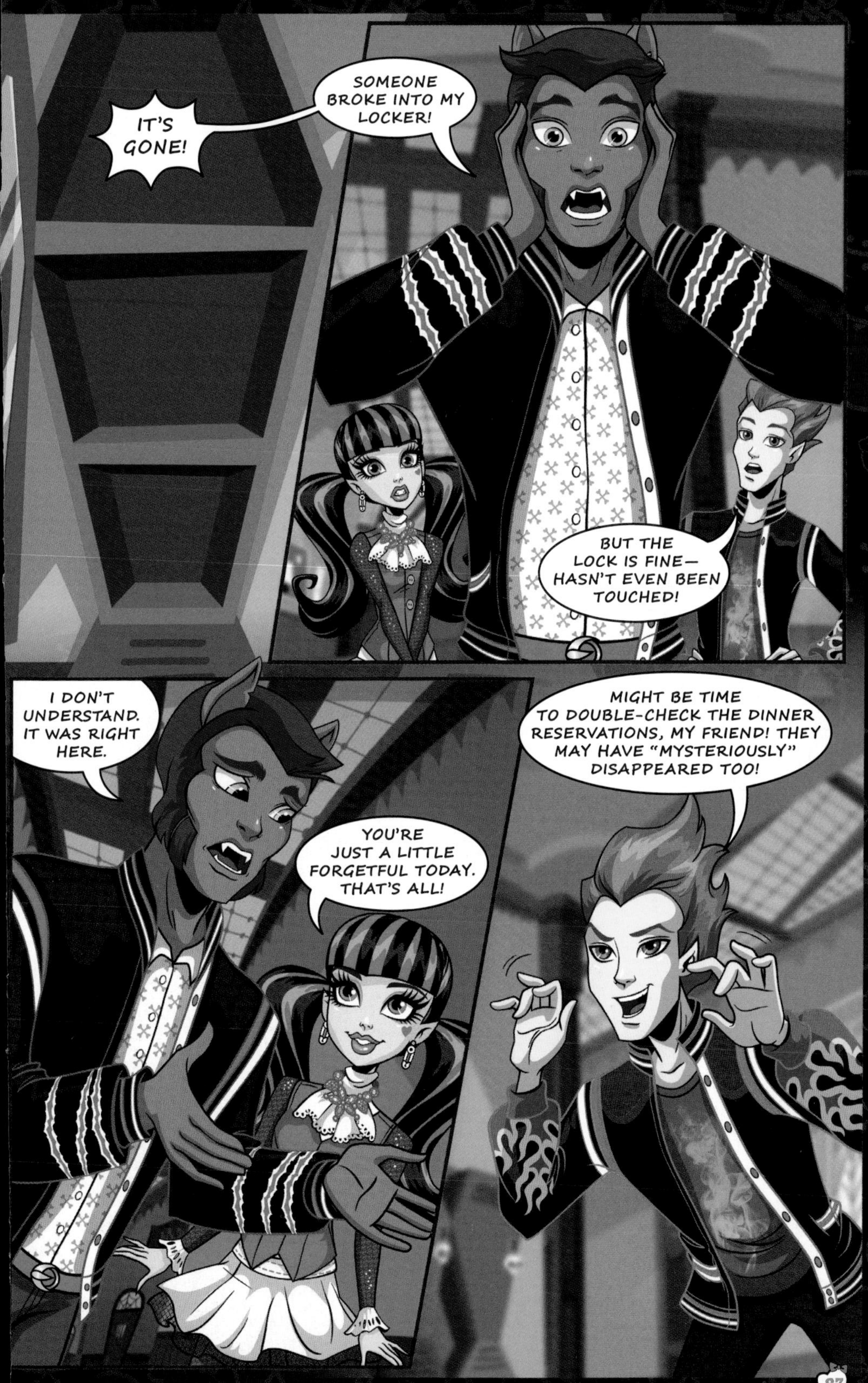
IT'S GONE!
SOMEONE BROKE INTO MY LOCKER!
BUT THE LOCK IS FINE—HASN'T EVEN BEEN TOUCHED!
I DON'T UNDERSTAND. IT WAS RIGHT HERE.
YOU'RE JUST A LITTLE FORGETFUL TODAY. THAT'S ALL!
MIGHT BE TIME TO DOUBLE-CHECK THE DINNER RESERVATIONS, MY FRIEND! THEY MAY HAVE "MYSTERIOUSLY" DISAPPEARED TOO!

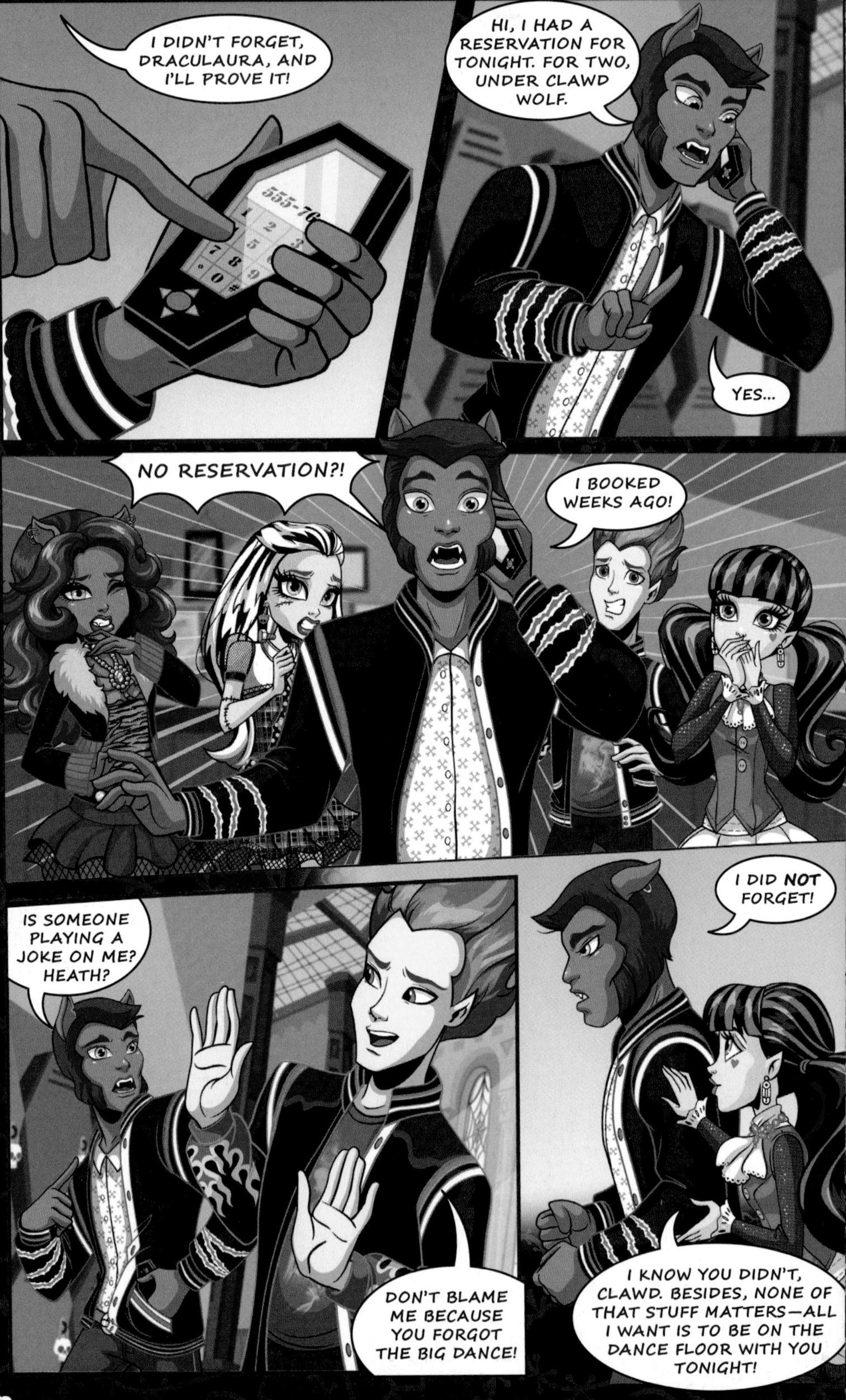
I DIDN'T FORGET, DRACULAURA, AND I'LL PROVE IT!
555-76
HI, I HAD A RESERVATION FOR TONIGHT. FOR TWO, UNDER CLAWD WOLF.
YES...
NO RESERVATION?!
I BOOKED WEEKS AGO!
IS SOMEONE PLAYING A JOKE ON ME? HEATH?
DON'T BLAME ME BECAUSE YOU FORGOT THE BIG DANCE!
I DID **NOT** FORGET!
I KNOW YOU DIDN'T, CLAWD. BESIDES, NONE OF THAT STUFF MATTERS—ALL I WANT IS TO BE ON THE DANCE FLOOR WITH YOU TONIGHT!

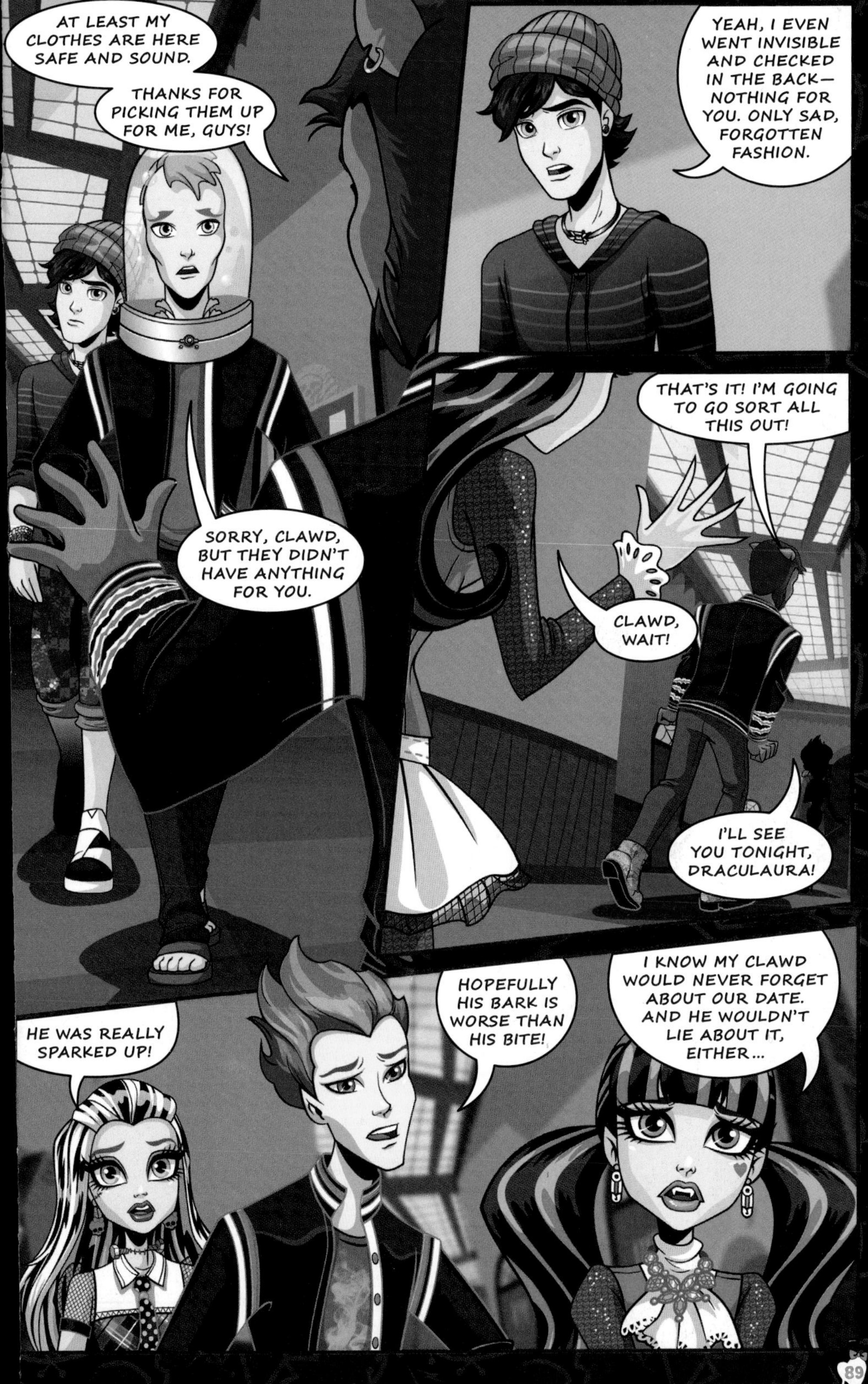

AT LEAST MY CLOTHES ARE HERE SAFE AND SOUND.
THANKS FOR PICKING THEM UP FOR ME, GUYS!
YEAH, I EVEN WENT INVISIBLE AND CHECKED IN THE BACK— NOTHING FOR YOU. ONLY SAD, FORGOTTEN FASHION.
SORRY, CLAWD, BUT THEY DIDN'T HAVE ANYTHING FOR YOU.
THAT'S IT! I'M GOING TO GO SORT ALL THIS OUT!
CLAWD, WAIT!
I'LL SEE YOU TONIGHT, DRACULAURA!
HE WAS REALLY SPARKED UP!
HOPEFULLY HIS BARK IS WORSE THAN HIS BITE!
I KNOW MY CLAWD WOULD NEVER FORGET ABOUT OUR DATE. AND HE WOULDN'T LIE ABOUT IT, EITHER...

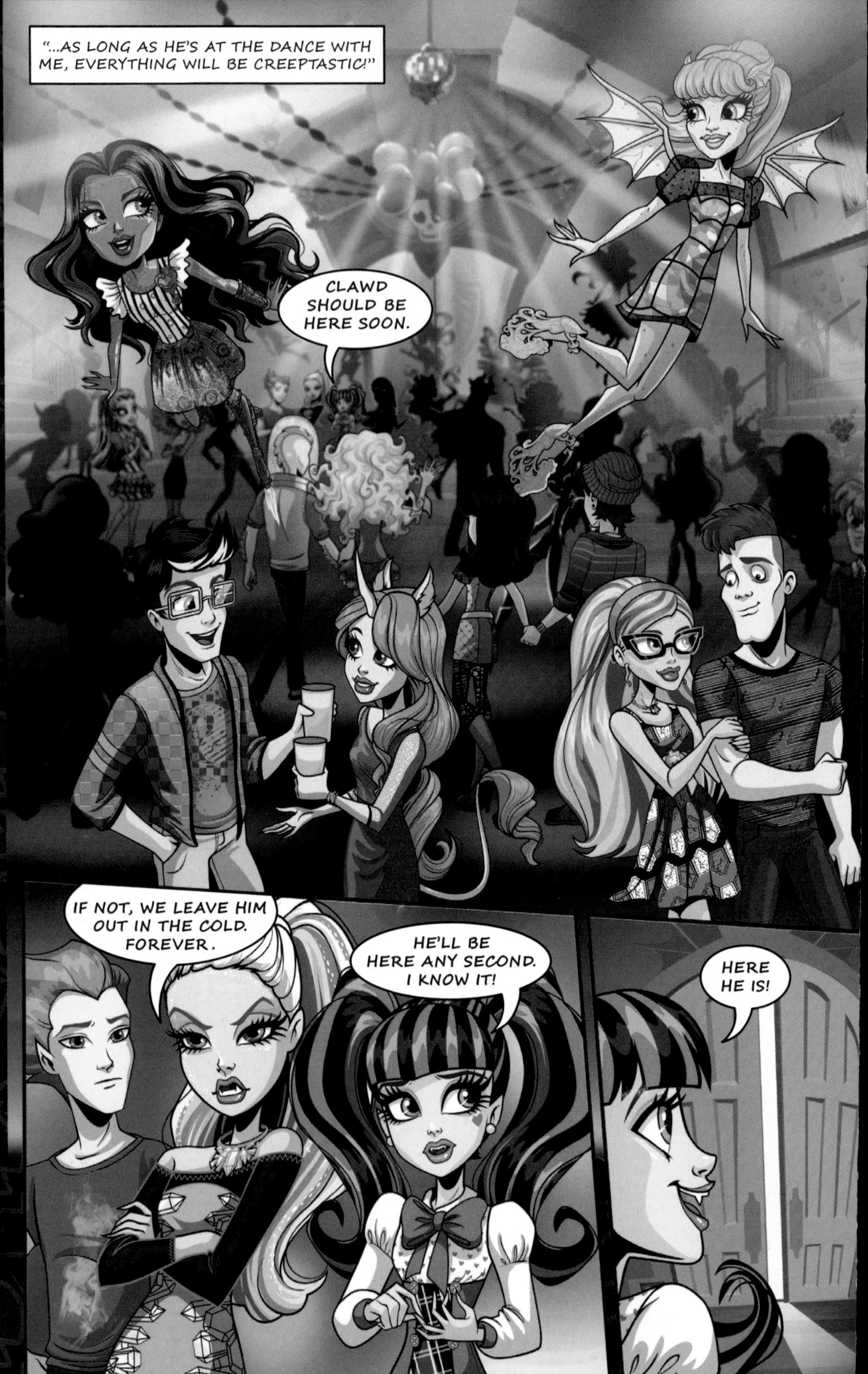
"...AS LONG AS HE'S AT THE DANCE WITH ME, EVERYTHING WILL BE CREEPTASTIC!"
CLAWD SHOULD BE HERE SOON.
IF NOT, WE LEAVE HIM OUT IN THE COLD. FOREVER.
HE'LL BE HERE ANY SECOND. I KNOW IT!
HERE HE IS!

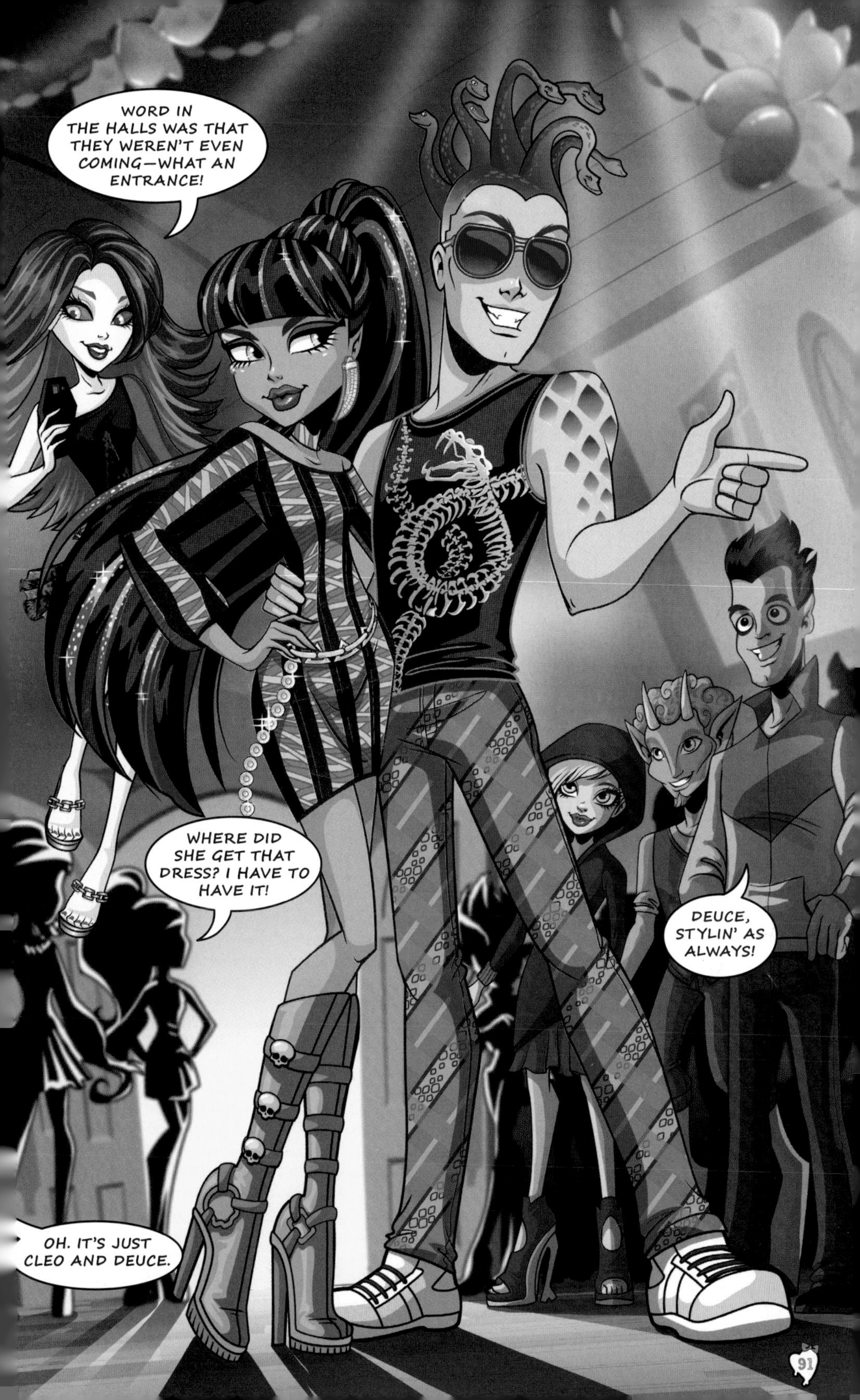
WORD IN THE HALLS WAS THAT THEY WEREN'T EVEN COMING—WHAT AN ENTRANCE!
WHERE DID SHE GET THAT DRESS? I HAVE TO HAVE IT!
DEUCE, STYLIN' AS ALWAYS!
OH. IT'S JUST CLEO AND DEUCE.

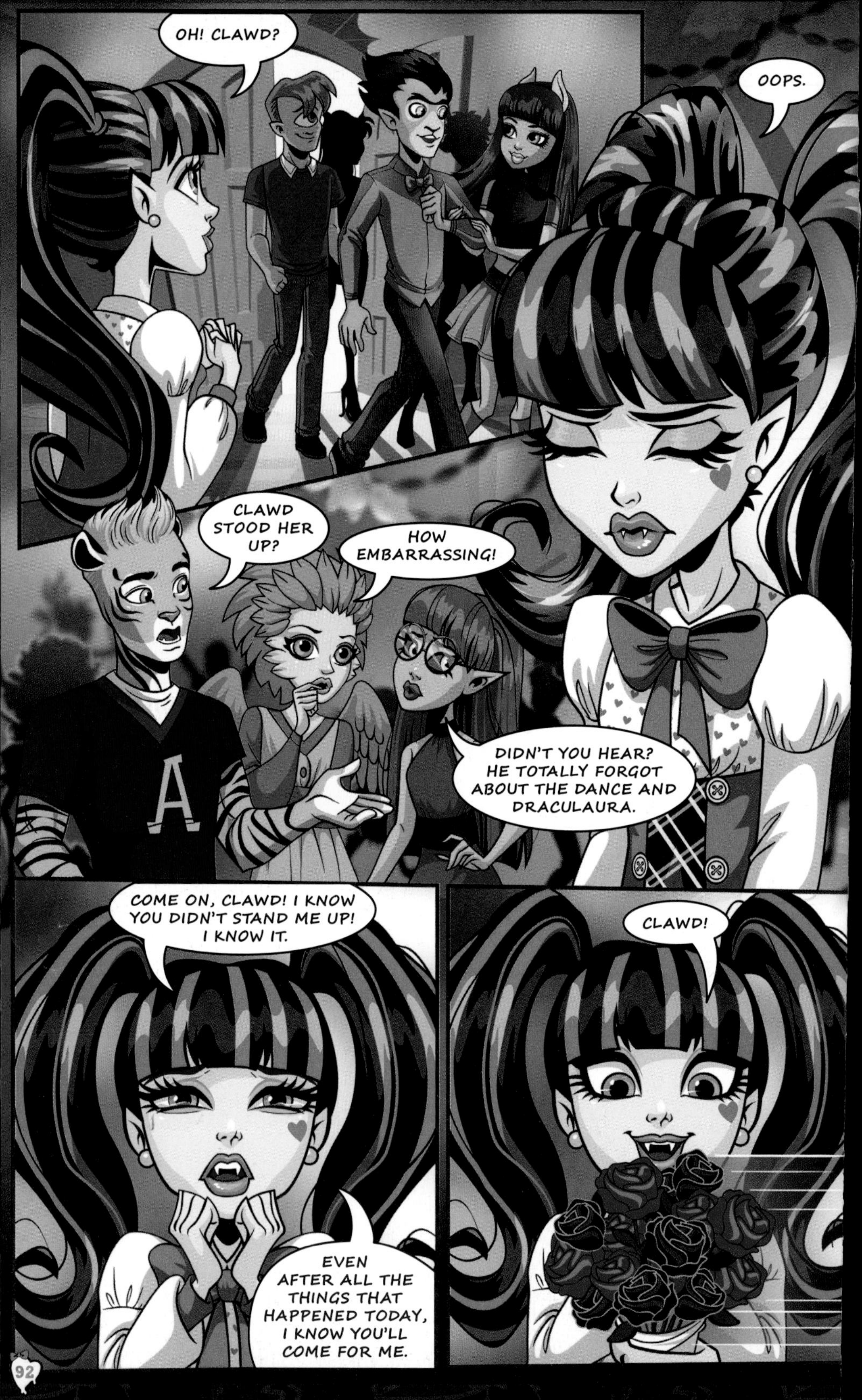
OH! CLAWD?
OOPS.
CLAWD STOOD HER UP?
HOW EMBARRASSING!
DIDN'T YOU HEAR? HE TOTALLY FORGOT ABOUT THE DANCE AND DRACULAURA.
COME ON, CLAWD! I KNOW YOU DIDN'T STAND ME UP! I KNOW IT.
EVEN AFTER ALL THE THINGS THAT HAPPENED TODAY, I KNOW YOU'LL COME FOR ME.
CLAWD!

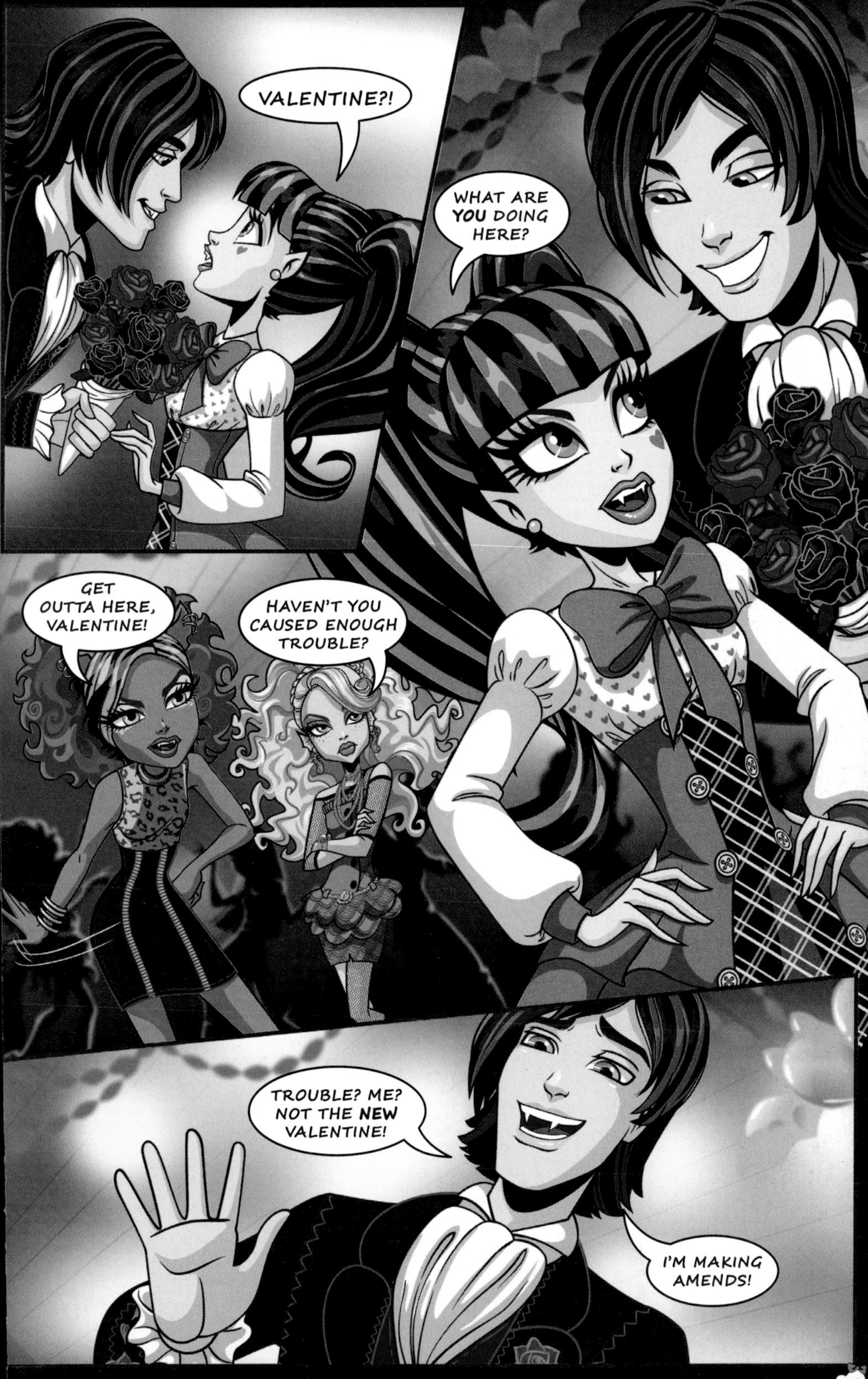
VALENTINE?!
WHAT ARE YOU DOING HERE?
GET OUTTA HERE, VALENTINE!
HAVEN'T YOU CAUSED ENOUGH TROUBLE?
TROUBLE? ME? NOT THE NEW VALENTINE!
I'M MAKING AMENDS!

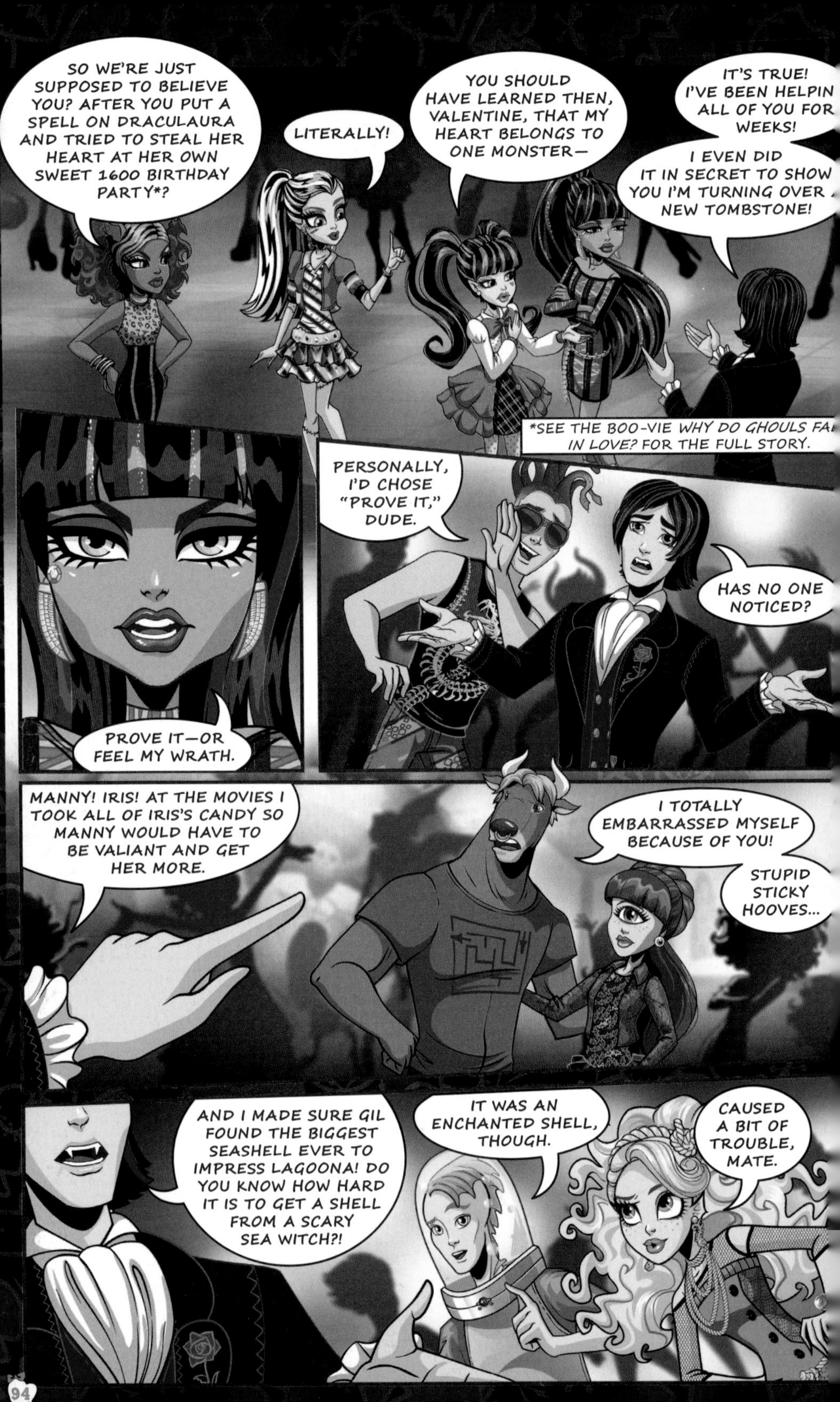
SO WE'RE JUST SUPPOSED TO BELIEVE YOU? AFTER YOU PUT A SPELL ON DRACULAURA AND TRIED TO STEAL HER HEART AT HER OWN SWEET 1600 BIRTHDAY PARTY*?
LITERALLY!
YOU SHOULD HAVE LEARNED THEN, VALENTINE, THAT MY HEART BELONGS TO ONE MONSTER—
IT'S TRUE! I'VE BEEN HELPIN ALL OF YOU FOR WEEKS!
I EVEN DID IT IN SECRET TO SHOW YOU I'M TURNING OVER NEW TOMBSTONE!
*SEE THE BOO-VIE *WHY DO GHOULS FA IN LOVE?* FOR THE FULL STORY.
PROVE IT—OR FEEL MY WRATH.
PERSONALLY, I'D CHOSE "PROVE IT," DUDE.
HAS NO ONE NOTICED?
MANNY! IRIS! AT THE MOVIES I TOOK ALL OF IRIS'S CANDY SO MANNY WOULD HAVE TO BE VALIANT AND GET HER MORE.
I TOTALLY EMBARRASSED MYSELF BECAUSE OF YOU!
STUPID STICKY HOOVES...
AND I MADE SURE GIL FOUND THE BIGGEST SEASHELL EVER TO IMPRESS LAGOONA! DO YOU KNOW HOW HARD IT IS TO GET A SHELL FROM A SCARY SEA WITCH?!
IT WAS AN ENCHANTED SHELL, THOUGH.
CAUSED A BIT OF TROUBLE, MATE.

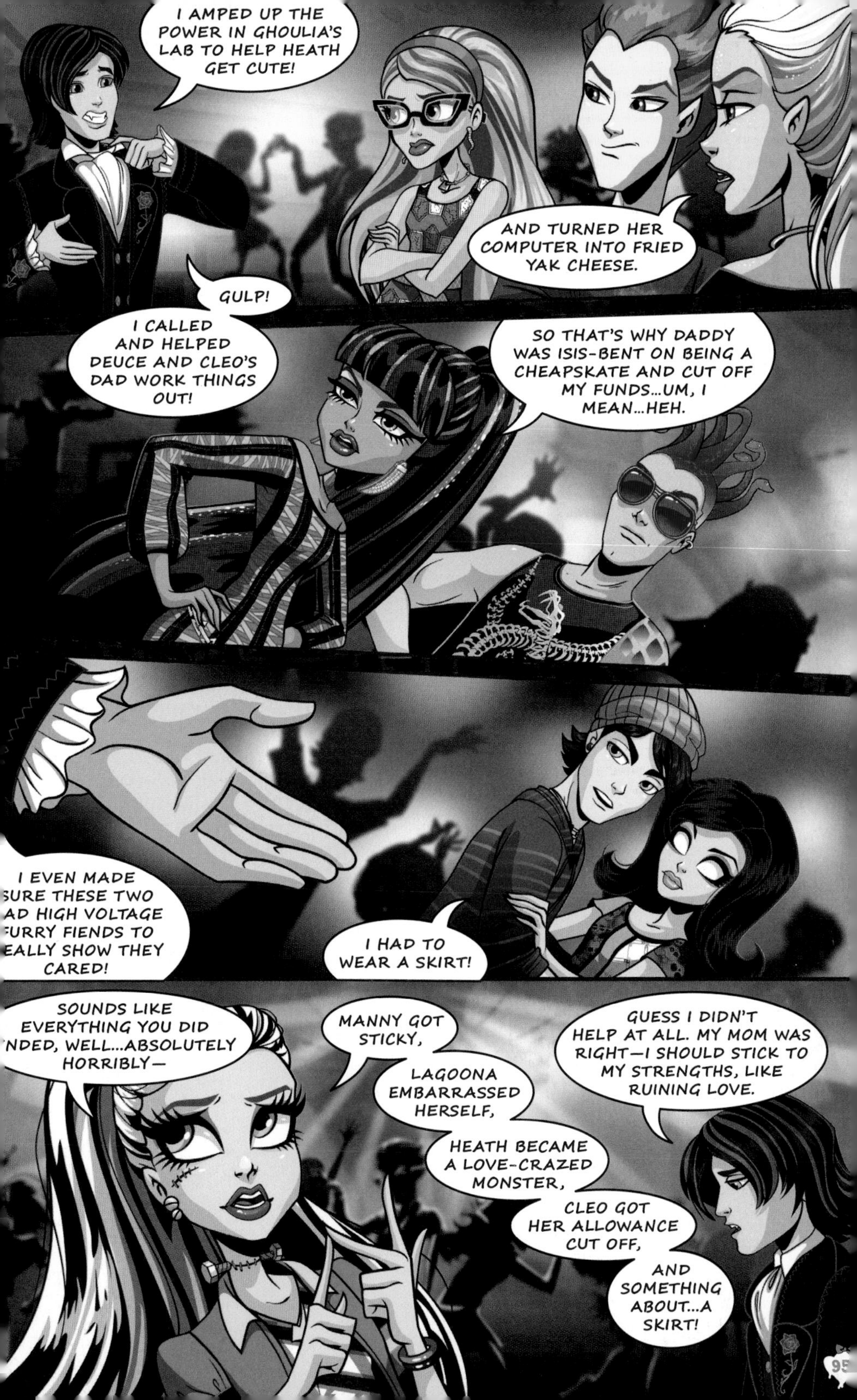
I AMPED UP THE POWER IN GHOULIA'S LAB TO HELP HEATH GET CUTE!
AND TURNED HER COMPUTER INTO FRIED YAK CHEESE.
GULP!
I CALLED AND HELPED DEUCE AND CLEO'S DAD WORK THINGS OUT!
SO THAT'S WHY DADDY WAS ISIS-BENT ON BEING A CHEAPSKATE AND CUT OFF MY FUNDS...UM, I MEAN...HEH.
I EVEN MADE SURE THESE TWO AD HIGH VOLTAGE URRY FIENDS TO EALLY SHOW THEY CARED!
I HAD TO WEAR A SKIRT!
SOUNDS LIKE EVERYTHING YOU DID NDED, WELL...ABSOLUTELY HORRIBLY—
MANNY GOT STICKY,
LAGOONA EMBARRASSED HERSELF,
HEATH BECAME A LOVE-CRAZED MONSTER,
CLEO GOT HER ALLOWANCE CUT OFF,
AND SOMETHING ABOUT...A SKIRT!
GUESS I DIDN'T HELP AT ALL. MY MOM WAS RIGHT—I SHOULD STICK TO MY STRENGTHS, LIKE RUINING LOVE.

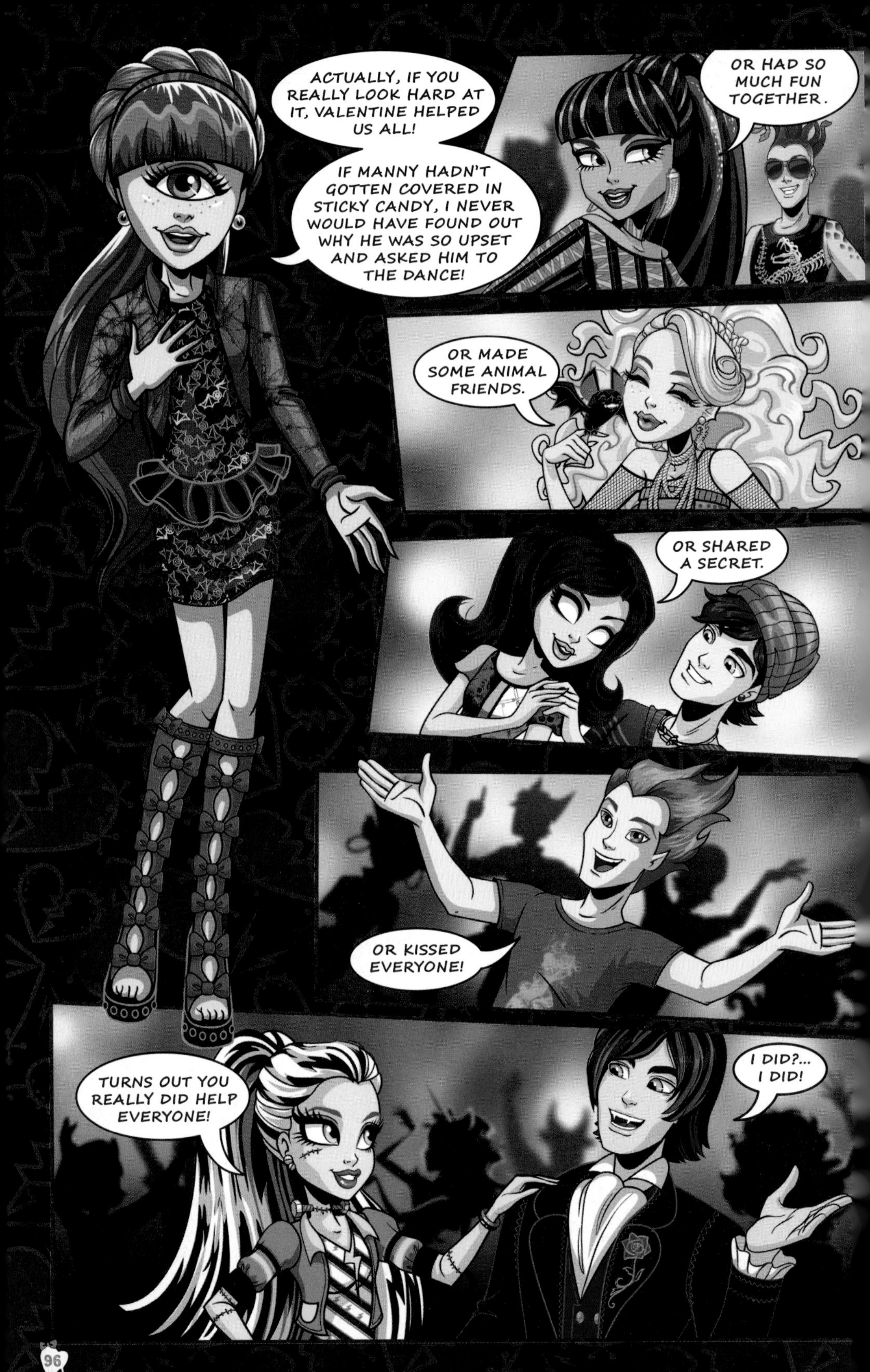
ACTUALLY, IF YOU REALLY LOOK HARD AT IT, VALENTINE HELPED US ALL!
IF MANNY HADN'T GOTTEN COVERED IN STICKY CANDY, I NEVER WOULD HAVE FOUND OUT WHY HE WAS SO UPSET AND ASKED HIM TO THE DANCE!
OR HAD SO MUCH FUN TOGETHER.
OR MADE SOME ANIMAL FRIENDS.
OR SHARED A SECRET.
OR KISSED EVERYONE!
TURNS OUT YOU REALLY DID HELP EVERYONE!
I DID?... I DID!

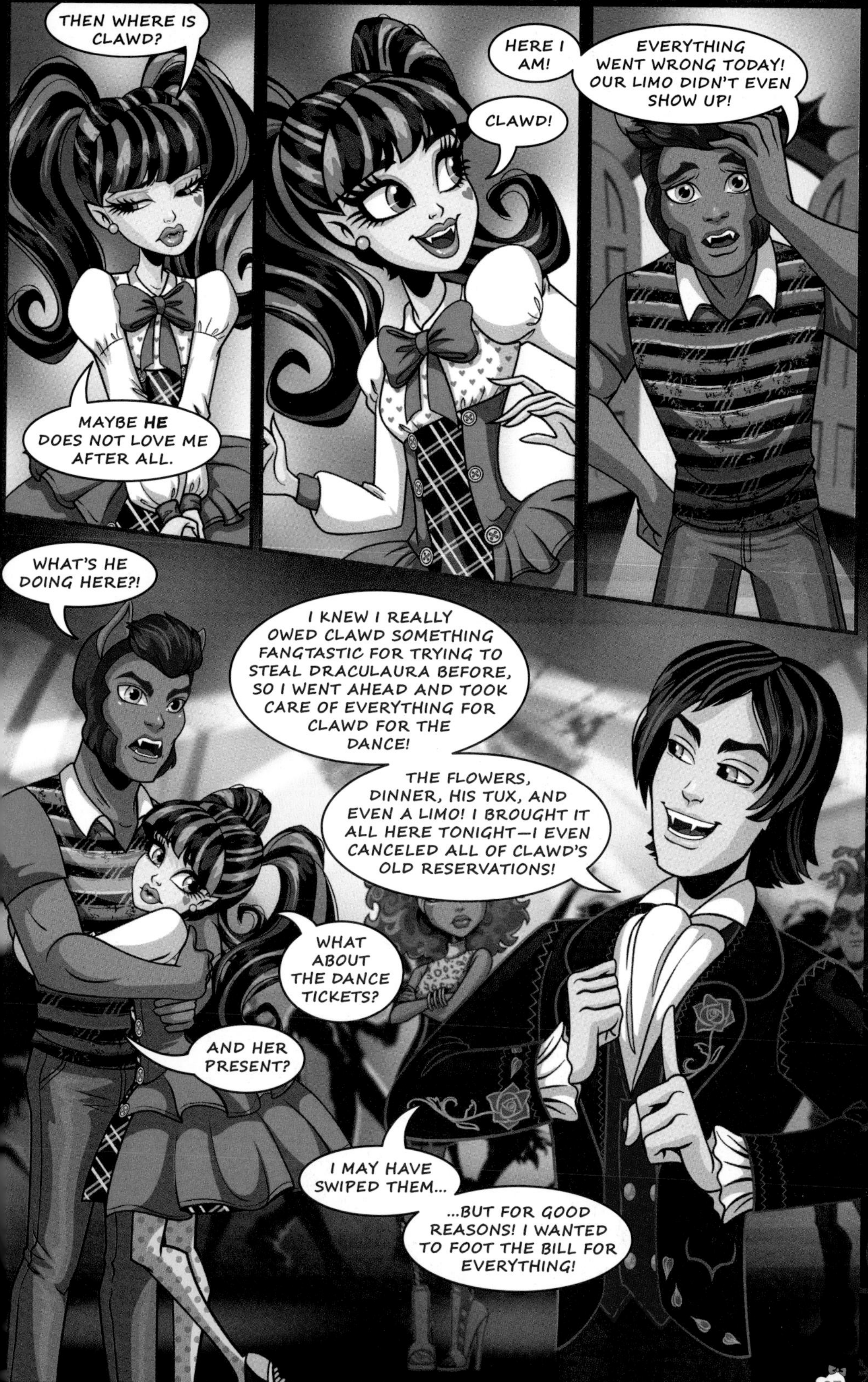
THEN WHERE IS CLAWD?
MAYBE **HE** DOES NOT LOVE ME AFTER ALL.
HERE I AM!
CLAWD!
EVERYTHING WENT WRONG TODAY! OUR LIMO DIDN'T EVEN SHOW UP!
WHAT'S HE DOING HERE?!
I KNEW I REALLY OWED CLAWD SOMETHING FANGTASTIC FOR TRYING TO STEAL DRACULAURA BEFORE, SO I WENT AHEAD AND TOOK CARE OF EVERYTHING FOR CLAWD FOR THE DANCE!
THE FLOWERS, DINNER, HIS TUX, AND EVEN A LIMO! I BROUGHT IT ALL HERE TONIGHT—I EVEN CANCELED ALL OF CLAWD'S OLD RESERVATIONS!
WHAT ABOUT THE DANCE TICKETS?
AND HER PRESENT?
I MAY HAVE SWIPED THEM...
...BUT FOR GOOD REASONS! I WANTED TO FOOT THE BILL FOR EVERYTHING!

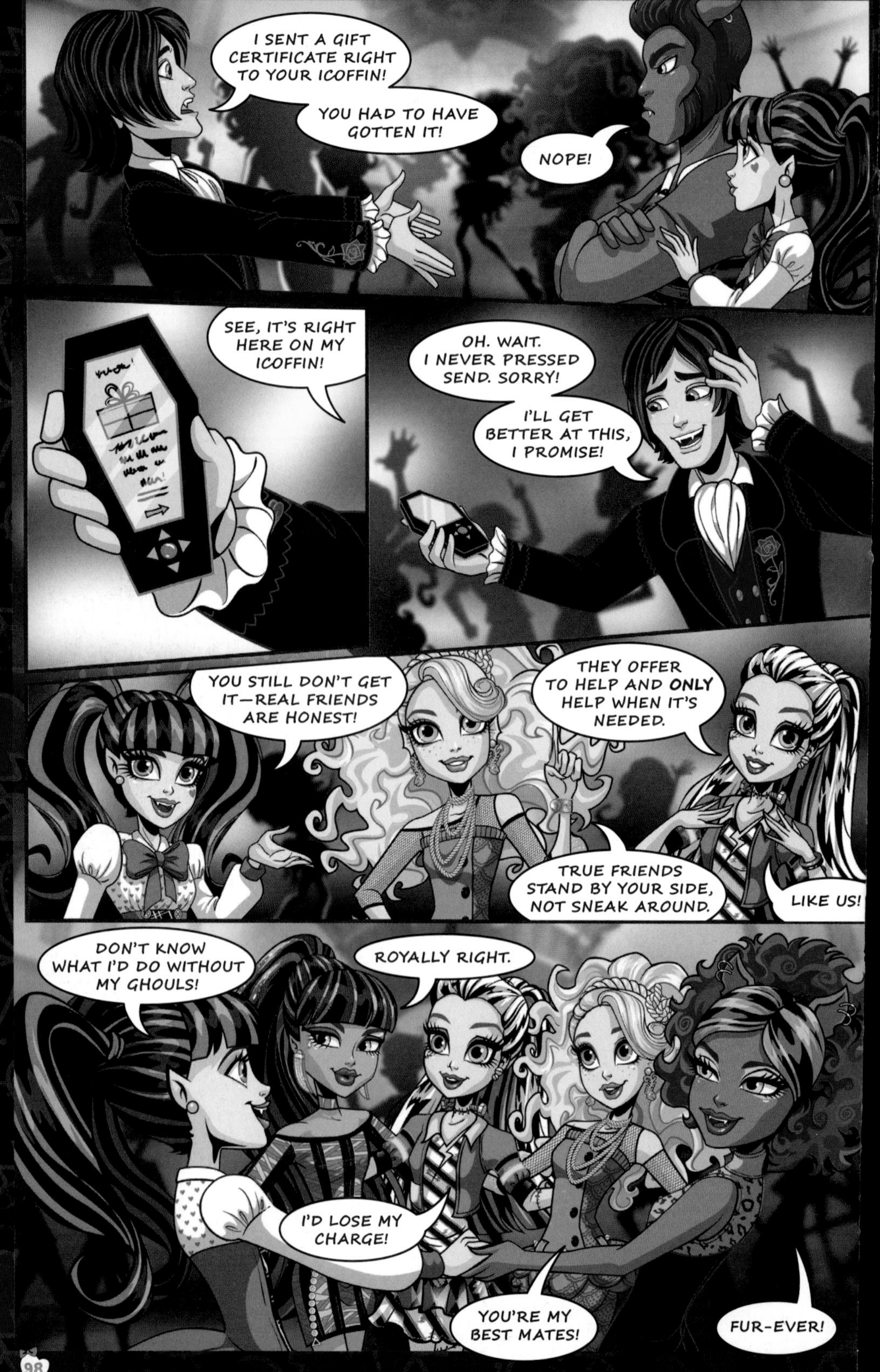

I SENT A GIFT CERTIFICATE RIGHT TO YOUR ICOFFIN!
YOU HAD TO HAVE GOTTEN IT!
NOPE!
SEE, IT'S RIGHT HERE ON MY ICOFFIN!
OH. WAIT. I NEVER PRESSED SEND. SORRY!
I'LL GET BETTER AT THIS, I PROMISE!
YOU STILL DON'T GET IT—REAL FRIENDS ARE HONEST!
THEY OFFER TO HELP AND **ONLY** HELP WHEN IT'S NEEDED.
TRUE FRIENDS STAND BY YOUR SIDE, NOT SNEAK AROUND.
LIKE US!
DON'T KNOW WHAT I'D DO WITHOUT MY GHOULS!
ROYALLY RIGHT.
I'D LOSE MY CHARGE!
YOU'RE MY BEST MATES!
FUR-EVER!

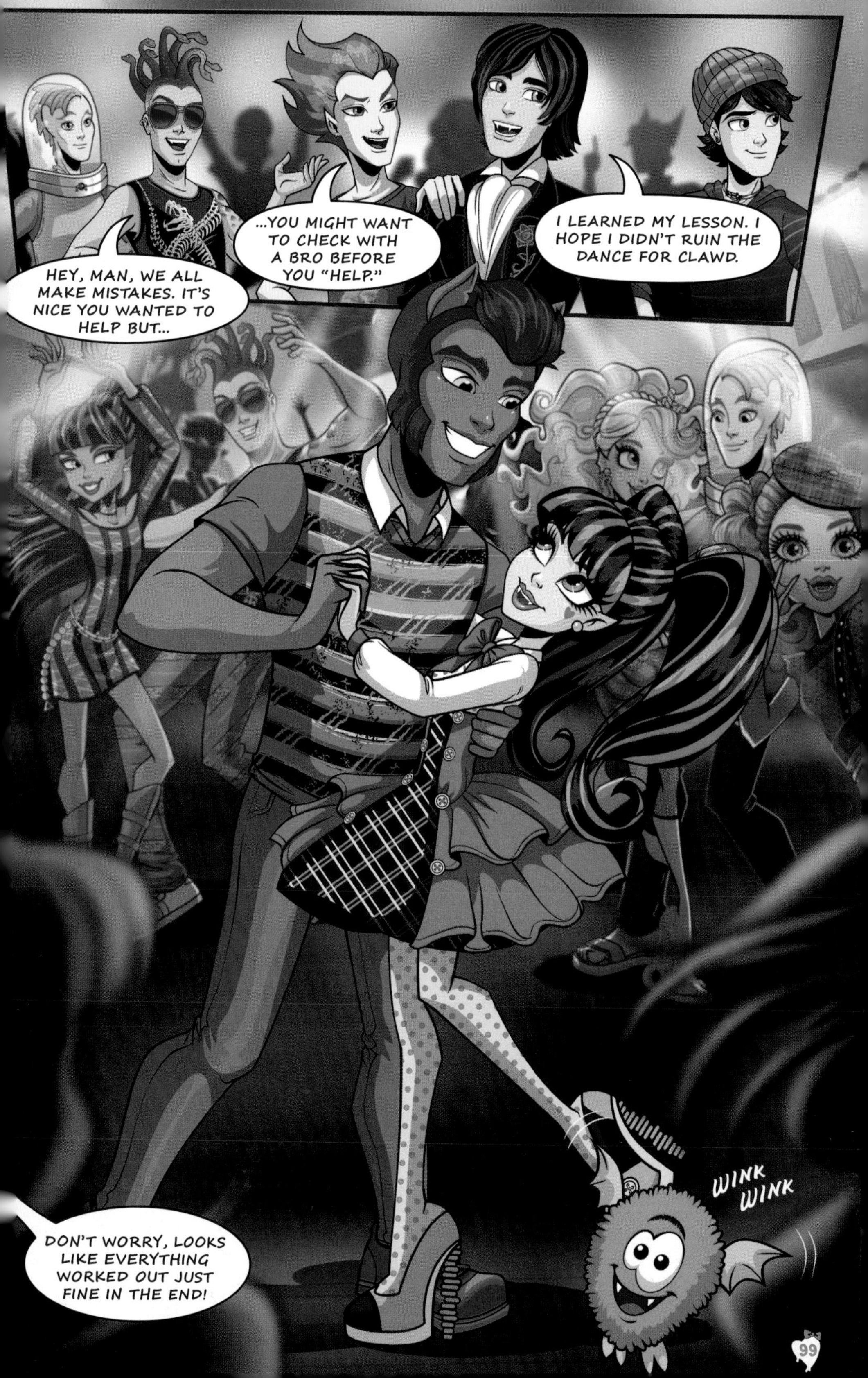
HEY, MAN, WE ALL MAKE MISTAKES. IT'S NICE YOU WANTED TO HELP BUT...
...YOU MIGHT WANT TO CHECK WITH A BRO BEFORE YOU "HELP."
I LEARNED MY LESSON. I HOPE I DIDN'T RUIN THE DANCE FOR CLAWD.
WINK WINK
DON'T WORRY, LOOKS LIKE EVERYTHING WORKED OUT JUST FINE IN THE END!

HEATHER NUHFER

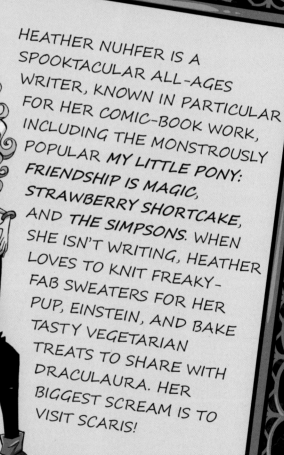

HEATHER NUHFER IS A SPOOKTACULAR ALL-AGES WRITER, KNOWN IN PARTICULAR FOR HER COMIC-BOOK WORK, INCLUDING THE MONSTROUSLY POPULAR *MY LITTLE PONY: FRIENDSHIP IS MAGIC*, *STRAWBERRY SHORTCAKE*, AND *THE SIMPSONS*. WHEN SHE ISN'T WRITING, HEATHER LOVES TO KNIT FREAKY-FAB SWEATERS FOR HER PUP, EINSTEIN, AND BAKE TASTY VEGETARIAN TREATS TO SHARE WITH DRACULAURA. HER BIGGEST SCREAM IS TO VISIT SCARIS!

About the Illustrator

KELLEE RILEY

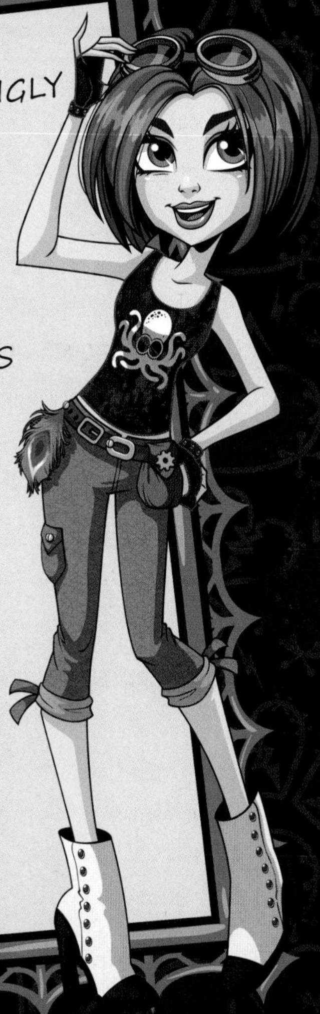

KELLEE RILEY IS A FRIGHTENINGLY BUSY ILLUSTRATOR WHO HAS WORKED ON OVER TWENTY MAJOR BRANDS, INCLUDING **BARBIE**, **MY LITTLE PONY**, **DORA THE EXPLORER**, AND MANY MORE. MOST NOTED AS THE ORIGINAL ILLUSTRATOR ON **MONSTER HIGH**, SHE ALSO HAS OVER FORTY CHILDREN'S BOOKS TO HER CREDIT. KELLEE LOVES COMICS, VIDEO GAMES, AND DRESSING UP IN FUN OUTFITS TO MATCH HER FANGTASTIC WIG COLLECTION.

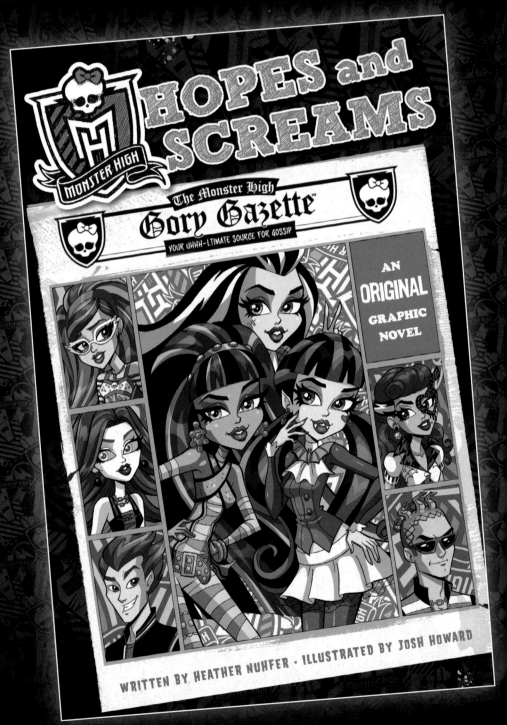

Read howl about

Frankie Stein and the

Gory Gazette in the first

Monster High graphic novel!

Turn the page for a peek at

Cleo de Nile's story from

Hopes and Screams!

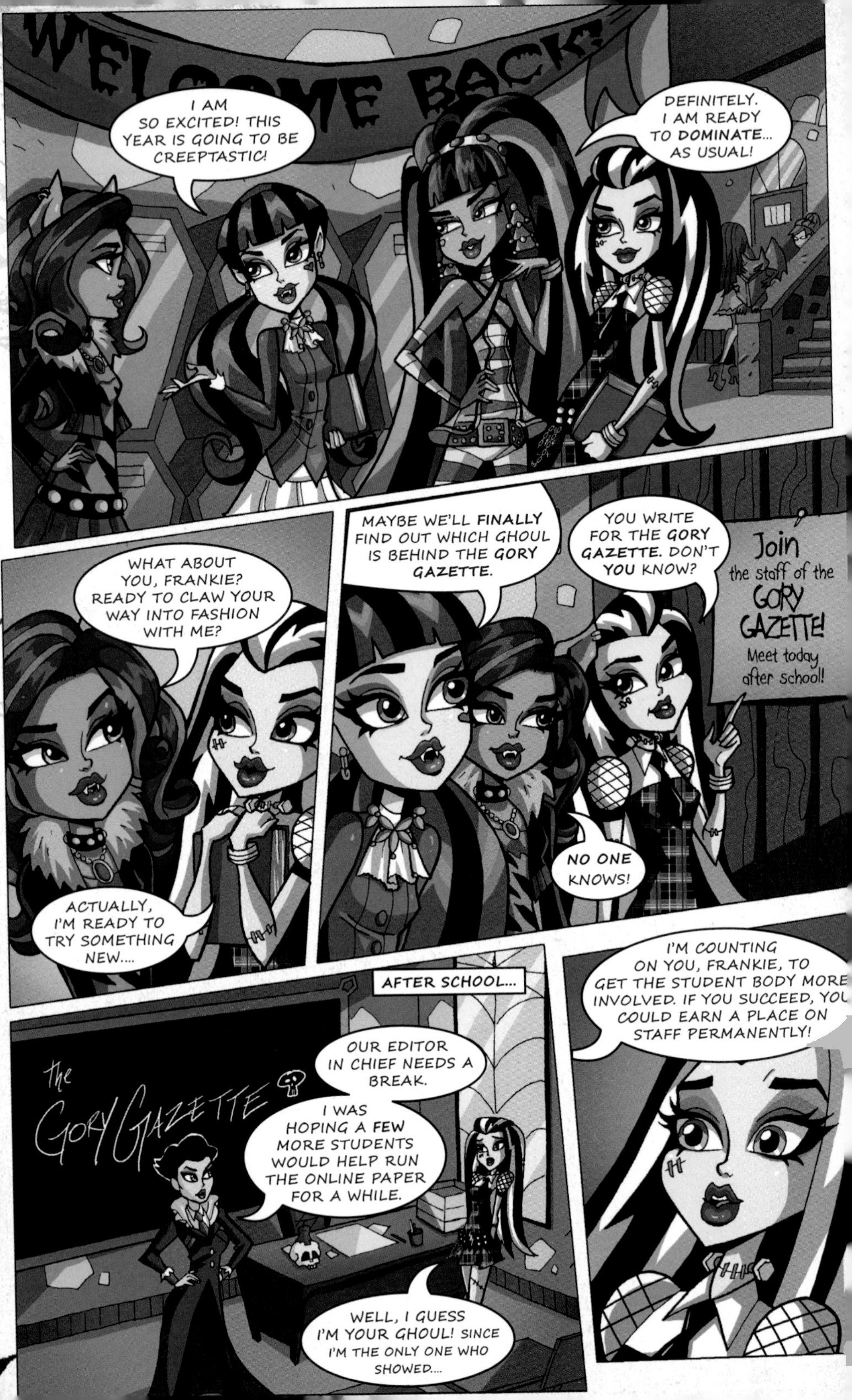
WELCOME BACK!
I AM SO EXCITED! THIS YEAR IS GOING TO BE CREEPTASTIC!
DEFINITELY. I AM READY TO DOMINATE... AS USUAL!
WHAT ABOUT YOU, FRANKIE? READY TO CLAW YOUR WAY INTO FASHION WITH ME?
ACTUALLY, I'M READY TO TRY SOMETHING NEW....
MAYBE WE'LL FINALLY FIND OUT WHICH GHOUL IS BEHIND THE GORY GAZETTE.
YOU WRITE FOR THE GORY GAZETTE. DON'T YOU KNOW?
Join the staff of the GORY GAZETTE! Meet today after school!
NO ONE KNOWS!
AFTER SCHOOL...
the GORY GAZETTE
OUR EDITOR IN CHIEF NEEDS A BREAK.
I WAS HOPING A FEW MORE STUDENTS WOULD HELP RUN THE ONLINE PAPER FOR A WHILE.
WELL, I GUESS I'M YOUR GHOUL! SINCE I'M THE ONLY ONE WHO SHOWED....
I'M COUNTING ON YOU, FRANKIE, TO GET THE STUDENT BODY MORE INVOLVED. IF YOU SUCCEED, YOU COULD EARN A PLACE ON STAFF PERMANENTLY!

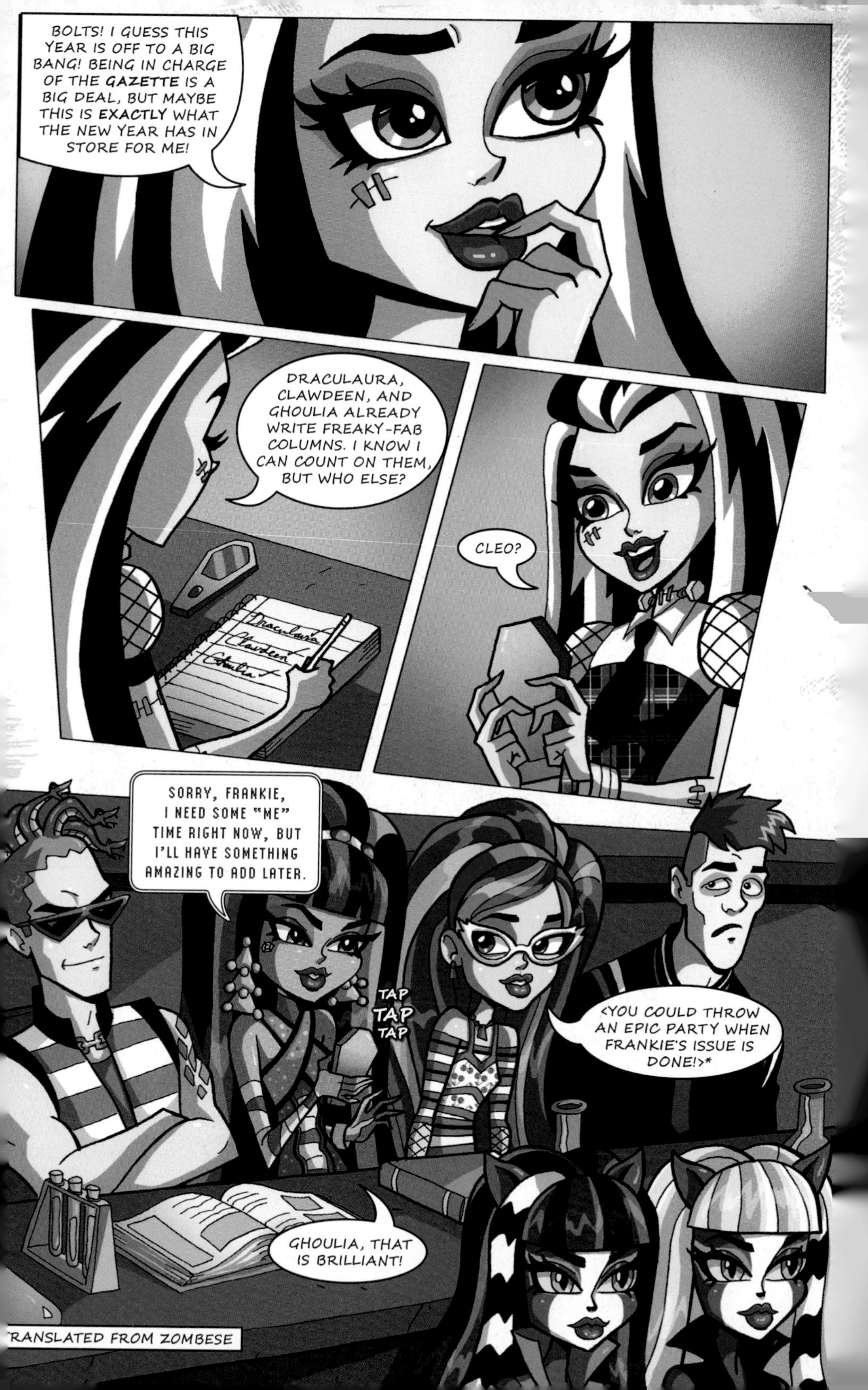
BOLTS! I GUESS THIS YEAR IS OFF TO A BIG BANG! BEING IN CHARGE OF THE **GAZETTE** IS A BIG DEAL, BUT MAYBE THIS IS **EXACTLY** WHAT THE NEW YEAR HAS IN STORE FOR ME!
DRACULAURA, CLAWDEEN, AND GHOULIA ALREADY WRITE FREAKY-FAB COLUMNS. I KNOW I CAN COUNT ON THEM, BUT WHO ELSE?
Draculaura
Clawdeen
Ghoulia
CLEO?
SORRY, FRANKIE, I NEED SOME "ME" TIME RIGHT NOW, BUT I'LL HAVE SOMETHING AMAZING TO ADD LATER.
TAP
TAP
TAP
<YOU COULD THROW AN EPIC PARTY WHEN FRANKIE'S ISSUE IS DONE!>*
GHOULIA, THAT IS BRILLIANT!
*TRANSLATED FROM ZOMBESE

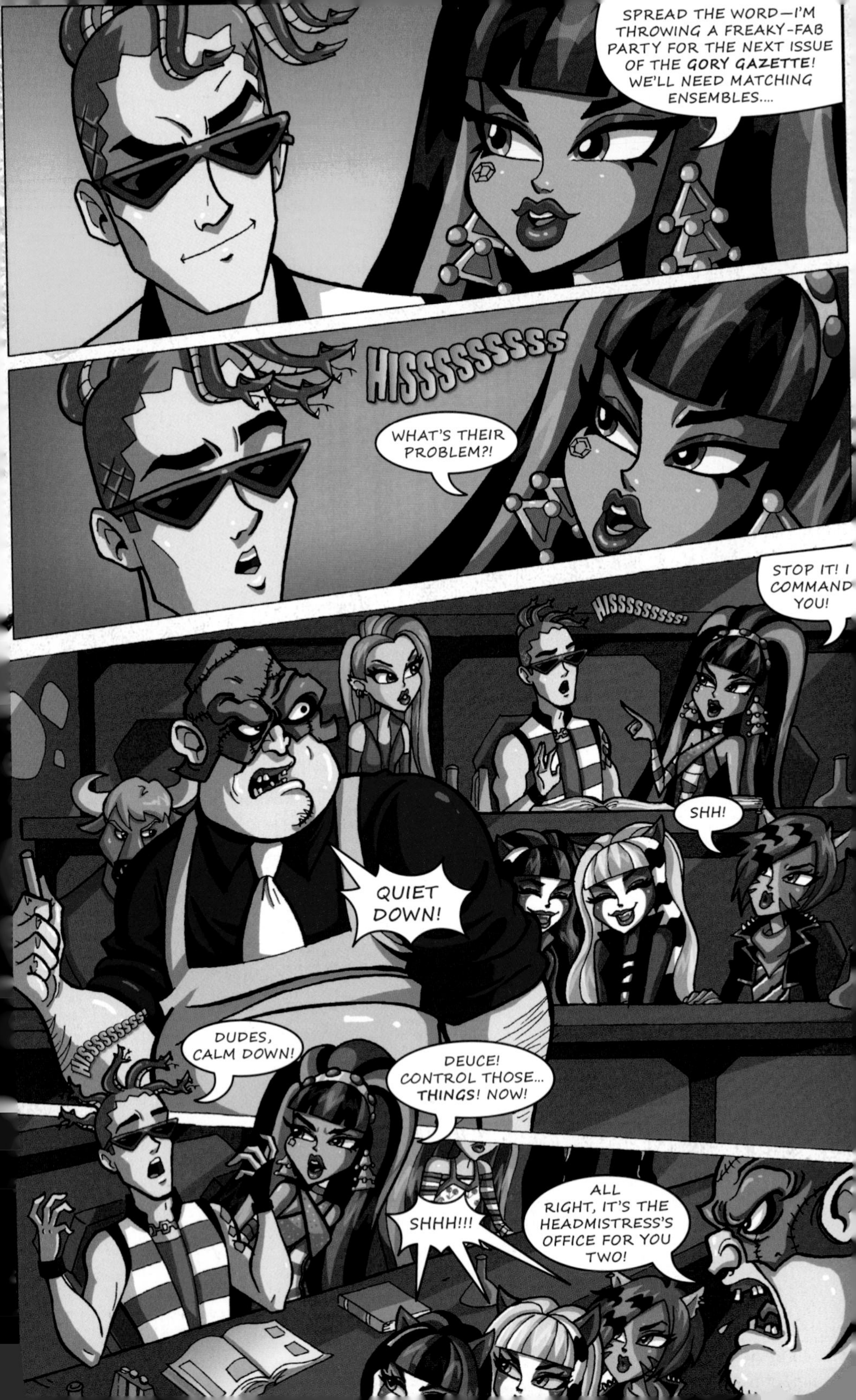
SPREAD THE WORD—I'M THROWING A FREAKY-FAB PARTY FOR THE NEXT ISSUE OF THE GORY GAZETTE! WE'LL NEED MATCHING ENSEMBLES....
HISSSSSSSSS
WHAT'S THEIR PROBLEM?!
HISSSSSSSSS!
STOP IT! I COMMAND YOU!
SHH!
QUIET DOWN!
HISSSSSSSS!
DUDES, CALM DOWN!
DEUCE! CONTROL THOSE... THINGS! NOW!
SHHH!!!
ALL RIGHT, IT'S THE HEADMISTRESS'S OFFICE FOR YOU TWO!

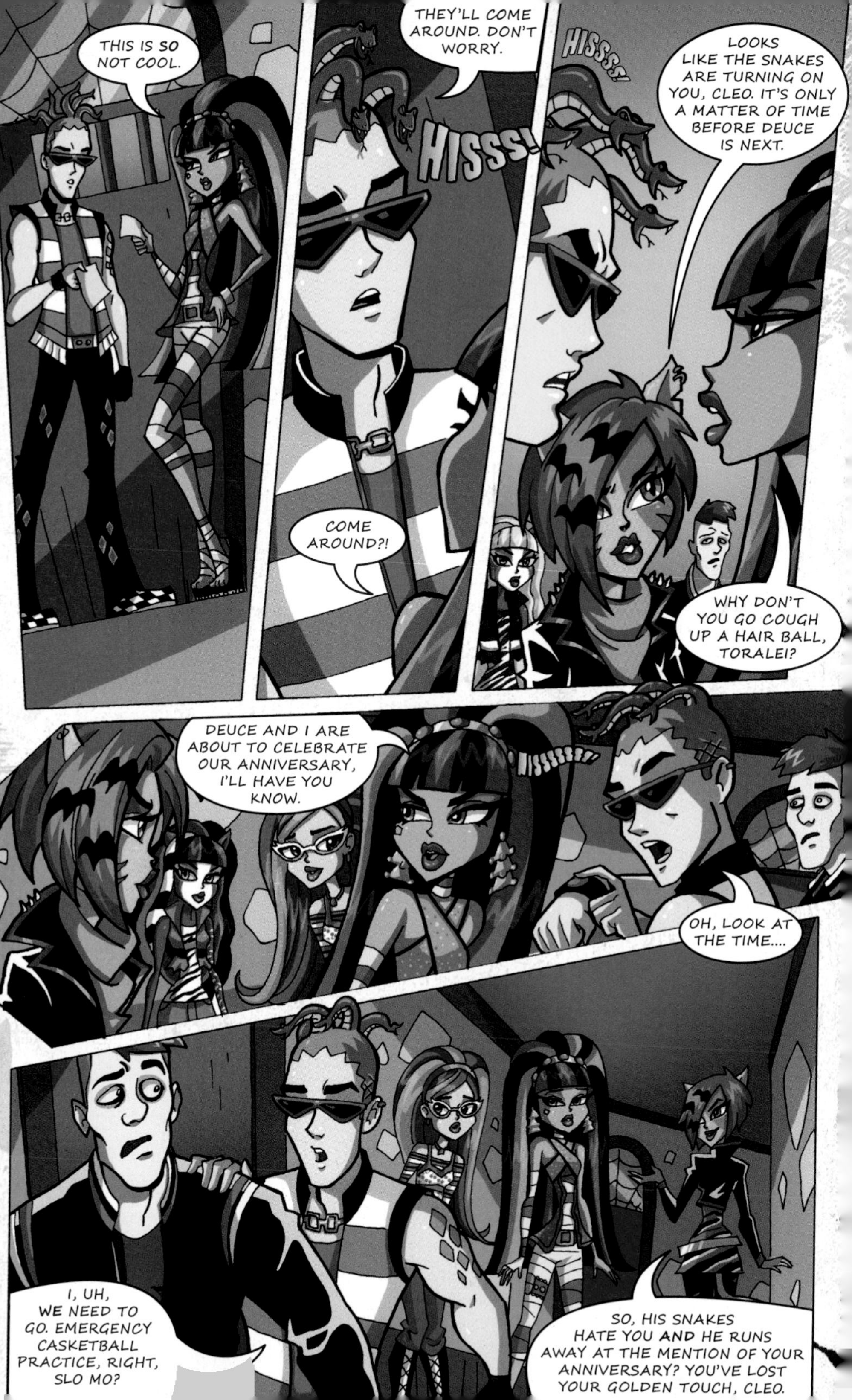
THIS IS SO NOT COOL.
THEY'LL COME AROUND. DON'T WORRY.
HISSS!
COME AROUND?!
HISSSS!
LOOKS LIKE THE SNAKES ARE TURNING ON YOU, CLEO. IT'S ONLY A MATTER OF TIME BEFORE DEUCE IS NEXT.
WHY DON'T YOU GO COUGH UP A HAIR BALL, TORALEI?
DEUCE AND I ARE ABOUT TO CELEBRATE OUR ANNIVERSARY, I'LL HAVE YOU KNOW.
HISSSSSSS
OH, LOOK AT THE TIME....
I, UH, WE NEED TO GO. EMERGENCY CASKETBALL PRACTICE, RIGHT, SLO MO?
SO, HIS SNAKES HATE YOU AND HE RUNS AWAY AT THE MENTION OF YOUR ANNIVERSARY? YOU'VE LOST YOUR GOLDEN TOUCH, CLEO.

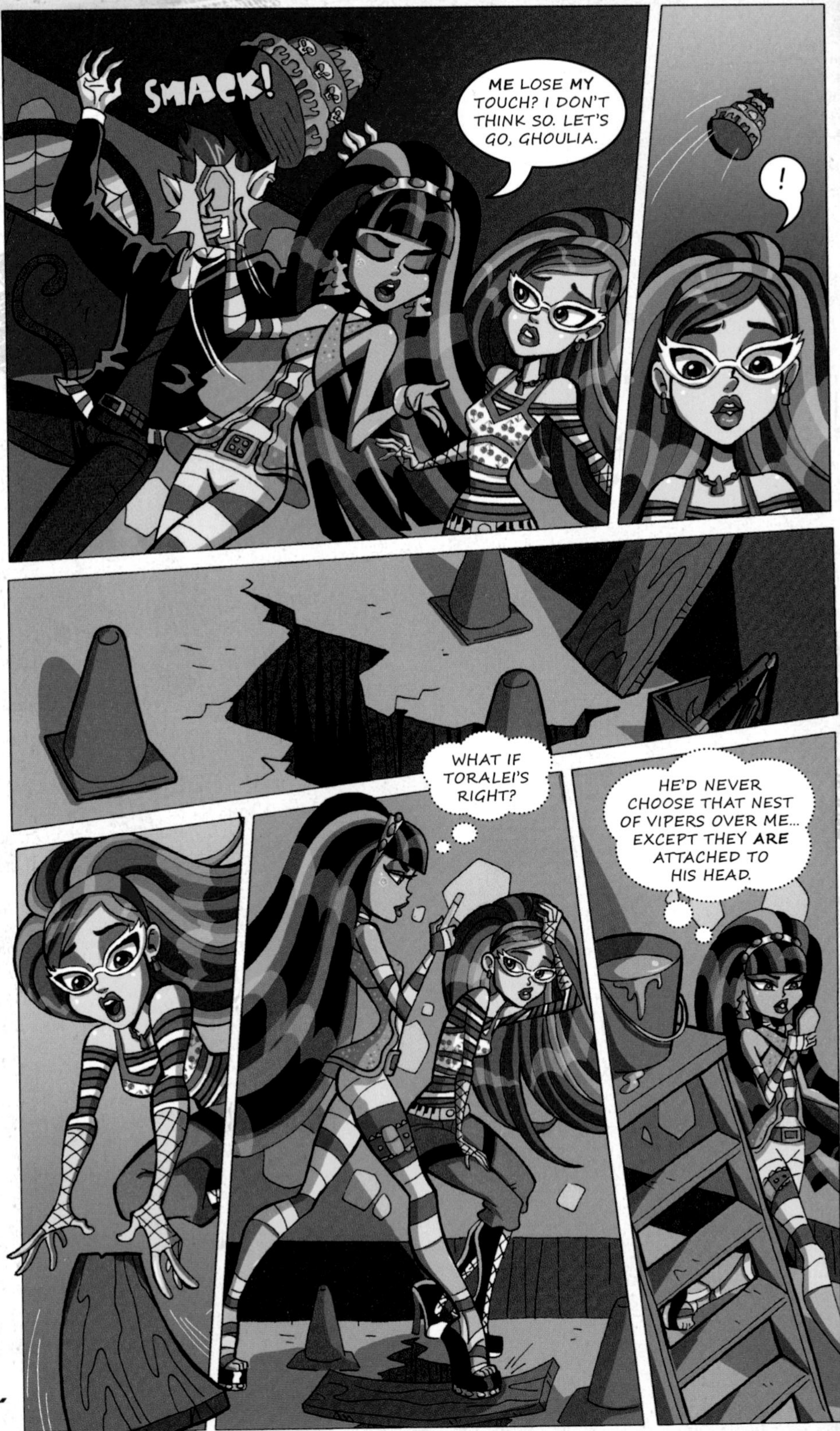
SMACK!
ME LOSE MY TOUCH? I DON'T THINK SO. LET'S GO, GHOULIA.
!
WHAT IF TORALEI'S RIGHT?
HE'D NEVER CHOOSE THAT NEST OF VIPERS OVER ME... EXCEPT THEY **ARE** ATTACHED TO HIS HEAD.

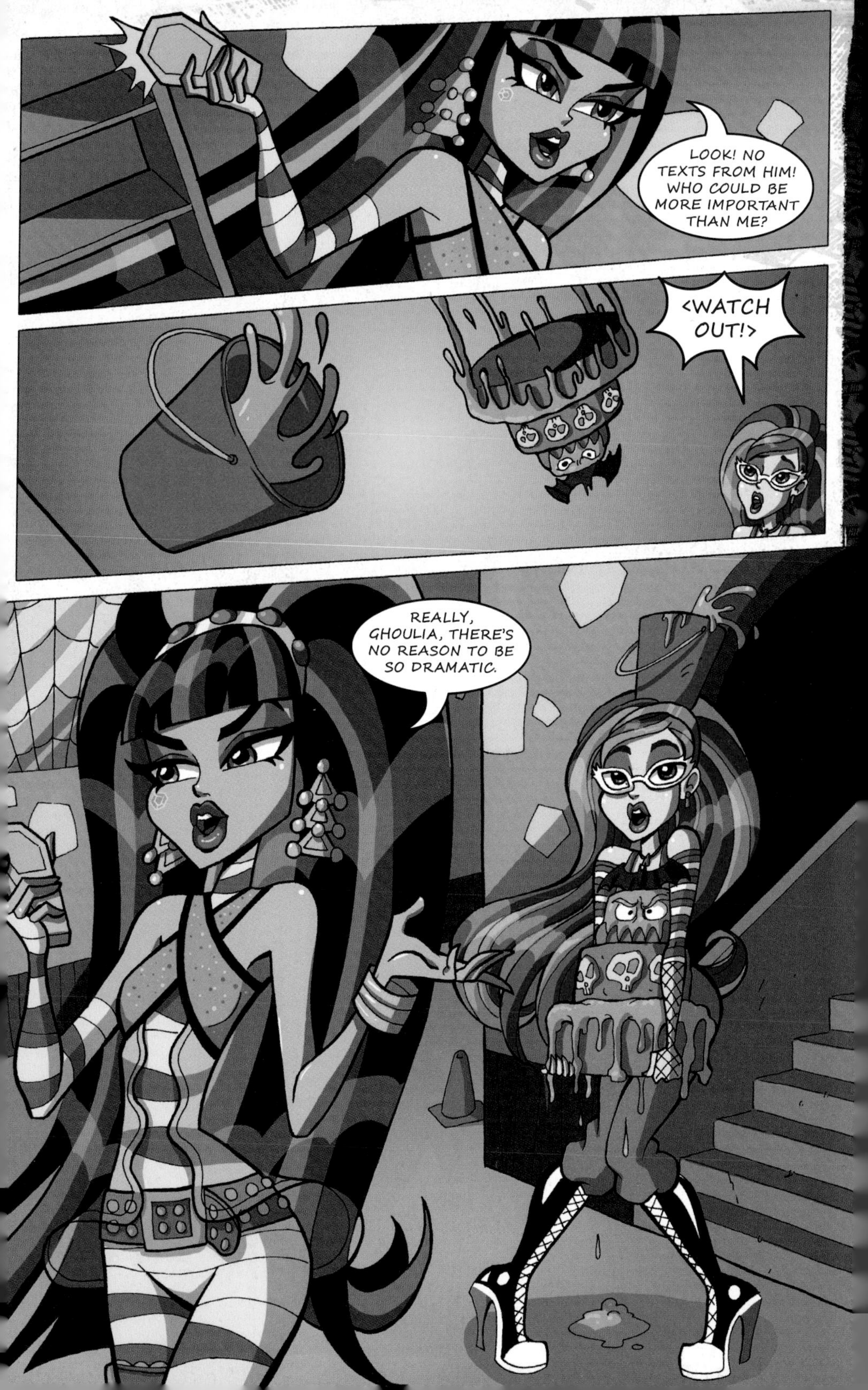
LOOK! NO TEXTS FROM HIM! WHO COULD BE MORE IMPORTANT THAN ME?
<WATCH OUT!>
REALLY, GHOULIA, THERE'S NO REASON TO BE SO DRAMATIC.

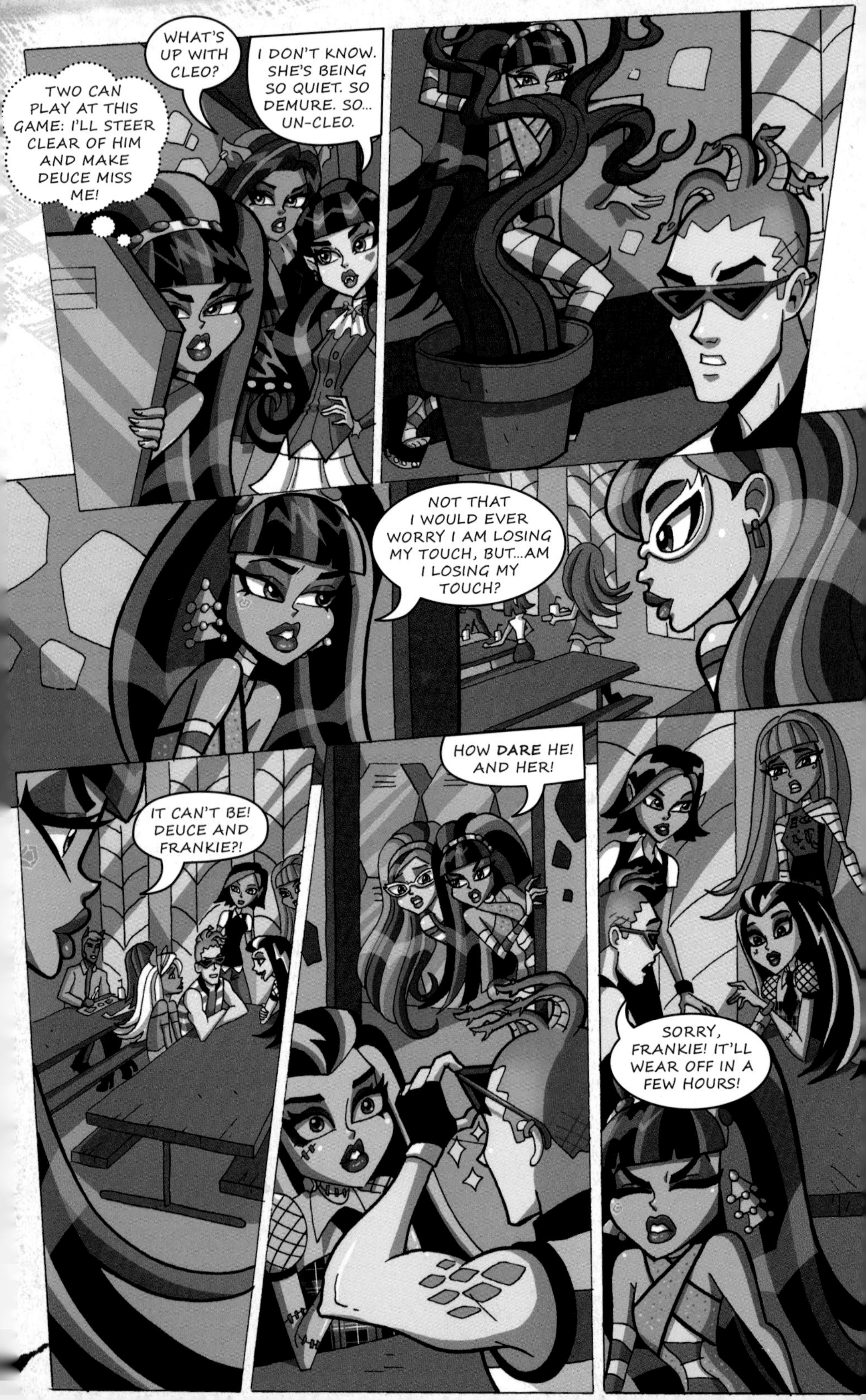
TWO CAN PLAY AT THIS GAME: I'LL STEER CLEAR OF HIM AND MAKE DEUCE MISS ME!
WHAT'S UP WITH CLEO?
I DON'T KNOW. SHE'S BEING SO QUIET. SO DEMURE. SO... UN-CLEO.
NOT THAT I WOULD EVER WORRY I AM LOSING MY TOUCH, BUT...AM I LOSING MY TOUCH?
IT CAN'T BE! DEUCE AND FRANKIE?!
HOW **DARE** HE! AND HER!
SORRY, FRANKIE! IT'LL WEAR OFF IN A FEW HOURS!

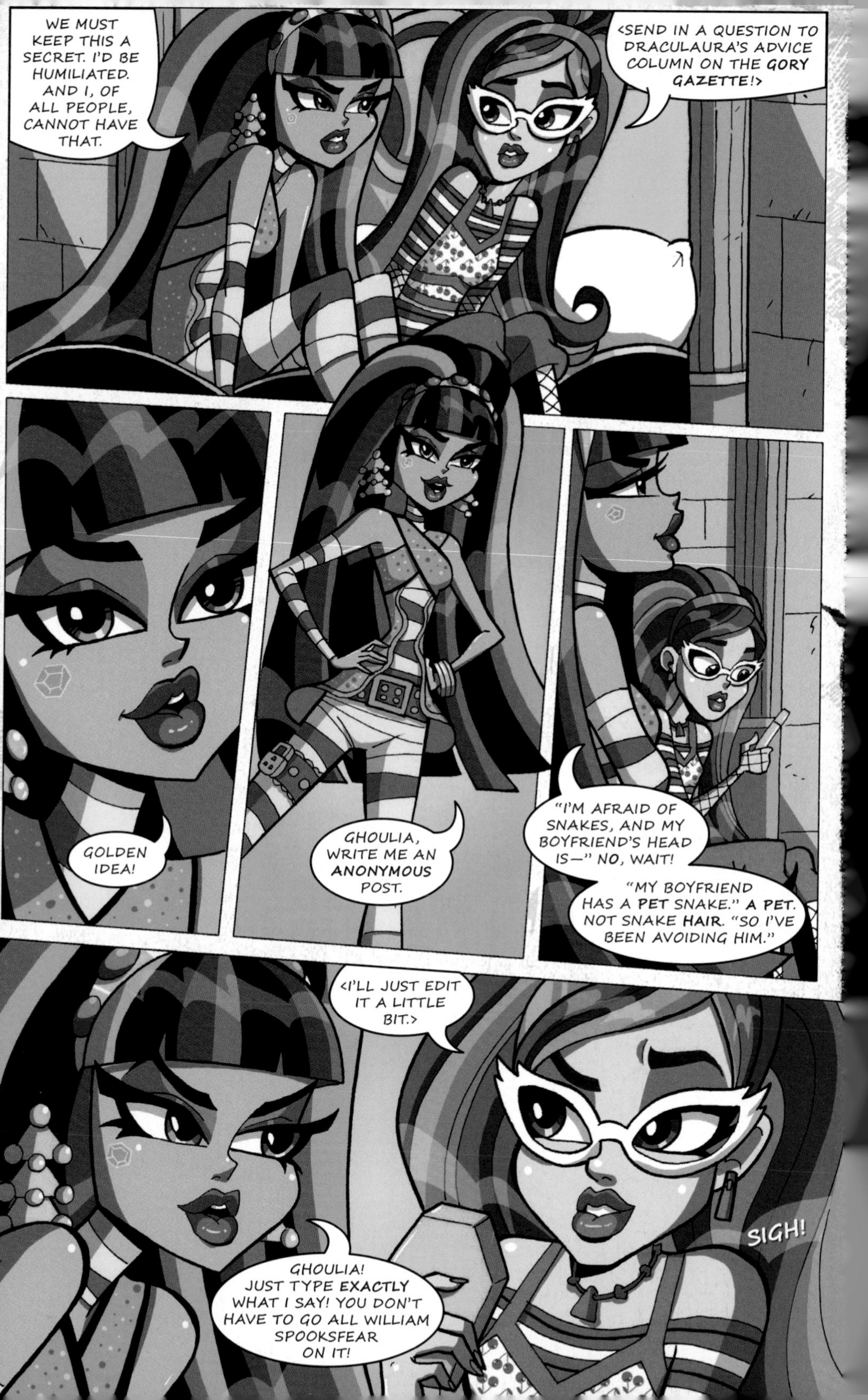
WE MUST KEEP THIS A SECRET. I'D BE HUMILIATED. AND I, OF ALL PEOPLE, CANNOT HAVE THAT.
<SEND IN A QUESTION TO DRACULAURA'S ADVICE COLUMN ON THE **GORY GAZETTE**!>
GOLDEN IDEA!
GHOULIA, WRITE ME AN **ANONYMOUS** POST.
"I'M AFRAID OF SNAKES, AND MY BOYFRIEND'S HEAD IS—" NO, WAIT!
"MY BOYFRIEND HAS A **PET** SNAKE." **A PET**. NOT SNAKE **HAIR**. "SO I'VE BEEN AVOIDING HIM."
<I'LL JUST EDIT IT A LITTLE BIT.>
GHOULIA! JUST TYPE **EXACTLY** WHAT I SAY! YOU DON'T HAVE TO GO ALL WILLIAM SPOOKSFEAR ON IT!
SIGH!

READ THE GHOULFRIENDS SERIES BY GITTY DANESHVARI!

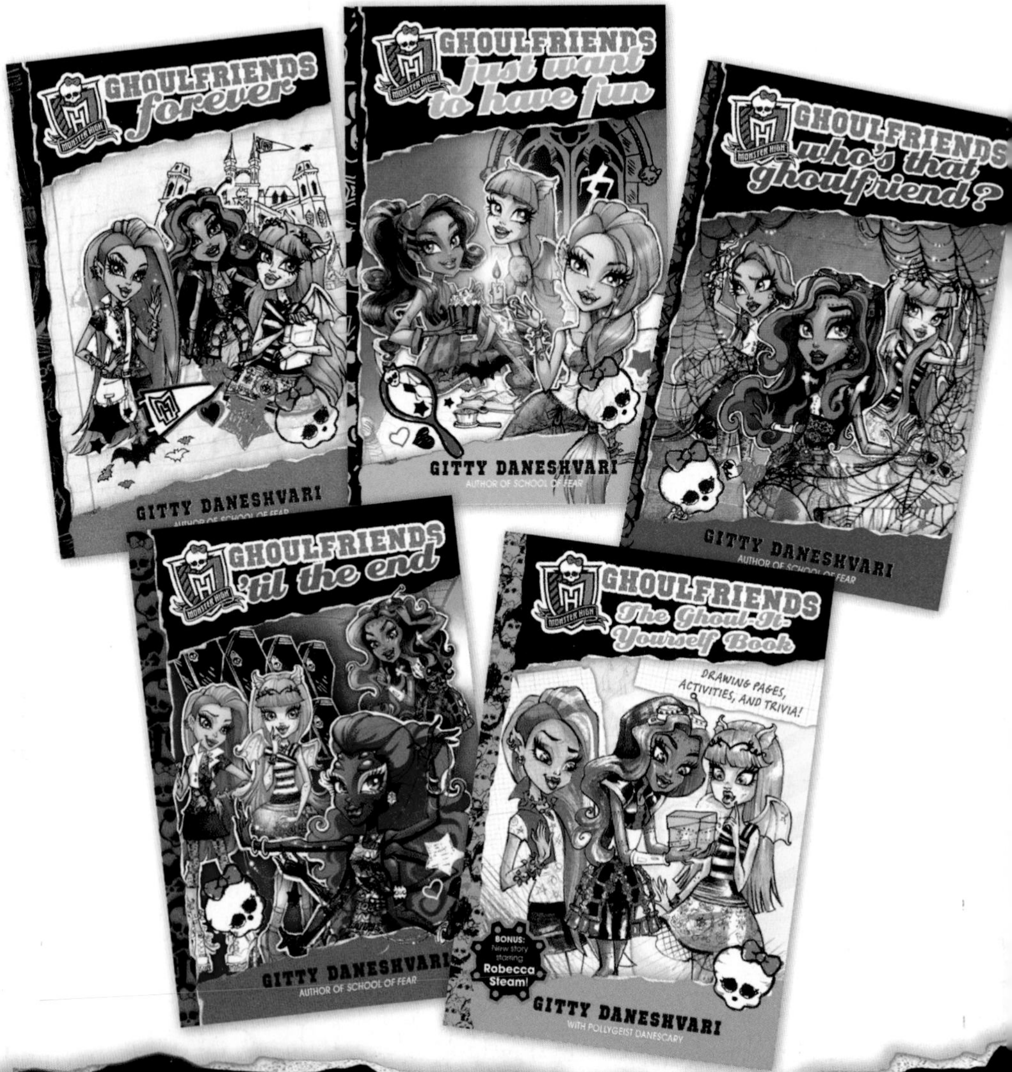
GHOULFRIENDS forever
GITTY DANESHVARI
GHOULFRIENDS just want to have fun
GITTY DANESHVARI
AUTHOR OF SCHOOL OF FEAR
GHOULFRIENDS who's that ghoulfriend?
GITTY DANESHVARI
AUTHOR OF SCHOOL OF FEAR
GHOULFRIENDS 'til the end
GITTY DANESHVARI
AUTHOR OF SCHOOL OF FEAR
GHOULFRIENDS The Ghoul-It-Yourself Book
DRAWING PAGES, ACTIVITIES, AND TRIVIA!
BONUS: New story starring Robecca Steam!
GITTY DANESHVARI
WITH POLLYGEIST DANESCARY